BREATHLESS

Amelia moaned softly, moving restlessly, wanting, needing something that remained just beyond her reach. What was wrong with her?

Lifting heavy eyelids, Amelia stared up at Colter, who was watching her with dark, passionate eyes. "Colt?" she whispered. "What's happening to me?" His hands cupped her breasts through the fabric of her chemise, teasing her nipples until they were tight as rosebuds too new to blossom. "Colt. What are you doing?"

"I'm loving you," he muttered. "Let me have your mouth, Amy. I have to know its taste."

Amelia lifted her face and his mouth covered hers in a kiss so exquisitely sweet that it rendered her almost mindless.

When he had kissed her almost breathless, Colter lifted his head and met her eyes. "I shouldn't be doing this, Amy," he muttered. "You need to stop me now."

"Stop you? Why?"

"Because you're an innocent. I'm supposed to be protecting you." His dark eyes were tormented, his voice harsh. "Tell me to stop or give me your mouth again."

She slid her arms around his neck and pressed her lips to his. "More," she breathed huskily, an expression of absolute bliss on her face.

His dark eyes gleamed. "Gladly," he whispered.

BOOK YOUR PLACE ON OUR WEBSITE AND MAKE THE READING CONNECTION!

We've created a customized website just for our very special readers, where you can get the inside scoop on everything that's going on with Zebra, Pinnacle and Kensington books.

When you come online, you'll have the exciting opportunity to:

- View covers of upcoming books
- Read sample chapters
- Learn about our future publishing schedule (listed by publication month *and author*)
- Find out when your favorite authors will be visiting a city near you
- Search for and order backlist books from our online catalog
- Check out author bios and background information
- Send e-mail to your favorite authors
- Meet the Kensington staff online
- Join us in weekly chats with authors, readers and other guests
- Get writing guidelines
- AND MUCH MORE!

**Visit our website at
http://www.zebrabooks.com**

TEXAS TREASURE

Betty Brooks

Zebra Books
Kensington Publishing Corp.

http://www.zebrabooks.com

ZEBRA BOOKS are published by

Kensington Publishing Corp.
850 Third Avenue
New York, NY 10022

First Printing: April, 2000
10 9 8 7 6 5 4 3 2 1

Printed in the United States of America

Chapter One

Texas Hill Country
March, 1865

Home.

Only a few more miles now and he would be home. That thought quickened Colter Morgan's steps. It was the thought of home and family that had kept him going when his body cried out for rest. His mother and father would be there ... at home. Waiting for him. And Annie, his little sister.

Home. Family. Colt tried to lengthen his strides so he would get there sooner, but his weary body would not obey. He was too damn tired.

Would his brothers be home yet? He prayed to God that they were, that they had been lucky enough to survive Gettysburg.

Sarah Morgan had already lost one son. It would break her heart to lose another one ... or two.

Forcing such thoughts from his mind, he allowed his hungry gaze to drink in the sight of the hills that rose steeply on the east and west sides of the valley. Covered with a thick growth of cedars, they were as unchanging as time. And Colt needed that now. Needed the sameness that was Morgan's Creek. His home. In his mind's eye, he could see it now as it had been when he'd left with his brothers. His father and mother had stood on the porch, watching them leave. And beside them stood six-year-old Annie, clutching a rag doll in one hand while the other was lifted to wave good-bye to the brothers who were leaving to join the Confederate Army.

It had been a useless fight that had lasted over four long years and consumed hundreds of thousands of lives and millions of dollars. It was a war where brother had fought against brother, father against son, but it was finally over. The time had finally come to lay down the weapons, to put aside all prejudice, and to get on with life . . . for those left alive to do so. There were so many who would not be returning home, Colt knew. He was one of the lucky ones.

His thoughts returned to his brothers. To Matthew. Sturdy, reliable Matt. Matt was so different from fun-loving Gabriel, who was three years younger than Colt. Gabe was the jokester, always laughing, making those around him smile. Had he been able to remain that way even through all that hell? There had been no word of him nor of Matt since Gettysburg.

Colt had seen Blake last year, though, but only for a brief moment. Blake had been wounded and was on his way to a field hospital. Blake had known the whereabouts of Benjamin, the fifth brother. It was the last time Colt had word of any of his brothers, and it had been longer still since he'd heard from home.

That was not so unusual, though. With battles raging all

around them, the people of the South had more to worry about than getting mail through the lines.

Putting aside the horrors of the war, Colt turned his thoughts toward home again. It was easy to do, because he could already hear the sound of water rushing over limestone as it made its way downstream. Morgan's Creek. Colt's heartbeat quickened. Just a little farther now and he would be home.

Even now he could smell the sweet perfume of wildflowers mingled with clear fresh air, untainted by the smell of burned gunpowder. The flowers were all around him, a glorious carpet of pink, yellow, red and orange, purple and blue, blooming in radiant glory. So many of them, so plentiful, each flower ablaze with its own rich hue.

It was a breathtaking sight—one that Cole had always taken for granted until it had been lost to him.

Never again, though, he silently vowed.

Suddenly Colt felt a tremendous sense of peace wash over him. He could finally believe it was over. The war had ended. And he had come home.

The *clip-clop* of hooves interrupted his reverie, and Colt turned to see a rider approaching. He stepped aside, narrowing his gaze on the Appaloosa stallion.

Good horseflesh. But it was obvious by the droop of heads that both horse and rider were bone weary.

The newcomer, like Colt, wore a tattered gray uniform. But there was something about him . . .

His large frame—lean, sinewy, almost haggard in appearance—was somehow familiar.

The rider reined up beside Colt, pushing back the brim of the Confederate cap he wore, and narrowed his gaze, studying Colter's features for a long moment. And when he finally spoke, his voice was a harsh rasp. "Colt?" he asked huskily. "Is that you?"

Colt's heart gave a quick jerk as he stared into familiar blue eyes. "Matthew?"

"Yeah," Matthew confirmed. "It's me." He sighed heavily. "You look as bad as I feel, Colt. Climb up behind me. We got a ways to go yet."

Before the war, Colt would have leaped on the horse, but his bones were too weary now, his body weakened by too little food and not enough sleep. Moving like an old man, he mounted behind his brother and the two men set off toward the homestead.

"Are you just now getting home, Matt?"

"Yeah. You heard anything about the others?"

"No. Not recently. I saw Blake last year, though. And he'd been in touch with Benjamin. What about Gabe? Have you heard anything from him?"

"No. Not since we joined up." Matthew sighed heavily. "It was a useless war, Colt. It should never have been fought. We didn't accomplish a damn thing."

Neither brother believed in slavery. They hadn't fought for that reason. They were only bent on saving their homes from Northern invaders, who had appeared intent on destruction.

"How long has it been since you heard from Ma?" Colt asked.

"I had a letter last year."

"They were all right?"

"Yeah. Nothing much changes in Morgan's Creek. Pa lost some of his stock to raiders, but they were mostly stragglers. Ma said there'd been deserters passing through the area on their way west. She hadn't seen any herself, but they ran stock off from the Bar-D Ranch. It's my guess the Bar-D was raided because it was closer to the Llano Road."

As they rounded a curve, Matthew drew back on the reins to slow the stallion. "Whoa, Thunder," he said softly.

"What's up, Matt?" Colt asked, peering around his brother's right shoulder.

A sway-backed mule carrying a stooped figure stood beside the road munching grass while at the beast's head, tugging on the reins with all his strength, a slender young man wearing jeans, a red-checked flannel shirt, and a straw hat that had seen better days, turned the air blue with his curses.

Pushing back the tip of his hat, the young man wiped his sweat-streaked face with one hand and jerked at the reins with the other. "Come on, you damned, stubborn, useless, flea-bitten, mangy nag! You're going with me whether you like it or not!"

"Need some help?" Matt inquired, stopping beside the mule.

The young man jerked, as though startled; then he uttered a short curse, apparently angry at being taken unawares. His expression, a mixture of frustration and confusion, quickly became one of hope.

"Matthew?" he questioned. Suddenly a smile spread across his face. "My God, it is you, Matt! And Colt too! Damned if the two of you ain't a sight for sore eyes!"

"Same to you, Benjamin." Matthew looked at the man astride the mule, who seemed unaware of what was going on around him. "Is that Blake?" he asked softly.

"Yeah." Benjamin's expression became grim. "We were together at the end. Blake got shot up real bad. Wasn't the first time neither. He needed to stay in the hospital but he wouldn't hear of it. I'm just trying to get him home to Ma so's she can fix him up."

"Looks like we'd make it faster without the mule," Matthew said shortly, dismounting. When Colt started to follow suit, Matt stopped him. "Stay there, Colt. Appears you're gonna have to hold Blake on the stallion." He turned to his younger brother. "Help me get him on the Appaloosa, Ben."

Blake appeared unaware of the brothers as they shifted him off the mule and onto the stallion. Moments later they resumed their journey.

Matt and Ben walked behind the stallion, leaving the mule to follow along or stay behind, whichever pleased it most. It wasn't the least bit surprising when the mule decided to accompany them.

Ben's gaze rarely left his wounded brother. "I ain't so sure Blake's gonna make it, Matt."

Although the wounded brother had been silent throughout the meeting, his voice was a low growl as he made his own thoughts known. "I'll damned well make it home. Just quit bellyaching and take me to Ma."

A silence settled over them then, broken only by the steady thud of hooves.

Soon they rounded the last curve that blocked their view and there it was. Spread out before them. Home. Even Blake, wounded as he was, sat up straighter.

The house was a big, whitewashed, two-storied affair, built by their grandfather at the turn of the century. It stood not more than a hundred yards from Morgan's Creek. The paint was peeling now, and some of the windows were broken. Nothing to cause real alarm, though. Pa had been working the land alone. Unless old Charley, who'd been with them ever since Colt could remember, was still around. Even then, with the two of them, there would have been no time for repairs. But there were other signs the brothers found even more disconcerting. The corral was empty, and the chicken yard bare of fowl. As they rode closer, there was an emptiness about the place that struck a chord of uneasiness in Colt.

Where was everyone?

His gaze swept the clearing, then went unerringly to the

lone pine tree that marked the spot where his grandparents had been buried. The headstones were there. But three more had been added.

"They ain't home." Benjamin's voice held a plaintive sound.

But Colt felt deep within his soul that his brother was wrong. He was aware of Matthew and Benjamin lifting Blake off the horse and carrying him to the porch of the big house. But instead of following them, he rode slowly toward the graveyard. He was vaguely aware of movement behind him, yet he did not acknowledge the presence of another. Dread weighed heavily on him as he stopped beside the pine tree and dismounted.

As Colt reined up beside his grandfather's grave, he became aware of Matt, who had followed him up the hill and stopped nearby.

"James Morgan." Matt's voice was husky, grating. "Born July, 1810. Died June, 1864."

No, Colt thought. The gravestone in front of him was his grandfather's. His name was John. Not James. Colt turned then and saw Matt kneeling beside one of the new headstones.

Pa's name is James. Colt silently cried. At that moment he admitted to himself what he'd already come to realize somewhere deep inside. *Pa is dead.*

Colt dismounted and went to the next headstone. "Sarah Morgan," he read. His eyes stung with unshed tears as he continued. "Born January, 1816. Died June, 1864. Raped and . . . murdered by the Kincaids."

Colt's skin, tough and leathery from the years in the sun, turned ashen beneath his perpetual tan. Of their own accord, his legs moved, taking him to the last headstone. "Annabelle Morgan. Born April, 1854. Died June, 1864. Raped"—*Oh, God, no!* Colt forced himself to go on—"and murdered by the Kincaids."

Horror swept over Colt and he left the graveyard to empty his guts on the ground. He was aware of Matthew stopping beside him, of leaning on his older brother's strength as they returned to the house, yet he couldn't escape the horror that continued to hold him in its grip.

His parents. His baby sister. Damn the Kincaids to hell! He would find the sons of bitches, and he would make them pay.

Hatred blazed in the heart of Colter as he made that vow. He would never rest until every last one of the Kincaid devils had met his Maker. They would answer for what they had done that day in June. A deed so foul could never be forgotten, nor could it ever be forgiven.

If it took the rest of his life, Colt vowed, he would avenge the deaths of his loved ones.

Chapter Two

New Orleans
April, 1866

It was late when Colter Morgan reached New Orleans and moonlight blanketed the cobblestone streets of the city. The big Appaloosa stallion he rode snorted and tossed his head impatiently as though to remind his master of his own needs.

"Easy, boy," Colt soothed. "You'll get your oats real soon."

Colt sympathized with the stallion. The day had been an especially long one since they broke camp before daybreak. And now it must be nearing midnight.

Although Colt wouldn't normally have asked so much of his mount—he had too much respect for good horse-flesh—he had done so today. And the reason was inexplicable, just a curious feeling he'd had ever since the sun had crested the eastern horizon. A feeling that he must reach his destination quickly before it was too late.

Too late. Colt had no idea where that thought had come from. Too late for what? For Grady Kincaid? Colt's mouth thinned and his dark eyes glinted with hate. He had no doubt there were others like himself who wanted the man to pay for his foul deeds. And he would pay. With his life. Colt would see to that. But Kincaid had some talking to do first. He had names to give: the name of every man who'd ridden with him that day.

Colt's hands clenched into fists and his fingernails dug into the flesh of his palms. He imagined his fingers wrapped around Grady Kincaid's neck and squeezing. He had waited a long time, had covered many a weary mile during his search for the men who had murdered his family. His father, his mother, and his sweet Annie.

Even now, after more than a year of searching, Colt wouldn't have known the whereabouts of even one Kincaid if he hadn't overheard a conversation in a Kansas City saloon. They had been casual words spoken by a cardsharp intent on distracting his opponent by carrying on a conversation while he dealt the hand.

But Colter wasn't just any opponent. He was a gambler so adept at cards that he knew when to play and when to fold. He'd known by the spread of his hand that it was time to fold if he didn't want to lose, but he wanted the information his opponent would innocently give if he kept on playing.

Colt lost over three hundred dollars to the cardsharp, but when he left the Red Garter Saloon, he went straight to the livery stable and saddled the Appaloosa. They headed straight for New Orleans, where Grady Kincaid had, according to the cardsharp, taken up residence in a mansion he'd supposedly bought for a song.

Colter had his own ideas about how Kincaid had

acquired his mansion. But however Kincaid had managed it, he wouldn't live to enjoy the fruits of his plunder, because Colt intended to see Grady Kincaid dead—about five minutes after they stood face-to-face. But first he would learn the names and whereabouts of the others who had taken part in the atrocities done to the Morgan family.

And then he would take great pleasure in sending the first, but not the last, Kincaid to hell!

Amelia Spencer woke with a start.

She wasn't sure what had caused her to waken . . . some slight sound or perhaps the sudden certainty that she was no longer alone in the room.

"Who's there?" she demanded, attempting to sound brave when she was quaking like magnolia blossoms in a brisk wind.

A husky laugh was her only answer, but it was followed by the sound of heavy footsteps crossing the floor.

Icy fingers played along her spine as fear streaked through her. She peered into the darkness, trying to determine the source of the sound, but the shadows were too dense, too thick to penetrate everywhere in the room except one place where a shaft of moonlight streamed through the open window and danced across the floor a few feet from her four-poster bed.

"Who's there?" Her voice trembled. "Answer me!"

A whisper of sound was her only answer. Someone was deliberately trying to frighten her.

Anger surged forth covering her fear, and she flung back the covers and scrambled off the far side of the bed, putting more distance between herself and whoever was approaching so stealthily.

"Who are you? What do you want in here?"

A harsh laugh was her only answer. She watched one of

the deeper shadows move and begin to shape itself into a human form as it neared the shaft of moonlight. Another step and the intruder's face was exposed. Sharp, angular, bony. In that instant Amelia recognized the face of Grady Kincaid, her employer.

"What do you want here?"

Grady Kincaid laughed harshly. "Don't be coy, Amelia." He detoured around the bed, his hand outstretched as though he were approaching a skittish colt. "Come back to bed and we'll talk about what I want."

"No!" Amelia's voice trembled as she fought to control her fear. "Please leave my room."

"*My* room." He smiled, appearing to take great pleasure in correcting her. "This is *my* house, Amelia. And don't you ever forget it. It's my house and you are my servant. Bought and paid for with hard-earned cash."

Bought and paid for? What did he mean by that? "I don't know what you mean. You pay my salary, but that doesn't give you the right to come into my room at night."

"I have the right to do anything I please with you, Amelia." He appeared amused. "Your father gave me that right when he sold you to me."

"Sold me?" She shivered. "I don't believe you."

His voice became hard. "Surely you know your own father well enough to know what he's capable of. He sold you, right enough. For two hundred dollars. A goodly sum in these times, I might add. I own you now, Amelia. Body and soul—you belong to me."

Amelia couldn't believe that her father could be capable of selling his own daughter. She wouldn't believe it. Her chin lifted defiantly and she glared at her employer. "You're lying!" She felt strong in her denial. "My father would never be so despicable."

"Oh, but he would," Kincaid said softly. "Do you want to know why, Amelia? I bought his mortgage from the bank. And I gave him a choice. He could keep you or the farm, and I'm afraid, my dear, he chose the farm."

Amelia or the farm. Given such a choice, which one would Karl Spencer choose?

The farm was her father's life. Had been ever since her mother's death. He had fought off raiders during the war, and somehow, even as farms around them had been destroyed, the buildings burned to the ground, the Spencer farm had remained intact. And when the war had finally ended, Karl Spencer had put all his energy into reclaiming what had been lost. He'd gone to the bank and secured a loan. Amelia had been aware of that fact. But he'd never mentioned that the loan had been acquired by her employer, nor the circumstances surrounding the sudden offer of a position in the Kincaid household.

The farm or his daughter.

An aching sadness caused a knot to form in her throat. She'd suspected her father had never loved her, and now she knew it for certain. But she was determined that her employer would never know how badly she was hurting.

"Did you really expect me to go along with such an arrangement?"

"I'm afraid you have no choice, Amelia. You'll go along with it or find yourself out on the streets."

"Then I'd rather be out on the streets!" She tilted her chin defiantly. "Just give me time to pack my belongings and I'll be on my way."

His gaze narrowed and his voice was cold when he spoke. "Make no mistake, Amelia. If you leave my house tonight, then you'll take nothing with you."

"You mean to deny me my possessions?"

"You'll take nothing," he repeated.

Realizing that he had the upper hand, and that she would do well to get away while she could, Amelia said stiffly, "If that is the way I must go, then I shall do so. Just get out of my room and allow me privacy to dress."

"No, Amelia." His lips curled in a cruel smile that chilled her soul as he sat down on the bed and watched her. "If you leave here, then you'll go just as you are."

In her nightdress? It would be bad enough, a woman alone on the streets of New Orleans at night in these troubled times, but to leave in her nightclothes was just asking for trouble.

Amelia shivered at the look in his eyes. He expected her to relent. But she would never submit to him. The danger that awaited her in the darkness of night was far more desirable than what lay ahead for her if she remained in this house.

Swallowing hard around the knot of fear that had lodged in her throat, Amelia said, "Very well." She stepped around the bed and moved cautiously toward the door. "If leaving tonight is the only way I can avoid what you have in mind for me, then so be it."

She was almost to the door when he sprang from the bed and caught her upper arm in a hard grip.

"You're going nowhere," he snarled, yanking her hard against his body.

For a moment fear immobilized her. But as Grady Kincaid lowered his head and pressed eager lips against hers, that very same fear lent her enough strength to wrench away from him. Then, before he could react, she darted toward the door, yanked it open, and sped down the hallway toward the staircase that led to the lower floor. Halfway there, he caught her, curling his fingers around her wrist and jerking so hard that Amelia lost her balance and landed on the floor with a hard thump that took away her breath and left her gasping for air.

Amelia lay on the floor, her heartbeat pounding loudly

in her eardrums as she struggled for air to relieve her burning lungs.

Oh, God, she silently prayed. *Please help me!*

Feeling a helpless sob rise in her throat, she bit her lips to hold it back, refusing to allow her employer to see just how terrified she was.

Thud! Thud! Thud!

Amelia recognized the sounds, and hope sprang within her breast. Footsteps. Running. Someone in the house had been aroused by the struggle. Even Grady Kincaid would never dare lay a hand on her while there were witnesses. But her hope was short-lived, she realized, when Grady Kincaid turned his head to face whoever had dared approach them.

"Get back to your room," he shouted angrily.

The thuds stopped, then sounded again, but they were becoming more distant with each passing moment. Whoever had interrupted them had quickly taken flight.

Suddenly Grady was bending over her, grasping her forearm and pulling her upright with so much force that she thought her shoulder might have been dislocated.

Kincaid's hold was brutal, his fingers digging into her forearm. There would surely be bruises when he'd finished with her . . . if she was still breathing.

Oh, God, *would* she be alive? Somehow the thought that he might actually take her life hadn't occurred to her before.

Perhaps, though, when he was done with her, she wouldn't want to live.

She shuddered with fear as he shoved her toward the nearest room—his bedroom, she realized, when the door slammed behind them and she saw the ornately carved four-poster bed.

"Don't," she cried, hating herself for pleading with him, yet desperate to escape her plight. "Please don't do this."

He laughed harshly, his gaze flickering between her pale face and the curve of her breasts. "Go on," he cajoled. "Beg some more. It's music to my ears."

It was then that Amelia realized he enjoyed hurting people, that the more she pleaded, the more he would hurt her.

Her gaze flicked back and forth as she searched the lamplit room for anything that would help her escape the madman who was bent on ravishing her. Her gaze swept over the four-poster bed and became fixed on the gun belt that was hanging on one of the posts.

Amelia looked away quickly, hoping her employer had forgotten the weapon hanging there. One look at his face was all she needed to realize that his only thought at the moment was to slake the lust that had him in its grip.

"Get on that bed!" he growled, shoving her so hard that she fell face forward onto the mattress.

Then he was on her, tearing at her nightgown, ripping the fabric away to expose the satin skin beneath. Amelia fought desperately, struggling mightily against his greater strength, but her efforts were puny against him. He turned her over easily, nudging her legs apart with his knee while he fumbled with the buttons on his breeches.

Although Amelia shuddered with fear, she realized she dared not give in to that emotion. Her only hope lay in holding that fear at bay, in using the wits that God had given her to escape the man who appeared bent on destroying her sanity.

Amelia flung her head from side to side, trying desperately to avoid the harsh lips that sought to claim hers. His breath was so tainted with the whiskey he'd consumed that it gagged her.

God, the man was so besotted that he should be incapacitated, but it was obvious he was not. His strength was that of a man gone mad. That knowledge only increased her fear.

Although Amelia was almost numb with fear, she continued to fight wildly, desperately. Her blood raced through her veins, her panic almost choking her. But she couldn't give in. She'd fight him as long as there was breath in her body.

Amelia's desperate gaze flickered to the gun belt hanging across the post again, then quickly returned. Although the six-gun was too far to reach, it was her only hope.

Grady laughed harshly, his mouth clamping over hers as she stretched her arm toward the weapon. His head hid the weapon from view, but she splayed her fingers, searching for the pistol as she continued to fight. His breath was gagging her, his tongue probing at the corners of her mouth. She gripped his hair and yanked hard.

"Damn you!" he howled, slapping her across the face with so much force that her ears rang.

Amelia ignored her tormentor, stretching out her arms again as she tried desperately to reach the six-gun that offered her hope. But it was too far. No matter how she stretched, she couldn't quite reach it.

Then, suddenly, fate took a hand in the shape of the very man who was bent on ravishing her. He slid his hands beneath her bared buttocks and shifted her slightly ... just mere inches, yet it was enough. As he probed at the apex of her thighs, her fingers closed over the pistol and she drew it swiftly toward her.

"Dammit, keep still!"

Grady Kincaid punctuated each word with a hard slap that almost knocked Amelia senseless.

Almost, but not quite.

With the weapon gripped firmly in her hand, she pointed it at her attacker. Her finger tightened on the trigger. A loud bang, split the silence of the night, and the acrid smell of burned gunpowder filled her nostrils.

As Amelia stared at her employer, Grady Kincaid's face took on a look of surprise. Then, his eyes glazing over, he slumped across the bed, pinning Amelia beneath the heavy weight of his body.

Chapter Three

Colt kept a silent vigil beneath the magnolia tree laden with fragrant blossoms, his eyes fixed unwaveringly on the lighted window.

He had been waiting for more than an hour, and his patience was beginning to wear thin, yet he realized he could do nothing except continue waiting there. He dared not enter the house until every occupant had retired for the night. He wanted to surprise Kincaid. He needed time alone with the man, and he was determined to have that time. He had come too far, searched for too long, to risk everything with his impatience.

In other circumstances Colter would have enjoyed the star-studded night. The moon rode high overhead, a huge yellow orb in the ebony sky that shed its pale light over the spacious lawns surrounding the mansion.

It was a beautiful estate Kincaid had acquired. It was too bad, Colt told himself, that the man wouldn't live long enough to enjoy it.

But perhaps the poor devil Kincaid had undoubtedly stolen it from could reclaim it.

Probably not, though. Some other equally evil man would probably wind up owning the estate when all was said and done.

Colt shifted slightly, trying to relax his body. All around him was silence, but it was an uneasy silence. Even the crickets, usually heard chirping from beneath the crepe myrtle and jasmine bushes, were silent tonight.

Suddenly a shot rang out. It split the silence with a resounding bang that seemed to shake the mansion with its intensity. Then, amazing though it seemed, the silence became absolute again.

Colter swore softly, his gaze flickering from one window to another as he waited for lights to come on and for the sounds of an aroused household. But there was nothing to be heard. And even more amazing, no more lamps were lighted. Only that one window remained aglow, shining as though it were a beacon lighting the way for a traveler as he made his weary way home.

Colt knew he had not imagined the sound. He was certain a weapon had been discharged somewhere in the large mansion. And he could not contain his anxiety for that fact, could not remain idle when every instinct told him that somehow his one link to the raiders he'd been searching for so long had suddenly been lost.

Bolting from his place of concealment, Colt moved quickly across the yard to the side entrance of the house. As he'd suspected, the door was locked, but that posed no problem to a man as determined as himself.

Colter shrugged out of his jacket and wrapped his six-gun in the heavy cloth, smashing it against the window. The jacket covered the sound of glass breaking, and it was only a matter of moments before he entered the mansion.

As Colt stopped inside the room and waited for his eyes

to adjust to the greater darkness, a grating sound froze him in his tracks.

Colter waited for a long moment, standing with his head cocked, listening to the silence, and knowing he couldn't afford to be caught unawares for even one moment.

Then the noise came again, grating harshly, and Colt breathed a relieved sigh as he recognized the sound for what it was: a branch of the magnolia tree outside grating against the eaves of the house.

Satisfied that no one was aware of his entry, he crept farther into the room, the thick carpet absorbing the sound of his footsteps.

Upon reaching the stairway, Colt climbed stealthily to the second floor. There was enough moonlight streaming through the window at the end of the hallway for him to see that the doors along the passage were all closed. And beneath one door there was a thin sliver of light.

Was that where the shot had come from?

Colter paused before the door. He gripped the door-knob and slowly turned it. A careful push allowed him to see through the narrow slit into the room. The four-poster bed was directly in his line of view. And on the bed a couple lay entwined, engaged in the age-old ritual of mating.

His lips curled slightly. It seemed obvious that there was no trouble inside that room.

He was easing the door closed again when his nostrils suddenly twitched. Colter sniffed, then realized what he was smelling. Gunpowder.

He sniffed again. Yes, there was no mistake. He d smelled burned gunpowder enough to identify it. He'd been wrong, he realized. There *was* something amiss in that room. Someone had just fired a weapon.

A muffled sound came from the bed . . . almost a groan. That was not unusual in the circumstances, but there was something else . . . a peculiar urgency, as though someone were in distress.

A cold chill crept over Colter, like spiders dancing along his spine, as he remembered the nature of the man he'd come to find.

Pushing the door wider, Colter entered the room, his long strides carrying him swiftly to the bed. The woman who lay there was obviously struggling to free herself from the man who was motionless atop her. And it was more than obvious that the man was too heavy for her to shove aside. She was well and truly pinned beneath him.

Colter strode quickly across the room and leaned over the bed, making his presence known. The woman gasped, her vivid blue eyes widening with horror. Then just as swiftly, her emotions changed. Sudden relief warred with rising anger.

"Well, don't just stand there!" she snapped. "Help me move him!"

Although Colt was surprised that a woman in her position would even considering voicing a demand, he lifted the man and shoved him casually aside. It was then he saw the blood. His eyes fixed on the woman who was bent on covering herself with the patchwork quilt. She waited until her breasts and thighs were decently covered, then shoved herself upright and met his eyes.

"I suppose I should thank you." She appeared embarrassed by her situation.

She was an exotic-looking creature, small boned, and not more than five feet, two inches tall. Her brilliant blue eyes were framed by dark lashes and brows, and her mouth was full, sensuous. Perhaps, though, her lips gave that appearance because they were swollen at the moment.

Damn the man who treated her so roughly! Colter was surprised at the fury that surged through him, but the woman was so fragile in appearance. Her pale face, scattered with freckles, was a striking contrast to the reddish-gold color of her hair. It was tousled, probably from the rough handling, and curled around her shoulders in a thick, silken mass.

"I take it you weren't a willing participant," he said mildly.

"I most certainly was not!" she snapped, her eyes brilliant with anger and, if he wasn't mistaken, unshed tears. "The damned beast attacked me."

"Then he deserved to die," Colter said mildly. "Who was he anyway?" Even as he asked the question, Colt was afraid he already knew.

"My employer," she muttered, her gaze flickering to the dead man, then quickly away again. "His name is . . . was . . . Grady Kincaid."

Colter's body tensed. His lips flattened and a muscle twitched in his jaw. "I was afraid of that."

Her gaze became fixed on his, and her fingers tightened on the quilt. "What are you going to do?"

"Do? Not a damn thing. It appears to me you've already done what I came to do . . . with one exception"

"I don't know what you mean. But if you're not going to turn me over to the law, then get out of my way. I have to leave here before somebody works up enough courage to investigate that shot."

"You can't be held responsible for shooting the man," he said. "It's obvious what he had in mind. All you have to do is explain to the authorities—"

Her expression was cold, as were her eyes. "Those people are his friends. My life would be forfeit if I left it in their hands."

"But surely the law—"

"Don't you understand?" she asked, trying desperately to control her panic. "Grady Kincaid was a big man around these parts. He managed to buy me even though slavery has been outlawed.''

Colt's brows drew together in a dark frown. "He bought you?" Perhaps he'd been wrong about her. But she didn't look like a woman of easy virtue. "Where will you go?"

"I don't know. But I can't go home. According to him"—she nodded at the dead man—"my pa sold me so he could keep the farm."

"Sold you!" A curious relief flowed through him as he realized he'd misunderstood her words. "No man—not even a parent—has the right to sell another human being. It's more'n likely Kincaid was lying to you."

"I would like to think so. But it's a fact that we were on the verge of losing the farm until Mr. Kincaid offered me a job. And now Pa appears to be buying up livestock and hiring on hands, when before he couldn't even afford to keep food on the table."

"Be that as it may, Kincaid's dead now. Whatever devil's bargain they made is over. You should be safe enough at home."

Her lips tightened. "A man who'd sell his daughter for money wouldn't hesitate to turn her in for more."

"You think there'll be a reward offered?"

She threw him a hard look. "You can bet on it. Kincaid has family that won't take his death lightly. They'll be looking for me."

His gaze narrowed. "They might be at that," he said gruffly. "I suppose you'd better find yourself another place to go."

"There won't be a safe place in all of Louisiana," she replied grimly. "If I stay here, then someone—either his family or the law—will find me."

"Then I imagine you'd better leave the state."

"And go where?"

A plan was already forming in Colter's mind. If he

couldn't find the Kincaids, perhaps he could make them come to him.

His gaze lingered on Amelia. Yes, perhaps that might be necessary. And if he was to set a trap for a coyote, then he would need bait.

Colter realized he could be putting the woman in jeopardy, but he consoled himself with the fact that he could take care of her. Anyway, the Kincaid bunch might not come after her.

Then again, he thought with a smile, they might decide to do that very thing.

But he couldn't rely on them coming. So he'd best search the house while there was time . . . if there was time.

Why in hell hadn't someone come to investigate the shot? Surely the woman had made some noise when she was fighting her employer.

Knowing he didn't have time to work it out in his mind, Colter crossed the room quickly and yanked out a bureau drawer, searching through the articles he found there for something that would provide a lead to the other Kincaid brothers.

Amelia, realizing she had been dismissed, gripped the quilt tightly around her body and left the stranger to do whatever pleased him most. Then she hurried down the hallway to her own room.

She discarded the quilt and donned a riding skirt and blouse. Amelia knew that she'd already wasted enough time, that she needed to get away, to leave this house as quickly as possible . . . before Grady Kincaid's body was discovered. He was a powerful man around New Orleans, and to remain nearby would surely prove to be disastrous, perhaps even fatal.

Amelia made short work of gathering her things together. She didn't have many possessions, which made it easy to put everything into her reticule.

When she finished packing, she shoved her employer's pistol in with her clothing. Then, hurrying as quickly as she dared, she descended the stairway and headed for the front door.

With escape only a few steps away, she was finally able to utter a sigh of relief.

But it was a moment too soon, she realized, when the intruder stepped from the library, shoving some papers into his vest.

"You'd better come along with me," he said, reaching for her carpetbag. "Give me that. It's too heavy for you to carry."

"Do you have a horse?" she asked.

At his nod, she handed over the satchel.

Amelia spared little thought for the man to whom she was entrusting her life. Every move she made was designed to put as much distance as possible between herself and her dead employer.

The rest could be worked out later.

She left the house, pausing momentarily to breathe in the fresh night air. Then, remembering her circumstances, she loped across the wide lawn, hoping she had made her escape without anyone being aware of it.

Chapter Four

The big Appaloosa nickered softly in welcome as Colter approached the stallion's place of concealment.

Having had no idea how long he would have to wait for the household to retire, Colter had left his mount ground-reined beside a pond where there would be both water and grass.

Amelia had been following so closely on Colter's heels that she'd remained unseen by the big horse, but suddenly the stallion caught her scent and threw up his head, tossing his mane as his eyes rolled wildly. The Appaloosa's muscles quivered as he tried to determine the newcomer's status, whether she be friend or foe.

"Easy, boy," Colter soothed. "Everything's just fine." He smoothed his hand over the long, quivering neck, his voice low, soft. "Reach out your hand toward him," he told Amelia. "But do it slow. Don't make any sudden moves."

It took a moment for Amelia to realize that Colter was

speaking to her instead of the stallion, and when she realized it, she was slow to react.

"That's right," he murmured. "No sudden moves. Thunder's been a bit skittish the past few weeks . . . ever since some idiot tried to steal him."

"He's awful big." Amelia kept her voice low so she wouldn't startle the stallion, which was studying her hand as though it might be something good to eat. "Maybe we should take one of the horses from the stable. There's plenty there to choose from."

"No. Too risky," he replied. "Too many folks around these parts might recognize Kincaid's horseflesh. Thunder has enough strength to carry the both of us without too much effort. And later, after we've put some miles behind us, we can see about picking up another mount."

Without another word Colter stepped into the saddle, making it appear as easy as mounting a step. "Come on," he said, reaching a hand down to her.

Amelia hesitated momentarily, wondering if she was doing the right thing by going with him. She threw back her head so she could study his shadowed features, but there was nothing to be learned from his expression.

She had no way of knowing if he could be trusted.

Wondering if she was being too hasty in accepting his help, Amelia turned to look back at the house, and saw the lighted window where she'd left the man she'd killed only moments ago.

Amelia realized then that she really had no choice. She must accept his help. Yet still, she was reluctant to do so. "I—I don't even know your name," she whispered.

He waited patiently, his arm extended, his palm outward, ready to give her a hand up. "Does it really matter?" he asked evenly.

Amelia sighed softly. She had no choice but to trust him.

"I guess not," she muttered. "Not in the long run. But what do I call you?"

"Colt."

Colt. Like the weapon. Strong, sturdy. It suited him. And it was the deciding factor. A man with a name like Colt would surely be a good protector if the Kincaid bunch decided to come after her.

Amelia reached out, gripping the hand he offered, and allowed herself to be pulled atop the horse. As she settled behind the saddle she took note of the stallion's wide back. It was wide enough to make her feel comfortable. At least for a while.

"Where are we going?" she asked.

"West," he replied.

West. She grimaced. She supposed that would have to do, since she had nowhere else to go. But did he have to be so terse in his answers?

He gave no indication of their destination, or what was going to happen once they got there. But surely, she told herself, what lay ahead could not be any worse than what lay behind.

"Hang on," he grunted.

Amelia tightened her grip around his middle. A good thing too, she realized, because a moment later they were galloping away from the mansion with a speed that lightened the weight that had settled in her chest since she'd watched Grady Kincaid's eyes glaze over and realized she'd shot him dead.

The stallion was strong and his legs swift, and as the hours passed and the miles behind them increased with no sign of pursuit, Amelia began to relax.

But she had plenty of time to think now, to consider her circumstances, and she began to wonder again if the man she rode with was completely trustworthy.

Amelia had yet to learn why he'd been in her employer's

house at that time. Who was he anyway? And why had he come in the dead of night? And more to the point, had she been foolish to leave with him? He was a stranger, one who might be even more cruel than the man she had murdered.

Murdered! Oh, Lord, she was a murderess. How could she possibly live with that knowledge?

Even as that thought occurred, Amelia quickly dismissed it, knowing she could live more easily with what she'd done than with the rape she would have suffered if her employer had accomplished what he'd set out to do. As her mind absorbed that fact, Amelia's guilt was swept away, as though it had never been. Grady Kincaid had been an evil man. And he had deserved to die.

Amelia put thoughts of Kincaid from her mind, becoming suddenly aware of the wind that whistled around her. The air had become colder. The wind stung her face like a nest of angry wasps. It seemed only natural to take refuge in the broad back that rose before her.

She marveled at the width of Colt's shoulders. They were wide enough to provide a windbreak if she snuggled close against him, and she quickly took advantage of that opportunity.

Where was he taking her? she wondered. He had told her they were going west. But that one word, west, covered a lot of territory. For all she knew, they might be headed for California.

Which might not be such a bad idea. It would most definitely put her out of reach of the law.

Why was he helping her?

After what she'd been through, Amelia couldn't help but be suspicious of his motives. Her mind imagined all sorts of things, some too horrible to contemplate, but that same imagination had her sitting up straighter, trying to put some distance between them. It was an impossible task, though, since she had to keep her arms wrapped around him in order to stay atop his horse.

Although she told herself he was a good man, she couldn't stop worrying about him. She could very well have jumped out of the frying pan into the fire. But if his intentions were evil, then he would find it hard going. She was not a squeamish miss. Had she been, she would still be at the mansion, her spirit broken, her body ravished, more than likely bruised, damaged. Instead, she had survived the attack, had slain the man who'd meant to use her so savagely.

And she could do it again if need be. Her eyes glittered at that thought. She *could* take care of herself! It wasn't necessary to depend on some man she knew nothing about.

Her mouth tightened and she squared her shoulders, all outward signs that she'd reached a decision. She would rid herself of the stranger who called himself Colt at the first opportunity.

He had not even asked her if she wanted to come with him, had just expected her to do so. Why? Why hadn't he just ridden out and forgotten he'd ever seen her? He'd been searching Kincaid's study when she went downstairs. What did he find there? There'd been something, she knew, because she'd seen him shove some papers into his pocket.

Amelia determined to keep on guard, to keep a wary eye on him, and if he even looked cross-eyed at her, she'd be ready for him. She'd be damned if she'd allow herself to be taken unawares again. She still had her late employer's pistol and enough gumption to kill a man, and she wouldn't hesitate to do so if the situation warranted it.

Hadn't she already proved that?

Oh, God, what kind of woman was she? She had actually murdered one man and was already considering shooting another.

Never mind that Kincaid had deserved it. She had shot him dead with his own pistol. The pistol that was in her satchel now. And when his body was discovered, the law would surely be on her trail.

A wanted woman. That was what she was. The constable would surely form a posse and they'd come after her. At that thought, Amelia was suddenly glad that she wasn't alone.

Her arms tightened around Colt's waist, and she pressed her face harder against his wide back, hiding her head in shame. What would her mother think of her now, if she had lived to see her daughter branded a murderess?

Colter felt the woman's arms tighten around his waist, and he frowned as his lower body stirred in response. Dammit! That was all he needed . . . to lust after the woman riding behind him. If only she wouldn't hold on so tight.

But even as that thought occurred, Colt realized he would not ask her to loosen her hold. Not when it felt so damned good. Her soft breasts were pressed tightly against him, and the gait of the stallion caused them to rub against his back. He could feel her taut nipples even through the thickness of his shirt.

It wasn't only her breasts that were driving him crazy. Her hands were doing a good job of it too. Locked together as they were around his hips, he couldn't help thinking that if she moved them just a little bit lower she would realize from his tight breeches the state he was in.

He gritted his teeth in frustration and tried to block the image that rose in his mind. But he kept seeing her on that damn bed, lying there with so much creamy skin exposed, her glorious hair spread out around her, mouth swollen as though it were begging to be kissed.

But she had already been kissed, he reminded himself. Viciously. By Grady Kincaid.

My God, how could he even imagine kissing her, after what she'd been through? She had barely escaped being violated.

Damnation! How could he entertain such thoughts? He was lower than Grady Kincaid. Lower than a snake's belly in a wagon rut for what he'd been imagining.

Feeling a real need to put some distance between himself and the woman who clung so tightly to his hips, Colter decided it was past time to rest the Appaloosa. And the stream up ahead looked to be a good place to do just that.

Amelia was surprised when Colt pulled his mount up beside the shallow stream. It couldn't have been more than an hour since he'd last allowed the horse to drink at a water crossing.

Leaning back slightly so he could dismount without her getting in the way, she waited to see what was expected of her.

"We'll stop here for a few minutes," he said gruffly. "Thunder needs to rest." He reached up and curled an arm around her waist, pulling her to the ground.

To Amelia's complete dismay, her legs immediately crumpled beneath her. She would have fallen if he hadn't realized her need and helped her to a fallen log. She sat there shivering while he paced back and forth beside the stream, his head down, his eyes narrowed on the rocky ground.

As tightly strung as she was, Amelia found the silence unnerving. She cleared her throat. "What are you looking for?"

"Tracks."

Her gaze narrowed on the moonlit ground. Could he

really see tracks in that shadowy darkness? "Oh." She
frowned. "Why?"

He threw her a quick glance, then went back to studying
the ground again. "There's a good possibility we're being
followed."

"Followed? By whom? A posse?" Icy fingers crept down
Amelia's spine. "Wouldn't they be somewhere behind us?"

"Maybe. Maybe not." He felt like a fool and wondered
if she'd know it was next to impossible to find any sign on
a bed of rocks.

He hoped that, like most women, she would know nothing about tracking. But even if she did know, he would
continue his bluff. At least for a while, because he refused
to ride with her again until he was able to work off some
of the tension that gripped him.

Amelia watched him pace for a while, his gaze continually on the ground. Then, "Is Colt really your name?" she
asked abruptly.

His head jerked up and he stared at her with a puzzled
expression. "Yes. Why?"

"No reason. Except it's unusual."

"It's really Colter. A family name, handed down through
the years."

"Colter what?"

"Morgan."

"Colter Morgan." She tested the name on her tongue.
"Unusual, but I like it."

He grunted but otherwise remained silent. But not for
long. And when he spoke, she realized he was as curious
as she was. "You haven't told me your name."

"You never asked for it."

His lips quirked slightly. "Then consider yourself asked
now."

"My name is Amelia."

"Just Amelia?"

The edges of her lips curled in a smile. "No," she replied. "It's not just Amelia. Like you, I have a last name. It's Spencer. Amelia Spencer."

His lips twitched again as though he were going to laugh. But his mouth quickly straightened again. "Well, Amelia Spencer," he drawled. "It's past time we were on our way."

Although the smile had gone as quickly as it had come, that mere twitching of his lips, that almost smile, reassured Amelia about the nature of the man.

There'd been a time, she guessed, when a smile had been second nature to him. But something had changed him, made him hard, angry. Still, she found herself trusting him, and she decided to try to get some answers to the questions plaguing her.

"Where are we really going, Colt?"

"Texas eventually," he said gruffly. "But right now I'm just trying to put some distance between us and the law. Or the rest of the Kincaid clan, should they decide to come after us."

Remembering why they were running from the law, Amelia rose quickly from the log. "You're right. We'd better concentrate on putting some more miles between us and New Orleans."

They mounted again and rode on, and even though the brief stop had helped to relieve Colt's tension, it wasn't long before Amelia's hair, playing against his neck like silken fingers, conjured up images of the way she'd looked when he'd first seen her. And within moments, he was in the same condition he'd been in before they stopped at the stream. Realizing he could do nothing but endure, Colt gritted his teeth and rode on.

As the long night wore on, storm clouds began to gather and there was a smell of rain in the cool night air. When thunder rumbled overhead, Colt decided it would be better to seek shelter and rest his mount.

Searching for a place where they could rest unseen, Colt's sweeping gaze narrowed on the cliffs ahead which rose sharply above the tops of the trees.

During his journey to New Orleans, Colter had followed the stream to those cliffs, where he'd rested and admired the rock formations he found there. He'd seen several cliff overhangs that would serve as shelter from the rain—a place where they would not be seen by travelers on the road.

He reined his mount in that direction and moments later stopped beside one of the cliff overhangs that was hidden from view by a thick growth of willows.

"We'll rest here," Colter said, dismounting and working at the straps that tied his bedroll to his saddle. "You'd better get some sleep while you can."

Amelia eyed the bedroll uneasily. "What about you?" she asked huskily.

His gaze was penetrating . . . knowing. "The duster will suit me well enough." His voice was gruff, almost harsh. "You can rest easy, ma'am. I'm too tired to do anything but sleep."

A lie, he knew, but it appeared to set her mind at ease.

Amelia wasted no time in crawling into the bedroll. She was dead tired, too weary to fight off another man now, even if he had been so inclined. But so far Colter Morgan had been a perfect gentleman. He had given her no reason to believe he would harm her.

Holding that thought to her breast, Amelia uttered a weary sigh, then closed her eyes. A moment later she was fast asleep.

Colter felt the first drops of rain as he hobbled the stallion nearby where several large oak trees would provide some shelter from the coming storm. He hurried back toward their camp as it began to rain in earnest. Water was coming down so hard he had to search a moment before he found the willows that hid the overhang. He parted the branches that concealed Amelia's resting place and found her curled up in the bedroll.

It took only a moment to determine that she was sleeping. He stood over her then, his gaze taking in the pale shadows beneath her eyes.

Amelia. He tested the name. It was too sophisticated for the woman who slept on the hard rock floor of the cavern, her silken hair spread around her in disarray.

Despite the ordeal she had suffered, there was a look of complete innocence about her. She seemed almost childlike, with her thick, dark lashes creating a half-moon against her pale, freckled cheeks, her hand clutching the covers beneath her dainty chin.

"Amelia." He muttered her name. "Amy. Yes. That suits you more."

She murmured in her sleep, as though aware of his eyes upon her. Was she feeling threatened by him? Lord, he hoped not. As he continued to watch her, she sighed deeply, her bosom rising with the breath, then falling again. Rising and falling. His body was quick to react, and he made himself look away.

Her appearance could be deceiving. She might not be the innocent she appeared. But whatever she was, Colter would not dishonor himself by touching her. No matter how much he desired her. With a weary sigh, he stretched out on the cavern floor a short distance away and pulled his long duster around his wide shoulders. The duster would keep him warm enough; it had done so many times in the past.

Closing his eyes, Colt courted sleep. But it wouldn't come so easily. He was bone weary, having gone without sleep for the past two nights in his hurry to reach New Orleans. His eyes felt as though they were filled with West Texas sand.

Colter knew how badly he needed to rest and, with the rain coming down in sheets, doubted that anyone would discover them hidden behind the willows. He told himself to relax; willed himself to do so.

He felt the tension draining away, felt his muscles relax, and sighed deeply. And only moments later, like Amelia he was fast asleep.

Amelia woke with a cry of fear on her lips. Clutching the blanket around her, she stared up at the rock ceiling as sweat dried on her body.

Where was she anyway?

Then she remembered. The dream she'd had wasn't a nightmare. It had really happened. Her employer, Grady Kincaid, had attacked her and she had killed him, then fled with the stranger who had come in the night.

Colter Morgan.

They had ridden most of the night, seeking shelter only when it looked like rain.

She rolled to her side and peered through the willows. Although they were wet, the rain appeared to have passed. Her gaze returned to the shelter, narrowing on the man who'd helped her leave New Orleans.

Colt.

His length was stretched out a few feet away, covered by the black duster that had been tied to his saddle. He was asleep. He was not the source of her unease. Yet Amelia knew there had been something . . . some sound, perhaps, that had disturbed her.

Suddenly she felt it . . . a subtle trembling of the ground beneath her.

Horses coming.

Making sure their shelter was hidden from view, Amelia hurried to where Thunder was hobbled. The stallion tossed his head and rolled his eyes, but made no sound as she approached. Whispering softly to the Appaloosa, she covered his nose to silence him.

The hoofbeats were louder now. They clattered over rock, thudded against hard ground . . . closing the distance between them and the stream where Amelia waited so quietly, hidden within the bushes.

She prayed the riders would ride on by without pause. But to her dismay, her prayer went unanswered. They stopped nearby to water their mounts.

As the horses drank their fill, one of the men, a heavyset individual, spoke to his companion. "My backside's getting mighty sore, Shorty. How far do you reckon it is to New Orleans from here?"

"Ten or fifteen miles would be my guess," the man called Shorty replied.

"Whereabouts is Grady's place?"

Grady? Horror swept over Amelia. Were they looking for Grady Kincaid?

Surely it was only a coincidence. There must be several men in New Orleans who were called Grady. After all, it was not an uncommon name.

"Hell, Clem!" Shorty exclaimed. "You know as much about it as I do. I already told you what Rusty said. Grady Kincaid lives in a mansion somewhere around New Orleans. And word is out that he needs some gun hands for a little job he has in mind."

One of the other riders, a scrawny, unwashed individual with dirt-colored hair, guffawed. "I heard all about that little job, Clem. And it ain't so little, to my way of thinking."

"What do you mean, Beau?"

"Way I hear it," Beau growled, "Grady Kincaid is aiming to get even bigger than he already is. He's looking to get himself elected mayor."

"New Orleans don't already have a mayor?"

Beau grinned and spat a long stream of tobacco toward the ground. "They got one. But I hear he don't have much longer to live."

"What's wrong with him?

"Nothing yet," Beau replied with a harsh laugh. "But 'spect there will be real soon. And I 'spect that some fellas might just take exception to the way he dies. And that's where we come in."

Clem looked troubled as he absorbed the news. "Sounds like Grady's just like the other Kincaids, and they're real sons of bitches ain't they?"

"Better not let any one of those Kincaids hear you say that," Beau advised. "I hear it ain't healthy to bad-mouth them folks."

"Sounds like it ain't real healthy to be around 'em neither," Clem replied.

"No. But we wouldn't stay healthy running away from 'em," his companion said. "I heard the whole bunch of 'em hold a long grudge."

"I heard something like that too." Clem spat another stream of tobacco. "Guess we're damned if we do and damned if we don't."

He appeared to be contemplating his words when a big, burly fellow sitting astride a large dun waved an arm at them. "Come on, boys! Let's ride!"

Amelia watched them ride away, then retraced her steps as quickly as she could. She knew she had to wake Colt. He needed to know what she'd overheard. Because it appeared they might have more than a posse to worry about.

Chapter Five

Deep anxiety had turned to extreme fear by the time Amelia pushed her way through the thick growth of willows that hid the cliff overhang. She stopped abruptly then, her gaze directed on Colt, who appeared to be immersed in a dreamless sleep.

Amelia felt a curious resentment that he could be so at peace when their situation was so desperate. But of course, she reminded herself, it wasn't his life that would be forfeit if they were caught.

Realizing in her mind that she was being unfair to the man who'd done everything he could to help her, Amelia silently chastised herself for having such uncharitable thoughts.

Amelia's fear of being caught and left to dangle at the end of a hangman's rope quickened her steps as she hurried toward the man who was proving to be her only hope of escape.

She leaned over the sleeping man and gripped his shoulder, intent on shaking him awake.

But there was no need. The moment she touched him, Colt's eyes flew open and he grabbed her upper arms, twisting at the same moment in such a way that Amelia suddenly found herself trapped beneath his thickly muscled body.

The fear that she'd been trying so hard to control suddenly erupted and Amelia uttered a sharp cry, striking out with both fists as she struggled desperately to free herself.

Muttering curses beneath his breath, Colter jerked his head aside to avoid her blows, his grip tightening for better control. "Be still, woman," he growled. "I'm not going to hurt you."

Instead of calming her, the sound of his harsh voice made Amelia feel even more desperate to escape his hold. "No! No!" she cried, smashing her fist against his face. "Let me go! Please, let me go!"

In some distant corner of her mind, Amelia was ashamed of her cowardice, yet she was unable to control it. She squeezed her eyes shut tight, flinging her head from side to side as she tried to shut out the sight of the man who continued to hold her captive.

Her breath came in short gasps, literally torn from her chest by her furiously beating heart, yet barely escaping around the huge knot of terror that had lodged in her throat.

Squirming desperately beneath him, Amelia kicked and bucked, like a wild horse trying to dislodge a rider, as she tried desperately to escape from the man whose intentions were so apparent to her fear-clouded brain.

She had to escape! Had to!

But no matter how she struggled, he continued to hold her captive. He held her . . . held her . . . just held her.

Suddenly that fact worked its way to her conscious mind

and she realized it was true. Colt wasn't retaliating in any way. He was merely trying to avoid her blows as he continued to hold her in place.

As her mind digested that fact, Amelia sucked in a calming breath and opened her eyes to a mere crack, staring cautiously up at him. Her heart continued to pound rapidly, like that of a rabbit when it lay trapped in the talons of an eagle.

"What in hell happened?" Colter growled, his dark gaze narrowed on hers.

"I—I—" Her voice quivered with remembered fear. "W-would you g-get off me, please?"

As though he'd merely been waiting for those words, Colter immediately rolled aside. He remained motionless then, watching her intently as she scrambled quickly away to huddle near the back of the cavern.

Although Amelia silently cursed herself for being so cowardly, fear continued to hold her in its grip. It might help if he would stop watching her with that narrowed gaze that, she imagined, penetrated to her very soul.

But that wasn't likely, she realized. It was more than that. He required some answers to the questions she'd raised in his mind.

"Out with it," he said gruffly. "What happened to set you off like that?"

"I—I . . ." She swallowed around the knot in her throat and tried again. "You were holding me so tight and I—I c-couldn't get loose. It-it was l-like before when Grady Kincaid . . ."

He swore softly. "I'm sorry, Amelia. I didn't think. I heard you coming in my sleep and just reacted when you touched me."

"I'm s-sorry," she whispered, her blue eyes wide with remembered horror.

He brushed her cheek with the back of his palm and

she jerked away from him. "Stop that," he said gruffly. "I'm not going to hurt you."

She looked away quickly, unable to hold his gaze. "I know," she replied, trying hard to relax her tense muscles. "It was just reflex."

He sighed heavily. "Yeah. I suppose it will take a while for you to get over what happened." His brows were almost touching with the frown that had formed there. "I guess you had a good reason for waking me."

Amelia nodded. "I—I—Yes. There were horses and men and—"

His large frame tensed and he looked toward the willows. "Riders? Where?"

"On the road." Amelia expelled a deep, shuddering sigh. She could rely on Colt to keep them safe now. "They stopped to water their horses at the creek, talked among themselves, then went on their way."

"Hell!" Colter exclaimed. "I must've been tireder than I thought." He studied her pale face. "There's really no need to worry, Amy. There's bound to be travelers on the road now and then."

"They weren't ordinary travelers, Colt. I'm most certain of that. They were headed for New Orleans, for Grady Kincaid's place."

Something flickered in his dark eyes. "How do you know that?"

Amelia shrugged. "I was worried about the riders, afraid the stallion would alert them to our presence. So I went down there to keep him quiet and I watched them from the bushes when they stopped to water their horses. They were talking about Mr. Kincaid."

"You did what?" Colter exclaimed. "Dammit, woman! Don't you have any sense at all? You should have woke me the minute you heard them." He rolled his eyes. "Lord save me from a nosy woman!"

Amelia took exception to his words, but before she could form a reprimand, he spoke again.

"You might as well tell me everything that was said."

She did, and he cursed again, rising quickly to his feet. "We'd better make tracks while we can."

Amelia was in complete agreement. "We could make better time if we had another horse."

"I agree," he replied. "And we'll get one just as soon as we reach Donaldsonville."

"Donaldsonville?" Amelia frowned. "But that's on the river. Won't they look there for us first, thinking we might have taken a boat out of New Orleans?"

"Probably. But we need another horse and there's no other place to get one. We'll just have to keep a watchful eye out while we're there, and maybe if we stay away from the docks, nobody will notice us."

She controlled a shudder at the thought of her employer. "Grady Kincaid has powerful friends in this state," she muttered. "It won't be safe for me anywhere in Louisiana."

"You're probably right," he agreed. "But we won't be staying here."

"You said we were going to Texas. Do you have any particular place in mind?"

"Yeah. We're going to Morgan's Creek."

"Morgan's Creek?" The name had a pleasant sound. "Where is that?"

"Smack dab in the middle of Texas." He grinned. "That's the hill country."

"The hill country," she repeated. "Will it take long to get there?"

"Too long to suit me." Her wide-eyed innocence might prove to be his undoing before they parted ways if he wasn't careful. He had to get her settled somewhere soon so he could go on about his business.

"You roll up the bedding," he ordered abruptly, "while I fetch the stallion."

Then without another word he pushed the willows aside and strode quickly away from the woman who was proving to be more trouble than he'd ever imagined she could.

Colt knew he'd have to watch himself closely. Amelia's emotions were more fragile than he'd expected. She'd done so well during the long, hard ride that he'd been taken completely by surprise at her show of fear. He'd thought for a while there that she'd completely lost her mind.

Damn Grady Kincaid to hell!

Colter hoped the man would endure the flames of eternity for what he'd done. To her. To his mother and sweet little Annie. And to how many others like them? Defenseless women and children who were unable to fight against the man's superior strength.

He couldn't help the others, Colt knew, but he could damned well help Amelia. First, though, he had to get her across the Sabine River. And he had to do it fast. Louisiana law had no jurisdiction in Texas.

His long strides carried him swiftly to the place where he'd left his mount. As he approached, the Appaloosa tossed his head and pawed at the ground.

"Yeah, I know," Colt muttered. "You're rested and eager for a run." He stroked the stallion's long neck, then reached for the saddle he'd dropped nearby. "Let's just hope we don't pick up a posse while you're carrying double. I don't think you'd particularly like that."

It was only a matter of moments before the stallion was saddled and Colt was reining the Appaloosa toward the cliff overhang. Halfway there they met Amelia, the bedroll slung over one shoulder. And moments later they resumed their journey.

Although the sky had cleared, they were headed in the

same direction as the rain clouds that had already passed over them.

Colt narrowed his eyes on the dark clouds that loomed in the distance. There was a good chance they'd have to seek shelter again. And the thought of being enclosed in some hidden spot with Amelia again had his body hardening and his pulse racing. He was both relieved and disappointed when the road suddenly curved and he realized the storm clouds were moving away.

As the hours passed, Colt's empty stomach made a loud protesting groan. He wondered if Amelia was feeling a need for food too. She never mentioned hunger when they stopped to rest the Appaloosa, nor did she utter any other word of complaint.

During the long hours of that day, Colt found many traits in Amelia to admire. She was a woman of rare courage, he realized. The kind of woman that many men would seek for a wife. If his own circumstances were different, he might be so inclined himself.

But they were not, Colt quickly reminded himself. He had made a vow to get revenge for his family, and, no matter what happened, he would damned well keep it. Only then would he feel free to live his own life.

It was almost dusk when they reached the outskirts of Donaldsonville, and as they passed a small farm where several horses were corralled, Colt reined in his mount and headed up the rough track leading to the house.

Amelia looked around his shoulder. "Are we stopping here?" she asked wearily.

"Yeah," Colt growled, without giving a reason.

He nudged the stallion toward the barn, where a large, gray-haired man wearing homespun was repairing a corral. The farmer looked up from his work as Colter urged the Appaloosa toward him.

"Howdy, strangers." The farmer's voice was as cordial

as his smile when he greeted them. "Get down off that horse and rest yourselves for a spell."

Colt stepped out of the saddle and reached up to help Amelia down. Then he turned to the farmer. "We could use a break," he said. "We're headed for the livery stable at Donaldsonville. Hoped we'd be able to buy a horse there. My wife, Amy"—he nodded toward Amelia—"well, her mount stepped in a gopher hole this morning and broke his leg. I had to shoot him, and she's getting mighty crotchety having to ride double with me."

Amelia barely controlled an outraged gasp. She glared at him. Crotchety, was she? And wife too! My God, the man lied with such ease it must be second nature to him.

The farmer nodded sagely, a smile pulling at the corners of his mouth as his gaze swept over Amelia's flushed face. "Wives can be like that," he sympathized, offering his hand. "Jed Crandal."

"I'm Colter Morgan." Colt slid an arm around Amelia's shoulder and moved his hand in a gentle caress. "And this is my wife, Amy."

Wife.

There it was again.

What was Colter Morgan up to anyway? Whatever it was, Amelia thought, throwing him a heated glance, she supposed she would have to go along with it. She certainly couldn't brand him a liar before this good farmer.

A grim smile tightened her lips. Colt had called her crotchety, but he hadn't seen crotchety yet. He definitely would, though, the moment they were alone.

Feeling the weight of his arm around her shoulders, she stepped back out of his reach.

"Couldn't help but notice that you got some mighty fine horseflesh over yonder," Colt commented. "Don't suppose you'd be willing to part with that bay."

"Might," the farmer agreed. "If the price happened to be right." He looked at Amelia. "You go on and rest yourself in the house, ma'am, whilst me and your husband do a little dickering here. My wife, Sadie, has got some vittles going on the stove. Should be about ready to put on the table. We'd take it right kindly if the two of you would stay and sup with us."

Amelia's stomach growled at the mention of food. She met Colt's eyes and he gave a quick nod, a wry smile curling the corners of his mouth. She turned toward the house just as a wiry-looking woman stepped through the door and watched Amelia approach.

The farmer's wife stuck out her hand. "Howdy," she said, pleasure lighting her work-worn features. "The name is Sadie Crandal."

"And I'm . . . uh . . ." Should she give her right name? Amelia realized that she could not, since Colt had introduced them as man and wife. She supposed he had a good reason for having done so. Perhaps it was to throw off anyone who might be on their trail. "My name is Amy Morgan."

"I'm mighty pleased to meet you, Amy." Sadie's smile was welcoming. "Go on in the house and set yourself down at the table. I was just coming out to holler at Jed." No sooner had the words left her mouth than she did exactly that. "Jed! Supper's on the table and gettin' cold. Bring that feller along with you."

The mouthwatering aromas drifting from the kitchen were absolutely wonderful, but Amelia hesitated. "I don't want to be any trouble."

"No trouble," Sadie insisted, tucking a wisp of gray hair into the knot at her nape. "There's plenty of vittles for all of us. Besides that, looks like rain. You folks had best wait it out here where you'll stay dry."

A quick glance at the sky told Amelia that Sadie was right.

The clouds had become even darker and were moving in fast. "Maybe we'd just better be on our way before the rain starts," she said.

The men were close enough to hear her, and Jed spoke up quickly. "Better to wait here, little lady, until the rain passes on by. Anyways, you can't leave now. Not when Sadie's got supper all ready and me and your man's got business to tend to afterwards."

"Colt?" She looked at him questioningly, expecting him to refuse, but instead he nodded abruptly.

"We've been on the trail a long time, Amy," he said. "And a woman in your condition needs more rest than you've been getting lately. Anyway, those victuals Jed's missus cooked up smell mighty good." He looked suddenly mournful. "I don't rightly see how I could walk out this door without even a sample."

Amelia and Sadie spoke at once.

"My condition?"

"Her condition! Does that mean . . ."

"Yep," Jed said gruffly. "You guessed it, woman. Amy's in the family way."

"Oh my goodness!" Sadie's face was flushed, her eyes glowing with sudden pleasure. "Why, you sit right down in that chair, honey. You should have told me." She shoved a speechless Amelia into the nearest chair and began to fill her plate with food. "Just think. A baby." Her gray eyes turned misty. "I remember when our first young'un was born. A girl it was. And we named her Martha May." She continued to pile food on Amelia's plate.

"Martha lives in Arizona Territory now," Jed said. "Went there after the war. Said she couldn't stand seeing what the carpetbaggers were doing to Louisiana."

Slapping the plate in front of Amelia, Sadie said, "Now you just go ahead and eat up, honey."

"Sadie," Amelia protested, staring at the overflowing plate. "I couldn't possibly eat all of this."

"Don't forget you're eating for two now," Jed growled. "You gotta eat plenty of good vittles to nourish that baby you're carrying."

Amelia muttered a quick thank you, then managed a dirty look toward Colt while the others weren't looking. What was wrong with him anyway? Why did he want them to believe she was pregnant?

A rumble outside interrupted her thoughts, and she looked through the window just as the rain began to fall. Soon it was coming down in torrents.

"There," Sadie said. "Isn't it lucky you stayed here? If you hadn't, you'd have been caught in the open and gotten soaked. That wouldn't be good for a woman in your condition."

"No, it wouldn't," agreed Jed, cramming a biscuit into his mouth. "You gotta watch her closer, Colt. Take good care of her during this time so's the little one will be healthy when it comes into the world. There's too many strikes already against a newborn without giving it another one when it could be avoided. Too many young'uns don't make it past the first month."

"Jed!" Sadie said sharply in quick reprimand. "You hush up now!" She turned to Amelia, who was quietly seething. "Don't you be fretting now, Amy. Nothing's gonna happen to your baby."

Amelia gritted her teeth and managed another hard look at Colt. When she saw Jed watching her, she forced her lips into a smile.

"Of course," she said sweetly. "And please don't worry about me. Colt takes such wonderful care of me." She threw him a look from beneath fringed lashes. "Don't you, sweetheart?"

He appeared startled, but quickly recovered. "I try." He

winked at her, then dug his spoon into the mound of mashed potatoes he'd heaped on his plate. "Yep, I sure do. I try my darnedest to look after her." A grin curled his mouth. "But it's mighty hard sometimes, because Amy has a temper. Something terrible to behold too. And sometimes . . . well, it's mighty hard to—"

"A temper!" Amelia set down her spoon and glared at him. "Colt Morgan! How dare you say that? I do not have a temper."

"Now, now, honey," he chided, obviously enjoying himself a great deal. "Don't get yourself all worked up again."

"Again?" Sadie frowned at her. "Amy," she said hesitantly, covering Amelia's hand with her own. "You know, honey, it ain't good for the baby if you let yourself get all worked up. I know it's hard during these times, but you gotta take things in stride, not let things bother you so much."

Amelia swallowed hard, clenching her hands into fists. She wanted to hit Colt, to wipe the smile off his face, but if she did, these good folks would think she'd lost her mind. "Could we just talk about something else, please?"

"Of course, honey." Colter seemed intent on stretching her control to the limits. He stroked her cheek with the back of his hand. "I surely don't want to see you upsetting yourself again."

She kicked him beneath the table and was rewarded by his suddenly pained expression. "I'm not upset," she gritted, barely controlling the urge to toss her coffee into his face.

"Of course you're not," he soothed. Then he turned to the farmer, who was beaming at them. "Now about that horse we were talking about, Jed. Is he gentle enough for a woman in her condition to ride?"

"Gentle as a lamb," Jed replied heartily. "And just as soon as the rain slacks off, we'll go out and put him through his paces."

But the rain didn't slack off, and when it became obvious that it would rain most of the night, they were invited to stay.

"We couldn't possibly impose," Amelia said, glaring at Colt.

"It won't be no imposition," Sadie said quickly. "In fact, I'd be mighty thankful for the company."

"But you don't have the room, Sadie," Amelia protested.

"Who says we don't?" Sadie was not to be dissuaded. "There's a perfectly good guest room in the back. It used to be Martha May's bedroom until she married. Now we just mostly use it when she comes to visit."

"But we really couldn't—"

"Of course we'll accept," interrupted Colt. "And we'll thank you kindly for the offer." He pulled his eyebrows into a worried frown. "I have to admit I've been concerned about Amelia traveling so far."

"Colt, it's not—"

"Now don't argue, honey."

When they were alone in the bedroom, she turned to glare at him. "How could you lie to such nice people?"

Colt gripped her shoulders hard and literally pushed her across the room, away from the door where they might be overheard. "Use your head, Amelia. It's because they were so nice that I lied. Just think what would have happened if we'd gone on to Donaldsonville. We would have been forced to stay in a hotel overnight, and it would have been easy to trace us there. But now, when we ride out of here, we can skip the town, and nobody will ever know we were along this way.''

His words made sense, Amelia knew. But she couldn't help but wonder how she was going to manage to spend the night alone with him. Completely alone . . . just the two of them in a bedroom where the quiet shadows of night made everything so intimate.

Chapter Six

It was a small room by any standards, and the four-poster bed took up most of the space. It stood there, slap-dab in the middle, shoved against a small window and flanked by a chest on one side and a dresser on the other.

Amelia's gaze measured the breadth and length of the feather mattress. It was big enough to hold two people comfortably. And it looked soft. It would be like sleeping on air.

As though reading her mind, Colt arched his back and stretched his arms over his head. "Oh, Lord," he groaned. "I'm so tired I could sleep for a month." He sat down on the feather mattress and tugged at his right boot.

Amelia raised an eyebrow. "You won't be sleeping on that bed," she said firmly.

He paused in the act of tossing the boot aside and frowned at her. "What?"

"I said you won't be sleeping on that bed, Colter Morgan."

"The hell you say!"

"I do." Her voice was prim as she stepped around him and tugged at the crazy quilt covering the bed. It wouldn't budge, since he was sitting on it. "Get off the bed, Colt. Right now."

He stared at her as though he thought she had taken leave of her senses. "What for?" he asked belligerently.

"So I can get this quilt off the bed," she said, tossing him a quick smile. "I'm not about to sleep there with you."

Colter shrugged. "Okay." He tugged his left boot off and tossed it toward the other one. "It's your choice."

Amelia felt her muscles relax. She'd been afraid he would put up a fuss, but apparently she'd been wrong. "Get off the bed," she repeated. "I need to get this quilt for you."

Colt rose to his full height and began to unbuckle his gun belt while Amelia removed the quilt and put it at the foot of the bed. There was only one pillow, but since she'd have the whole bed, it was only fair that she allow him the use of it.

As she started to toss it toward the foot of the bed, Colt snatched it out of her hand. "Whoa," he said. "That pillow is mine."

"No need to grab," she reprimanded. "I was going to give it to you."

Colt looked doubtful for a moment, then shrugged his massive shoulders, as though willing to accept her words as the truth.

Amelia pulled down the covers and smoothed her hands across the cool, starched sheets. Heavenly. A smile of pure pleasure spread across her face. She couldn't wait to stretch out on the bed.

Her fingers went to the buttons on her shirtwaist, then paused. "Would you put out the light, Colt?"

"Sure." He blew out the lamp, leaving the room in complete darkness.

Amelia worked swiftly, unfastening her shirtwaist and hanging it over a post, then quickly worked at her skirt. Other sounds nearby told her that Colt also was divesting himself of his clothing, but she paid little attention, intent on discarding her own and climbing into that inviting bed.

When she'd stripped down to her chemise and pantaloons, she climbed in. But she'd barely stretched out on that wonderful mattress when she felt the bed give on the other side.

"What are you doing?" She sat up and frowned into the darkness.

A sigh was her only answer, yet it was enough, accompanied as it was by a long, hairy leg moving along her bare flesh.

"Colt!" she hissed, clutching the covers to her breasts. "Get out of this bed!"

"What?" He sat up abruptly. "What the devil for, Amelia?"

"Because I'm in it."

There was a long pause, as though he were digesting her words; then he said, "I thought you didn't want to sleep with me."

"I don't."

"Then what are you doing in my bed?"

"It's my bed," she said furiously, trying to keep her voice low so that Sadie and her husband would not hear their conversation.

"How do you figure that?"

"Because . . . because . . . Dammit, Colt! I'm the woman here!"

A husky laugh sounded. "You damn sure are. But what's that got to do with anything?"

"I shouldn't have to sleep on the floor."

"Did I ask you to?"

"No," she admitted. "But . . ."

He sighed wearily. "Amelia. Go to sleep."

"Not in this bed with you."

"As I said before, you can sleep wherever the hell you want to. It makes no difference to me."

"I want to sleep in this bed."

"Then, dammit, woman!" he growled, "go to sleep. Just leave me alone!"

"You're no gentleman, Colter Morgan!"

"Never claimed I was."

Realizing that he had no intention of leaving the bed, Amelia flounced off the mattress and snatched up the quilt she'd left at the other end.

After wrapping herself in the quilt, she stretched out on the floor. The hard floor. It was like stretching out on rock. Even the bedroll had more padding.

Amelia tried to relax, but her muscles were knotted after the hard riding she'd done for the last two days. She turned on her right side, trying to get comfortable, but there was a sore spot there, so she turned on her left side. It was sore as well.

Darn it! Maybe the floor wouldn't feel quite so hard if she slept on her stomach. Amelia turned over again. She was still tossing and turning an hour later when she heard Colter begin to snore softly.

Damn him! she silently cursed. How could he do this? He'd told their hosts she was in a family way. What would they say if one of them entered the room and discovered her sleeping on the floor? And they might very well do that, too. If she and Colt overslept, one of the Crandals just might open the door in the morning and find her on the floor, and then they would surely know they'd been lied to. And Jed might be so angry that he would refuse to sell them a horse.

That thought had Amelia jerking upright. They couldn't take the risk. Too much depended on their acquiring a horse and getting away without leaving a trace of their having been there.

No. They most certainly could not take that risk. There was nothing else to be done but to give in and share the bed with Colt. That wonderful, soft bed that had felt so good to her aching body when she stretched out on it for that brief moment.

After all, she consoled herself, there was plenty of room for two people. And Colt was fast asleep. He'd never even know they'd shared the bed if she woke up before he did and pretended she'd slept on the floor. She wouldn't have to lie, either. She just wouldn't say anything.

With her decision made, Amelia rose to her feet and quietly pulled back the covers, climbed in, and stretched out on the feather mattress.

Colt sighed heavily and rolled toward her, pulling her firmly into his arms so her head was resting beneath his chin.

Amelia lay there stiffly, frozen, waiting for whatever he would do. But after a time when he hadn't made another move and continued to breathe evenly, she decided he was fast asleep and had acted involuntarily, and her tense muscles relaxed. She snuggled closer and was soon fast asleep.

Colt lay quietly, listening to the sound of Amelia's even breathing. He'd been afraid she would change her mind and insist that he sleep on the hard floor after all. But her good sense—or perhaps it was only her weary body—had finally persuaded her to share the bed with him.

He'd felt her fear when he took her in his arms, had even known the exact moment when she realized she was not going to be attacked and began to relax. He'd been stretched out on the bed, damning Grady Kincaid's soul to hell, when that had happened. The man surely had plenty of sins to account for when he reached that place, but whatever he suffered there would never be enough to atone for what he'd done during his lifetime.

Colt thought of the day when he'd ridden into Morgan's Creek with his brothers and found the new gravestones on the hill. The pain of that day would be a long time leaving him, if it ever did. Home would never be the same again, now that there were only him and his brothers left.

How were his brothers managing anyway? He'd received a letter from Matthew when he was in Yuma, in which he'd said that the others had found jobs away from home to help restock the homestead. According to Matt, Blake had become a lawman and Ben was breaking horses for the Bar-D Ranch. He would be good at that. Ben had a way with animals. He could damn near talk them into being tame. Yeah, Ben would make a helluva wrangler.

Colter's thoughts turned to Gabe, who was still missing. He must have been killed during the war, and that thought caused immeasurable pain. Gabe had been the jokester, always playing tricks and making people laugh. It was hard to think of him being gone forever, of never seeing him again. They had been so close, the two of them. Whatever had ended his brother's life, Colt hoped he hadn't suffered before he passed on. Like his brother Trent must have done. And his mother and Annie. That thought caused a stab of pain that twisted in his gut. Hard, wrenching pain.

Don't think of Mother and Annie, a silent voice deep within his mind advised. *Trent. Think about Trent instead. If you must dredge up sorrow, remember the tragic way Trent died.* It had all been so unnecessary. So useless. And it wouldn't have happened if Trent hadn't got himself mixed up with that wild bunch of kids. He wouldn't have become an outlaw . . . a wanted man. It had taken time, but eventually Trent's name had been cleared. Too late for him, though. He'd become involved in a shoot-out and had taken a bullet in the stomach. Gut shot. The most painful way to die.

Don't think about it, the silent voice commanded again. *Think about the woman in your arms.*

Yeah. That was best. She was soft, rounded in all the right places . . . feminine to the core. And she had gumption too. Plenty of gumption. She'd make some man a damned good wife.

Too bad it wouldn't be him, but he had a job to do before he could ever settle down, and by then she'd have been snatched up by some lucky man.

He thought of Matthew, alone at the ranch. And that was where he was taking Amelia. Matt needed a wife to help on the homestead, but the thought of him marrying Amy was nothing short of painful for Colt.

No. Amy wasn't for Matthew either. If she was to marry any man, then she'd need to be far enough away that Colt wouldn't be likely to run into her. Because if he did, he wasn't sure he could keep his hands off her.

He tightened his grip and pulled her closer, and she stirred in her sleep and snuggled against him. Colt felt his lower body stirring and he moved slightly, knowing that if she wakened she would be alarmed.

But she slept on, completely unaware.

Colt smoothed his palm across her silky hair and forced his mind and body to relax the way he had learned to do during the war.

And moments later he was fast asleep.

When Amelia awoke, the room was bright with morning sunlight. Her nostrils twitched at the smell of bacon cooking, and she stirred and stretched. Something hairy stirred beneath the covers, and she let out a piercing scream.

A muffled cry jerked her eyes toward the curious hump beside her. It was huge, an enormous mound covered by the woolen blanket. She yanked back the covers just as the bedroom door was abruptly shoved open. "Colt!" she exclaimed. "What—"

"What's wrong?"

The high-pitched voice jerked Amelia's head around. She saw Sadie in the doorway, staring at her with wide eyes, a butcher knife held high as though she were prepared to attack whatever might be threatening her guests.

Hurriedly, Amelia tugged the covers around her shoulders to hide her bare flesh. "I—I thought something moved in the bed," she said quickly.

Sadie smiled. "You must not have been married very long, honey, else you'd know that when you got a husband in bed, there's always something moving around come morning."

Amelia was puzzled at her words but made no comment. The moment the door closed behind Sadie, Amelia rounded on Colt, who had raised himself to his elbows, a wicked smile playing across his face.

"What did she mean?" Amelia asked.

His smile widened. "I don't think you really want to know."

By the look in his eyes, Amelia suspected he might be right. "Get out of bed, Colt," she ordered. "I need to help Sadie with breakfast."

"Go right ahead," he replied cheerfully. "I wouldn't dream of stopping you."

"Well, I can hardly get out of bed with you watching me."

"Why not?"

"Because I'm not dressed!" she hissed. "Now get up from there."

"I'm not dressed either," he said, shoving back the covers and exposing naked flesh down to his hips. "But if that's what you want, then I'll—"

"No!" Her eyes were glued to his wide, muscular chest. Oh, Lord, he was beautiful. Powerful too, if the rest of him was equally muscled. Was he completely naked? "Colter Morgan," she squeaked. "Don't you dare get out of this bed!"

He leaned back and pulled the covers up to his chest. "Make up your mind," he said cheerfully.

"Cover your eyes while I get dressed," she commanded, waiting until he had done so before she slid from beneath the covers.

Although her trembling fingers slowed her down, it was only moments later when she had dressed and closed the bedroom door with a quick snap, which was designed to let Colt Morgan know exactly what she thought of his ungentlemanly behavior.

Chapter Seven

Sadie looked up as Amelia entered the kitchen. "You didn't need to get up so soon, Amy." The woman's welcoming smile warmed Amelia's heart and made her smile in return. "You could've stayed abed with that man of yours until breakfast was ready."

"I wouldn't think of lazing abed while you did all the work."

"I don't mind," Sadie replied. "I'm used to it. Anyways, I imagine your man would've appreciated a little more time."

Puzzled, Amelia asked, "What do you mean?"

Laughing softly, Sadie said, "I know how husbands are, Amy, having been married to Jed these forty years now. And it was plain as the nose on your face your man was feeling his oats this morning." She smiled gently. "Time was when I couldn't leave my bed so easy either, but Jed's settled down a mite since then."

Amelia felt her cheeks heating and knew they must be

awash with color. To hide her embarrassment, she scooped up the plates and began to set the table. But she didn't fool Sadie for one moment, she knew, as was made obvious when the other woman spoke.

"No need to be embarrassed, lovey." Sadie's voice held a gentle humor. "It's the way of things. And that's as it should be. It's all part of God's plan. He made man strong enough to protect his woman and his family, and He made him smart enough to figure a way to feed 'em—even when times were rough. The Lord was on our side when He did that, Amy," she went on. "It's only right that we do everything possible to keep our men happy . . . to make their lives as pleasant as we can." She laughed suddenly. "That's not to say I don't enjoy a little fooling around myself sometimes."

Amelia wondered how she was supposed to respond, then was spared when the door opened abruptly and Jed entered the kitchen, carrying a milk bucket foaming with froth.

"How're you feeling this morning, young lady?" he asked, hefting the bucket to the cabinet.

"I'm feeling just fine," she replied. "Could I help you with that?"

"No. You set yourself down and rest awhile."

"I don't need to rest," she said with a smile. "I just got out of bed."

"Should've stayed there longer."

Darn Colter's hide for making the Crandals worry about her! "I'd like to help do something," she insisted.

"No need," Sadie said. "But if you want, you could set the butter and jelly on the table." Sadie pushed back a tendril of hair that had escaped her bun, then turned her attention to the eggs she was frying.

Amelia set the required items on the table, then reached for the tableware, counting out four of each and setting them beside the plates. "I feel lazy letting you do all the work, Sadie," she grumbled.

"Lord love you, if you ain't something," Sadie laughed. "Most folks I know wouldn't give it another thought. Anyway, there's nothing left to be done. Breakfast is just about ready to be served."

Having finished straining the milk, Jed pulled out a chair and pushed Amelia into it with gentle hands. "You just rest yourself there, little mother, whilst I get you some coffee," Jed said, hefting the coffeepot and reaching for a cup. "How do you like it? Black? Sweet? With cream?"

"With cream, please. No sugar."

Sadie paused in the act of turning the eggs and frowned at Amy. "Are you sure you oughta be drinking that coffee, lovey?"

Jed was just about to set the steaming cup before Amy, but at his wife's words he paused, the cup hovering only inches away.

"Tarnation, Sadie!" he exclaimed. "I never thought of that." He frowned at Amelia. "Maybe you ought not have coffee."

Not have coffee? Not have that steaming, creamy, reviving drink that she so badly craved? Why?

The cup that had been so near was suddenly snatched away as Jed set it at the end of the table where he would soon be seated. "Sadie's right." His gray eyes glinted with humor. "As usual. Drinking coffee is a sure way to bring on morning sickness."

"Oh, no!" Amy said quickly. "I'm sure I—"

"Anyway," he went on, "I never thought stimulants were very good for a woman during the months she was carrying her babe. Might make the young'un take a notion to just come on out before it was time."

Sadie laughed heartily and went back to dishing up the food. She forked thick slices of bacon onto a platter that already contained several eggs done to perfection and set it on the table. Then, opening the oven door, she removed two pans of the most perfectly browned biscuits Amelia had ever seen and brushed the tops with butter before adding them to the feast.

Amelia was so hungry that she sat there, her eyes feasting on the laden platter. She hoped she wouldn't appear too eager, too greedy, but she'd always had a hearty appetite and she could already taste those scrumptious biscuits, the eggs with golden yellow centers, and crisp bacon.

At that moment Colter joined them in the kitchen looking like a new man. His dark hair had been brushed away from his face, and he had shaved away the growth of beard. He had a fresh, scrubbed look about him despite having donned the same clothes he'd been wearing.

Her pulse picked up speed as he eased himself into the chair beside her and gave the room in general a beaming smile.

"Sadie," he said, "my mouth has been watering for the last fifteen minutes. I can hardly wait to bite into one of those biscuits."

Jed had the biscuits in front of him and had already sliced and buttered every one.

"You don't have to wait," Sadie said gruffly, her pleasure there for all to see. "Just help yourself, Colt, and dig right in."

Colt wasted no time in doing just that. Amelia was about to do the same when Sadie stopped beside her and, with a flourish, set a bowl in front of her. "Here's your breakfast, lovey. Oatmeal. Guaranteed to stick to your bones and give you the strength you need during your journey. Good thing, oatmeal. Always ate it myself every single morning when I was carrying. It's chock full of nourishment."

Oatmeal? Amelia looked at the contents of the bowl and tried to hide her distaste. It wasn't that she couldn't eat oatmeal. She'd certainly done it enough times. But not when there was a veritable feast of bacon, eggs, and hot biscuits slathered with melting butter on the table.

Noticing the confused expression on Colt's face, Sadie explained. "You haven't been seeing to that young'un of yours, Colt. Amy needs food like this to make that babe grow like it ought to."

"There's something wrong with bacon and eggs?" he inquired with raised eyebrow.

She nodded. "Too greasy. In her condition it would be coming up almost as soon as she swallowed it, and that would be hard on the babe."

Amelia glared at Colt, and he fidgeted slightly beneath her gaze. "Like coffee," she gritted out. "I can't have that either. Too stimulating. Might make the baby pop right out before its birthing time."

"Oh."

Was that an apology she saw in his eyes? Perhaps. But it was only there for a moment; then he was digging into the food on his plate, sipping that wonderful-smelling coffee, and then scooping more food into his mouth.

Amelia looked at the oatmeal for a long moment and then picked up her spoon, pausing long enough for somebody to realize they'd made a mistake when they'd denied her that wonderful breakfast. But when no word was spoken, she scooped a spoonful and carried it to her mouth. Although it wasn't really bad, it still wasn't bacon and eggs . . . and hot buttered biscuits. And it would probably be a long time before she had a chance to have those again, traveling the way they were and trying to avoid civilization.

Conversation flowed around the table as they ate, but Amelia remained silent, eating slowly as though to savor the meal when in reality it was an effort to finish her food.

Suddenly Jed frowned at Amelia, then looked pointedly

at his wife. "Sadie," he growled. "Didn't you forget something?"

"Forget something?" Sadie was obviously puzzled. "What?"

He pointed his fork at Amelia's bowl, and Amelia's spirits lifted. Perhaps they had forgotten to offer her one of those delicious-looking biscuits. Yes. That must be it. After all, there must be something nourishing in biscuits, something that she needed to promote growth in her unborn child . . .

. Darn it! Now she was doing it herself, and she wasn't even pregnant! This was all Colt's fault, and there he sat, enjoying a delicious breakfast while she had to make do with a bowl of oatmeal . . . and maybe a biscuit.

But instead of motioning toward the pan of biscuits, Jed pointed toward the bucket on the cabinet. "Milk," he said shortly. "You didn't give her any milk, Sadie." He looked at Amelia. "Milk makes for a healthy babe. Builds strong bones and teeth."

"Jed's right, lovey. Don't know how I could have forgot to pour you a glass." Sadie shoved back her chair and hurried to remedy the oversight. "Must be my age," she muttered. "Everybody knows milk's important to an expectant mother. Just what you need the most."

No, Amelia silently told herself. *What I need more than anything else is a hot cup of coffee. And some bacon and eggs. And a handful of hot buttered biscuits.*

But since it was obvious that none of those things would be forthcoming, she gratefully accepted the glass of milk—so fresh it was still warm—and tried hard to pretend it was a cup of steaming coffee.

* * *

Since Colter insisted on helping Jed with the morning chores before they dickered for the horse, it was mid-morning before they said their good-byes.

It was obvious that the older couple had developed a fondness for their guests—Sadie was dabbing at her eyes with a corner of her apron, and Jed kept repeating his invitation to stop by anytime and stay longer—and Amelia felt sad as she and Jed mounted their horses and rode away.

When they reached a bend in the road, Amelia turned for one last look and saw that the couple hadn't moved at all. Jed had an arm around Sadie's shoulders, and she was waving at them.

"I wish we hadn't lied to them," Amelia said.

"I know," Colt replied. "I feel the same way. But we couldn't take the chance of telling them the truth. Anyway, it's best if they don't know. They would worry about us if they did."

"I suppose so." She sighed heavily. "They were nice people, though, weren't they?"

"Yeah. Real nice."

"Do you think we'll ever see them again?"

"Who knows?" *We.* She had lumped them together, as though they really were a couple. He liked that. Liked it a lot.

They rode in silence then, intent on reaching the Texas border as soon as possible. But even so, when darkness finally covered the land they were still in Louisiana.

Knowing it would be dangerous to continue their journey when he wasn't sure of his direction, he reined his mount toward a thick forest of pines. They wound their way through saplings and over fallen trees and stumps until they heard the sound of rushing water.

Suddenly they emerged from the dense forest into a

small moonlit glade. In the midst of the glade was a waterfall that cascaded into a natural pool where the clear waters reflected the glittering stars overhead.

"Oh, it's beautiful," Amelia said. "Can we camp here, Colt?"

"Don't see any reason why not." He dismounted, then helped her to the ground. "You gather some wood while I hobble the horses. And, Amy . . . don't go far."

By the time he'd taken care of their mounts, Amelia had several armloads of wood waiting for him.

Colt knelt on the ground and stacked kindling, then added a few limbs that were no thicker than three inches.

Turning to Amelia, he said, "Amy, go look in my saddlebag and see what you can find in the way of food."

Amelia obeyed, coming up with a can of beans and some coffee. Coffee. Oh, God, she could finally have a cup of coffee.

She pulled out a pan and a coffeepot, then returned to where Colt had a small fire going. "I'll fill the coffeepot," she offered, handing him the beans and the pan.

She took the coffeepot to the creek and dipped it into the water. Moments later she rejoined Colt, who was emptying the beans into the blue enameled pot. It was only a matter of minutes before the beans had been heated and the coffeepot was boiling steadily, making her nostrils twitch at the delicious aroma.

When they were seated together at the fire, each holding a plate of beans and a cup of coffee, Colt reached into his slicker and pulled out a brown package tied with twine and handed it to her.

"What's this?" she mumbled, scooping another spoonful of beans into her mouth before opening the package.

The wrapper fell away to expose four perfectly browned, buttered biscuits.

"Colt!" she squealed with delight. "You devil! You

brought me some of Sadie's lovely biscuits! How on earth did you manage that?''

"Sadie gave them to me. Thought we might need them on the trail. And I'm glad she did." His eyes glinted with amusement. "I've been feeling real guilty about that breakfast you missed. I'm afraid beans and coffee won't make up for it, but it's the best I could do. You could heat the biscuits if you set them near the fire."

Amelia reached out and placed the back of her hand against his cheek, feeling his muscles tense beneath her touch. "What a sweet man you are," she said softly. "Who'd ever think there was such thoughtfulness beneath that gruff exterior?" She held the package out. "Here. You take two of them."

His throat worked, and there was something undefinable in his dark eyes. "No," he said gruffly. "I saved them for you. You eat them."

She laughed. "I can't eat four biscuits, Colt. Not even to make you feel better."

The tension she'd felt in him slowly seeped away. He smiled at her. "Oh, well. If you insist. I guess I'd better help you eat them after all."

It was a pleasant meal they shared. And there in the moonlight, with the firelight casting flickering shadows across Colt's face, Amelia found she wanted to know more about the man she rode with. But she had no wish to change the pleasant mood he was in. Still, she knew it was past time she had some answers to the questions that had been plaguing her.

Chapter Eight

Although Colt watched the flickering flames while he sipped his coffee, his thoughts were on the woman seated across from him. It had been years since he'd spent time with a woman and he'd almost forgotten how pleasant it could be. The war had taken several years of his life, and since then, his pursuit of the Kincaid Raiders had left him no time to meet a good woman.

Oh, he'd met plenty of the other kind, since he'd spent so much time in saloons, questioning—without appearing to—those individuals most likely to know the Kincaids' whereabouts.

But those women held no interest for him. Not like Amelia. She was a woman a man could live with, could spend his life with, a woman who would be loyal to the man she gave her heart to.

And dammit! Colt told himself, that man would be one lucky devil, whoever he was.

His gaze lifted to find her watching him.

"Colt," Amelia said hesitantly. "You never did say how you came to be in Grady Kincaid's house that night."

Somehow he wasn't surprised that she'd broached the subject. "No. I guess I never did."

She waited for a long moment, then said, "Are you going to tell me what you were doing there?"

Although his expression was suddenly grim, his voice was matter-of-fact, showing no emotion when he spoke. "I went there to kill him."

Amelia sucked in a sharp breath, her blue eyes widening slightly. "Why?" she whispered. She'd already guessed that Colt had had no liking for the man, but she had never sensed that his dislike ran so deep.

He told her about the raid that had killed his parents and sister, and she was horrified. "How awful! How could they murder a child and live with their conscience?"

His voice was cold, deadly. "They have no conscience, no sense of guilt whatever. Men like that live for the moment with no thought for their immortal souls. And it's past time someone stopped them . . . sent them on their way to hell!"

"And you've made yourself responsible for sending them there."

"Yes."

"I'm sorry." The words seemed somehow inadequate. "And now I've taken away your only lead by killing Grady Kincaid."

"No," he said gruffly, staring into the fire.

"No? But I thought you needed to question him, to learn the names and whereabouts of his companions."

"There are still the other brothers." He lifted his cup to his mouth and met her eyes over the rim. "Two of the Kincaid brothers are in Austin."

"In Texas?" Amelia wondered how he had come by that news. "I thought Grady Kincaid was your only lead, Colt."

"He was . . . until I got there. When I searched his office, I found a letter from one of his brothers. It was very enlightening. And it was postmarked in Austin . . . just last month. They were there all the time," he mused. "So close to home, yet we had no idea." He took a long draught of coffee, then tossed the dregs aside.

Amelia wanted to wipe away the harsh look that had settled upon Colt's countenance, wanted to go back to that moment in time . . . before she had asked about his reasons for being in the Kincaid mansion. But they couldn't go back. That time had passed, would never come again, and now she would have to deal with the results of her actions.

Her wish now was to divert his thoughts from those horrible men who'd plundered the family home and killed his loved ones.

"Tell me about your brothers, Colt," she said softly as she reached for the coffeepot to refill her cup.

He arched a dark brow. "My brothers?"

"Yes. You spoke of your brothers. As though there were several of them."

He laughed abruptly. "There are," he replied. "Five of them. Or at least there were . . ." His expression became pensive again. "I guess . . . now there are only four of us left."

Amelia realized immediately that she'd made a mistake. Colt's harsh expression had been replaced by one of sorrow. Perhaps, though, she told herself, she could lead him past the sadness to a happier time in his life.

"What happened to the other two?" she inquired softly.

"The war." He sighed deeply. "It was the war that killed Gabe . . . at least we believe that's what happened. Gabe, short for Gabriel, joined up with the rest of us, but he never came home." Colt's thoughts turned inward. "Gabe was always funning." He smiled sadly. "One time when we were boys, Gabe decided to liven things up a bit, something he was always doing. Anyway, he put a burr under my saddle. It just so happened that Trent saw him do it and told me, so I finagled things around so that Gabe wound up riding that horse instead of me."

His smile widened, his dark eyes sparkling with memory. "You should have seen his antics, Amy. Since he'd been the one to saddle that bronc, he didn't want anyone to know there was anything amiss, so he tried to ride with his weight on the opposite side of the saddle." He laughed huskily. "It didn't work, though. Eventually that burr dug into that stud and he took off like a whirling dervish. The rest of us were laughing so hard we could barely see that boy and the stud top the rise in the distance."

"What happened?"

"Oh, Gabe was finally tossed off. Just barely escaped a good stomping, too."

"And did it teach him a lesson?"

"Hell, no! Just taught him to be more careful while he was at his pranks."

"What about your other brother?"

"Trent?"

"If he's the other brother you lost, then yes. Trent. Did he go off to war, too?"

"No," he said softly. "Trent never went to war. We lost him before the war began."

"If you'd rather not talk about him . . ."

He sighed heavily. "It's not that, Amelia. It's just that it's been a long time since I heard Trent's name mentioned. That has always bothered me. Seems like somebody ought to be talking about him to keep his memory alive."

"Then *you* talk about him. You tell me about your brother Trent Morgan."

"Trent was always different from the rest of us."

"In what way?"

"Well, for one thing, he was quiet, kept to himself most of the time."

"Even with such a large family?"

"Yeah." He frowned at his coffeecup. "Trent didn't much cotton to being a rancher, said he wanted something more out of life than living his days out in Morgan's Creek."

"Morgan's Creek is your home?"

"Yeah."

"What happened to Trent?"

"He fell in with bad companions. Got to drinking and carousing around, hell-bent on having a good time." Colt sighed heavily and his hands clenched around the tin cup. "I tried talking to him but it did no good."

"You're the oldest?"

"No. That's Matt. Matthew. He's the oldest. But I understood Trent better than any of the others did, knew how he was feeling." He sighed again. "Anyway, when he was just sixteen—still a kid—his companions decided it would be fun to steal old man Gray's racehorse for a few days. It was supposed to be a joke . . . they had every intention of returning the horse a few days later. But old man Gray . . . well, he heard the noise and met them with a shotgun. The kids got scared, and one of them killed the old man."

Amelia's eyes widened with horror. "Not Trent!"

"No. Not Trent. But he was no idiot. He knew the law would be after every last one of them. So he just took off . . . rode out that same night, and none of us ever saw him again."

"Then you don't really know he's dead, Colt."

"Yeah. I do know." He met her eyes. "We got word of him occasionally. Word was he left the state, went to Colorado Territory, where he took up trapping. He might've been okay but he earned the reputation of a gunman. And in the way of such things, he had to fight to stay alive.''

"Why was that?"

"Young punks looking to make a reputation by outshooting the known experts. Old hands looking to stay top gun, ready to challenge anyone and everyone. It's always been that way . . . always will be."

"He was killed by one of them . . . the young guns?"

"Not so young, as it happens. But, yeah, he was killed . . . gut shot by a man who wanted to be known as top gun."

She shuddered. "I'm sorry," she said. "I wanted to cheer you up and instead I've made things worse for you."

"You want to cheer me up?"

"Yes."

"Then tell me about yourself."

"There's not much to tell." She held his gaze. "You saw my circumstances. Already know about my pa and what kind of man he was."

"What about your mother?"

"She died when I was ten years old. The fever took her."

"And you have no more family? No aunts? No uncles? Grandparents or cousins?"

"No. My mother's parents died of cholera. She was an only child. I have no idea what happened to my father's parents. He never said, and he made it clear he didn't like me asking about them."

"Did he give you a reason?"

"No. But I think . . . from what my mother told me . . . that he ran away from home when he was a boy. I suppose they must have been harsh, to make him leave so young."

"You're an only child, then?"

She smiled sadly. "I had a sister once. But it was a long time ago."

"What happened to her?"

"I don't know. I was so young then. Not more than two

or three. But I remember her. Her eyes were blue, like mine, and her gold hair would glitter beneath the light of a candle when we went to bed."

"You remember that, but you don't remember what happened to her?"

She nodded. "But I know it must have been something terrible."

"Why do you think that?"

"When I was seven or eight years old I asked Mother to explain what happened to my sister, and she burst into tears and her body began to shake so hard I thought she would do injury to herself. I never asked her again."

"Did you ever ask your father?"

"Yes. And he slapped me. Said I never had a sister. That I just imagined her." She looked at Colt. "I did have one, though. I know I did. And I don't even remember her name." She blinked away tears. "I don't know why he denied it, but he put the fear of God into me when he threatened to beat me with his belt if I ever mentioned her again."

"Was he in the habit of beating you?" Colt asked softly.

"Yes."

"Damn him!" Colt wondered at the hatred that blazed through him at the thought of Amelia's father laying cruel hands on her. He set aside his cup and reached for her, pulling her into his arms.

"I've a good mind to go back and make him pay for the way he treated you." He stroked her bright, silky hair, and something shifted in the region of his heart. He wondered if that organ that had shriveled into a hard knot the day he'd found the graves of his loved ones was actually coming alive again.

Amelia smiled against Colt's shirt, finding comfort in his embrace. She couldn't help but admire this side of Colter . . . the protective man who would keep her from harm. With him beside her she would have no reason to fear anyone, or anything.

As though he'd guessed her thoughts, Colter set her aside. "It's past time we went to bed," he said gruffly.

"Yes," she agreed. "It's late and I'm tired." She looked at the bedroll and the quilt that lay beside it. "It was nice of Sadie to give us the quilt," she said.

"Yeah," he agreed. "The night is likely to get cold."

They fell quiet, each busy with their own thoughts.

Amelia wondered about the night to come. Would they share the bedroll, or would he give it to her?

All around them were the sounds of night. Frogs croaked by the stream. Crickets sang in the bushes. And somewhere in the night there was the flutter of wings as an owl went about the business of hunting for food.

Finally, Colt rose to his feet. "We'd better get some rest," he said gruffly.

"Yes," Amelia agreed.

She rose and stretched her arms high, arching her back as she did so, and her blouse stretched tautly over her bosom, making Colter's breeches tighten across his thighs as his loins stirred in response.

Realizing he needed to cool his heated blood before retiring, Colter said, "I believe I'll go for a swim. You go ahead and climb into that bedroll, Amelia. The night air is cooling down real fast."

Apparently he wasn't planning on their sharing a bed this night. She felt a curious sense of loss at that thought. "I hate to take your bedroll," she said quietly. "I could wrap up in the quilt instead."

"No," he said, his voice suddenly harsh. "I'll take the quilt, Amy. You use the bedroll."

Then he was gone.

* * *

The water sparkled and shimmered in the moonlight, but Colter didn't notice the beauty of the waterfall. He stood on the rock stripping the clothing from his body, his thoughts turned inward.

He thought of the life Amelia had been forced to live, unloved since her mother's death. And what had happened to her sister, he wondered, that was so horrible that her father threatened to beat her if she so much as spoke of her?

It was obvious to Colt that Amelia's father had something to hide, since he apparently wanted to make her forget that her sister ever existed.

But what was it?

"It's a damn shame," he muttered.

Amelia would never know what happened since her mother—who might have told her—was long dead.

But perhaps she *could* know. Perhaps there was a way to discover what had happened. When this was over, if Colter survived, he might just return to Louisiana and seek out her father.

"Yes," he said aloud. "I just might do that."

Then he dove into the cold water and emerged farther out in the pool, moving with the skill of an accomplished swimmer.

The water rippled turbulently around his muscular body as he cut through it with powerful strokes. He was a good swimmer, having learned when he was a boy.

Colter's mouth was drawn into a thin line as he tried to ease his frustration by tiring himself out before he returned to the camp and the girl who occupied so many of his thoughts these days.

Chapter Nine

They broke camp early next morning and crossed the river into Texas around noon. When they were safely on the west side of the Sabine River, Colter dismounted and helped Amelia to the ground.

"We'll rest here awhile," he said, offering her a strip of beef jerky.

Amelia took the jerky and studied it for a long moment. But she really wasn't seeing the dried strip of meat. Instead, she was remembering what had gone on before and wondering if the Kincaid gang was already riding after them.

"Do you really believe we're safe now?" she asked quietly.

"We're safe enough from the law," he replied. "They have no jurisdiction here in Texas. But as for Kincaid's men . . . well, it's hard to say. They might come after us, Amy. You have to be prepared for that. I've heard they're a relentless bunch. But you're safe with me, even if they do come."

"Those men I saw at the stream were headed for Kincaid's place. But I'm not so sure they were hired by him. I got the impression he had sent for them, but they might not have been on his payroll yet."

He smiled at her. "In that case they'd have no reason to follow us, would they?"

Amelia ran her fingers through her tangled curls. "Unless they were after the bounty the law put on my head."

"As to that ... well, I believe I'll wire Blake. He's a lawman. He might find out something for us from the constable in Louisiana."

"Are you sure that's wise?" she asked nervously. "He might make them wonder why he was asking. They could send bounty hunters after us if they knew which direction we're headed."

"Blake knows his business. He'll word the inquiry so as not to make them suspicious."

"If you're sure." She wasn't so sure. She was afraid of being separated from Colt.

"I am." He sighed, rose to his feet. "What I wouldn't give for a hot meal."

"Me too." She cast him a mournful look. "A meal just like the one Sadie set on the table and I wasn't allowed to eat."

Colt threw back his head and laughed. And then he immediately apologized. "I really am sorry about that, Amelia. I don't suppose you're ever going to let me live that down."

"Not likely."

Amelia knew why he'd done it, and if the truth be known, she really didn't mind being taken for an expectant mother. It had felt good to be cosseted. Something that she'd never been before.

How would it feel to be pregnant? she wondered. She

had seen women big with child, and although she'd thought being so cumbersome would make them unhappy, most of them had had a glow about them that made her think of the Madonna.

What would it be like to have a child with Colt? That thought made her lower her eyes, afraid he would know what she was thinking. But he seemed unaware of the turn her thoughts had taken. She peeked at him from beneath her lashes and studied his firm, strong jawline.

Colter Morgan would make some woman a wonderful husband, if he would forget his vow of vengeance and stay at home with his wife. But he was so determined to find the Kincaids, so set on exacting vengeance, that Amelia didn't think he'd ever take a wife.

Why had Colt been the one to go after the men who'd murdered his family? Matthew was the oldest. Why shouldn't he be the one?

Amelia thought about asking him, but remembered the way he'd looked last night when he'd spoken of his family and decided she didn't want to bring the subject up again.

One day, perhaps, he would tell her. If they stayed together long enough.

Just how long would they be together anyway? Colt was so determined to get her to safety. What was to happen now that they were in Texas?

She put the question to him.

"Why, you'll stay at the ranch with Matthew, of course."

"Stay with Matthew? But ... doesn't he live there alone?"

"Yes. With a couple of hands."

"Men?"

He arched a dark brow. "Certainly they are men."

"Colt! I can't stay there."

"Why ever not?"

"Because there are no womenfolk around."

Colt frowned at Amelia. Why in hell hadn't he thought of that? Of course she was right. She couldn't live at the ranch when there were only men around. It wouldn't be proper.

But he had nowhere else to leave her.

"We'll worry about that later," he said firmly. "Right now we have to get there. And I'm so hungry I could eat a horse."

Amelia looked at the stallion grazing a short distance away. "Better watch it, Thunder," she advised. "Your master just gave you notice."

Colt grinned when the horse snorted and pawed at the ground as though he'd understood her words. "As it happens, Thunder is not really mine."

"Oh, really?" She arched a delicate brow. "Stole him, did you?"

His grin widened. "He belongs to my brother Matt. He's on loan until I find a better mount."

"A better one? I guess he belongs to you then, because that will never happen."

"That's the way I figured it, too."

They mounted and rode on their way.

When they reached town they left the horses at the livery and headed for the local cafe. Colt pushed open the door and they stepped inside.

Amelia's nostrils twitched as she took in the aroma of fresh-baked bread, of cloves and cinnamon and strongly brewed coffee.

It was a pleasant room, brightened with whitewashed walls. The floors were made of smooth planks, and along each side of the room was a long table with benches made for communal dining. Several smaller tables paired with hide-bound chairs were placed in strategic spots where couples with a need to be alone could dine in comfort.

Several people were there—a young couple who only

had eyes for each other, an elderly couple who had just finished their meal, and a grizzled old man who was busy shoveling food into his mouth.

"I'll be with you in a minute," called a cheerful voice from across the room. "Just set yourselves down anywhere."

Amelia had only a glimpse of a blue calico dress covered with a crisp white apron before the woman disappeared through a door that obviously led to the kitchen.

Colt pulled a chair out from the nearest table and seated Amelia before he took the seat across from her. Moments later the woman in the blue dress was asking for their order.

Amelia enjoyed the hot meal, the first she'd had since they left the Crandals' farm. They finished it off with apple pie, and when they'd eaten the last bite and swallowed the last drop of coffee laced with cream, Colt paid for the meals and they left the establishment.

"Guess we'd best get our supplies now," he said. "And another sleeping bag too. The general store should have everything we need."

As they passed the stagecoach office, Colt paused, then looked at her.

"You go on to the store, Amy," he said. "I'll join you presently."

"What should I get?" she asked.

"We should be on the trail for another five days or so, so buy accordingly."

"But I'm not sure—"

"I'll be along in a few minutes," he interrupted. "I just need to send a telegram."

"All right then." Amelia headed toward the general store across the street. She was almost there when she noticed the horses waiting outside the bank. There were five of them, and a bristle-faced man was there holding the reins to all five.

As Amelia passed the man, his gaze swept over her womanly curves before lingering on her breasts. Not one to be intimidated easily, Amelia raised her chin and glared at the man, silently reprimanding him for his impertinence.

She'd be darned if she'd go through life cowed, fearful that she'd be recognized. Her gaze slid over his length the way his had done with her; then she pushed open the door to the store and went inside.

At the jangle of the bell the proprietor looked up. "Help you, miss?" he inquired.

"I need some things . . . supplies," she said, meeting the merchant's gaze. "Enough food to last two people five days on the trail."

"You planning on cooking or opening tins?"

She laughed at that, her blue eyes sparkling at the thought of preparing a decent meal on the trail. "I don't know much about cooking over an open fire, so I guess we'll be opening tins."

"Then you'll be needing beans, coffee, sugar, tinned milk, and—"

"The works," she told him. "And add some canned peaches. I think Colt would like that."

He nodded and began to gather the items, placing each one on the counter for her approval.

But Amelia paid little attention to her purchases. She couldn't stop thinking about the man across the street and the horses he was holding. Right in front of the bank, too. You'd almost think he had some designs on the money there.

Funny.

She turned and looked at the merchant, who had begun to tally up her bill. "Do you know what time it is?" she asked.

"Sure enough, little lady." He made a great show of pulling out his watch and studying the face for several moments. "Why, according to my watch, it's just about half past three."

"Three-thirty," she mumbled. "Shouldn't the bank be closed then?"

"That's right. It closes at three o'clock."

"And they're usually punctual about closing at that time, aren't they?"

"Mighty particular they are," he agreed. "They lock those doors right on the dot of three. You can stake your life on it."

"Then I wonder why they're still open now."

He looked at his watch again, as though to make sure of the time before he spoke. "They're not, little lady. Not at half past three."

"I just saw someone go in there."

Puzzled, he joined her at the door and looked across the street. "Are you sure?"

"Yes."

"Well, maybe it was the banker's wife."

"No. Not a woman. It was the man who was holding the horses a moment ago."

"Horses." He appeared to notice the horses for the first time. "By golly, there are horses there." He scratched his grizzled head. "Now I wonder . . ."

Amelia didn't hear what he was wondering. She had stepped outside, intent on alerting the sheriff to what was going on. And as she stepped into the road, several men ran out of the bank and leaped on their horses. She realized, too late, what a big mistake she'd made by leaving the safety of the store.

She stepped back, intent on retreating into the store, but the horses were galloping toward her. She turned to run, but the man who'd been holding the horses suddenly veered toward her.

Before Amelia could escape, the gunman leaned over and snatched her off the ground, pulling her into the saddle with a hard, painful thump.

Amelia struggled against his hold, lashing out with her fists, and caught the man's nose with a hard thump.

She saw his fist coming down; then she felt a blow on her chin that snapped her head back, and then she knew no more.

The noise in the street reached into the telegraph office and jerked the clerk, who'd been reading the message Colt had handed over, around. "What in tarnation is going on out there?" he muttered.

Colt thought at first the racket was caused by a drunk cowboy who was feeling his oats. But suddenly he wasn't so sure.

He strode quickly to the door, just in time to see several horses with riders galloping past him. Something about one of the riders caught his attention. The man was too burly, his frame too bulky, almost as though there were two people astride his mount.

The man seemed to be struggling with himself. Then Colt saw the bright flash of gold flowing over the man's shoulder, and he could scarcely believe his eyes.

"Dammit!" he roared. "They've got Amelia!"

His six-gun was already in his hand, appearing there as if by magic, yet it might as well have been a limp noodle for all the good it did. There was no way he could get off a clear shot with the man holding Amelia in front of him. Even a shot in the back might go all the way through and penetrate the woman.

Colt's heart raced with fear as he ran toward the livery

stable. He couldn't let them get away. With Thunder beneath his legs, he would surely overtake Amelia's abductors before they could go very far.

At least he hoped so.

An hour later he wasn't so sure. The men who had taken Amelia hostage seemed to have completely disappeared.

Chapter Ten

Colter continued searching through the long afternoon, but as twilight settled softly over the countryside, he realized he was no closer to finding Amy than when he first started his search. It seemed a useless task. The outlaws had ridden on rocky ground whenever possible, and for the past two hours Colt had been riding back and forth, trying to follow tracks that appeared to go in every direction.

It was obvious that the outlaws had split up in groups to confuse the posse they knew would be following them.

So where in hell was the posse?

Even as that thought occurred, Colter heard the sound of thundering hooves. It was only a matter of minutes before the posse reached him, circling around him with dust boiling up around the horses.

"Thought we'd be catching up to you before much longer," the man wearing the star commented. "Find anything?"

The sheriff was an older man, wide of girth. His beard was streaked with the same dirty gray that colored the hair showing from beneath his flat-crowned hat.

"Yeah!" Colt snarled, angry because they'd taken so long to follow. "There are tracks all to hell and gone. Too many for one man to cover alone." He glared at the sheriff. "Where in hell have you been anyway?"

The sheriff held his hand palm outward in a placating gesture. "Now don't get all riled up, son," he said. "We've been through this too many times before to hope we'll ever catch that bunch. It's getting harder each time the bank gets robbed to find men willing to spend their time chasing after the wind."

Colt's gaze narrowed on the sheriff. "Are you saying you've been robbed before?"

"Hell!" the nearest man, clad in black from head to toe, exclaimed. "Bandits rob that bank on a regular basis . . . every couple of months or so. That's the reason nobody gets in a hurry to ride after 'em when they do. We always lose 'em along about here. They split up and run us around in circles; then they double back and head straight for the big thicket. Like they prob'ly done today. And once they're in the thicket, there ain't no man amongst us that can find 'em."

"Don't make no sense to keep ridin' out after 'em, neither," another man, hidden from sight by those who surrounded Colt, grumbled. "It's a fact that they don't get much loot anyways. Not since that first time they robbed the bank."

"No," said another man. "Ain't nobody gonna be fool enough to leave their money in the bank now. Don't know why Ezra don't just close the doors."

The sheriff's expression hardened. "It ain't the same this time, boys. Charles Huckabee—the bank clerk—said Ezra got it in his head to fool 'em this time. Had some sacks all ready for 'em, just in case they hit the bank again. But the sack wasn't full of money. It had wads of newspaper stuffed in the bottom, with a few bills—small ones—stacked together on the top. I figger that bunch couldn't have got away with more'n a couple hundred dollars. But they left Ezra dead.''

"They killed Ezra?'' one of the men said.

Obviously, everyone wasn't privy to that fact.

Then another man voiced his thoughts. "Heck,'' he said, "I guess them robbers is gonna be mad enough to eat dirt. Or make somebody else eat it. Guess it's a good thing old Ezra didn't make it. Them outlaws is likely to be out for revenge.''

"Uh, Sheriff,'' said the man in black, "why don't we just go on back now? My wife is waiting supper and she's sure to be riled if it gets cold.''

The sheriff rubbed a hand through his beard. "Guess we might just as well,'' he said. "It's a cinch we ain't gonna find 'em in that wilderness. At least they didn't get away with much.''

Colt's hands clenched into fists as rage surged through him. "Dammit, man! They got away with more than a couple of hundred dollars this time! This time they kidnapped a woman!''

The sheriff frowned and edged his mount closer, his gaze narrowed on Colt. "What woman? Nobody reported a woman missing.''

"My woman!'' The moment the words left Colt's mouth he realized he had begun to think of Amelia that way. As his woman.

"Well, that puts an entirely different slant on things,'' the sheriff said. "Robbing a bank is one thing, but stealing a woman is something else.''

"Aw, hell!'' the man in black said. "I reckon that means

we'll be going into the thicket. My woman is going to be mad enough to throw my supper out to the dogs.''

"Charlie," the sheriff snapped. "Would you stop your bellyaching?''

"Ain't going to do no good atall to go into the thicket looking for them, Sheriff," Charlie said. "You know we useta go in there, done it more'n a hundred times I'd bet, and every time we find our way back out I count myself lucky. A man could lose himself so bad in there he might never be found.''

The sheriff sent a searching gaze around the group of men. "Nobody has to keep looking," he said gruffly. "But I'm the law around here. It's my duty to go. If I don't at least try to find that woman, then I reckon I ain't doing what I'm paid to do and the lot of you would need to vote me out come next election.''

"Dammit to hell," muttered a man who had remained silent up to that moment. "I reckon the sheriff is bound and determined to go in there.''

"Well, I damn sure ain't." Charlie reined his mount around. "I'm goin' home to supper.''

He set spurs to his mount, and as he rode off, several men went with him. That left only Colt, the sheriff, and three others to enter the thicket.

"It's too dark to see anything now," the sheriff said, looking at the massive oaks and tangled vines that marked the beginning of the thicket. "Guess we might just as well wait until daybreak." He dismounted. "We'll make camp here.''

Although Colt knew the sheriff was right, he felt a sense of urgency to find Amelia as quickly as possible. He realized, though, that he could do nothing but get lost in the darkness, which would do Amelia no good. But how could he even think about sleeping when Amelia was being held by outlaws? She had to be frightened; perhaps even hurt.

The thought of Amelia being harmed caused a stab of pain in Colter's middle. He'd promised to keep her safe, to take her to his home in Morgan's Creek, where the Kincaid gang would never find her. Although it wasn't the Kincaid gang that had taken her, she'd surely be just as terrified as though it were. And the men who had kidnapped her might very well be just as bad as the Kincaids.

Oh, God, what was happening to her?

Nearby, one of the young men, barely out of his teens, spoke hesitantly. "Sheriff?"

The sheriff turned to meet the young man's eyes. "What is it, Randy?"

"I don't want to leave, Sheriff. Not when you need help so bad, but my ma is gonna be powerful worried about me and . . ."

The sheriff's face softened. "Yeah," he said gently. "Ruth's already lost too much to risk losing another son. You should have stayed with her." He gripped the young man's shoulder. "Go on home, Randy. There's nothing you can do here anyway."

The young man's Adam's apple bobbed up and down. "If you're sure . . ."

"I'm sure." The sheriff looked toward the towering oaks. "Those trees are just the beginning, son. There's pines growing so thick in there that a horse can't squeeze through. It's gonna be mighty hard to find that girl."

Randy shifted his feet, obviously embarrassed. "I don't want you to think I'm a coward or nothing like that."

"I won't think that, Randy. No. I wouldn't ever think that. You're not a coward. But you'd best go on home to your ma. She's had enough heartache, losing your brother so recently."

Still the young man hesitated. "You'll let me know if there's anything I can do? If you find them and need help bringing them in?"

"Yeah. I'll sure do that, son."

The young man was on the verge of mounting up when Colt stopped him. "Randy, could you do something for me when you get back to town?"

"Yes, sir," Randy said eagerly, glad there was a way to redeem himself. "You just name it, mister."

"I need a telegram sent."

"If you got some paper, you could write it out for me, and I'll make sure Hal sends it off right away."

Although Colt had no paper or pencil, one of the men who considered himself something of a poet produced both items. Colter wrote his message, and then Randy set off toward Nacogdoches, carrying Colt's message tucked deep in the pocket of his breeches.

Amelia regained consciousness slowly, opening pain-racked eyes to see the moon wavering fuzzily overhead.

Squinting at the pale orb circled by brilliant stars in a dark velvet sky, Amelia wondered about the dark streaks that crossed it. A moment later she realized she was seeing the sky through a thick tangle of vines. Even so, the moon's silvery glow filtered though, casting pale light on the bushes that surrounded her.

She lay motionless where she'd been dropped, every muscle in her body aching. As she tried to straighten her legs, she discovered they'd been tightly bound. As were her wrists.

Amelia wondered about her circumstances. Numb with pain and fatigue, half frozen by the chill night air, she felt dull-witted, barely able to think. She shifted slightly, trying to ease the ache of her position, and pain flared along her rib cage.

Her reaction was immediate, and she moaned low in her throat.

"Hey, Slade," a rough masculine voice somewhere nearby said. "She's waking up."

"So she is," another voice, also definitely male, said. "I was beginning to think I'd hit her too hard."

Someone had deliberately struck her?

Why? Amelia turned her head toward the nearest man, and her memory returned with a jolt. He was the one who'd been holding the horses in front of the bank. He bent over her and brushed a tangled streamer of hair from her face, and she flinched away from his touch, watching him from beneath lowered lashes.

"Why are you doing this?" Amelia asked, feeling a dull pain in her jaw as she spoke. It was probably swollen from the blow he'd dealt her. "What do you want from me?" she went on. "I have nothing of value."

The man called Slade smiled thinly, his gaze traveling over her soft, feminine form. "You're dead wrong, honey. You got plenty of value."

She felt chilled by his words, but refused to let him see it. For some reason, she felt there was no immediate danger to her person.

Suddenly a shiver shook her frame, and she looked longingly at the fire. The heat from the flames didn't reach far enough to warm her.

"You cold, honey?" Slade asked, kneeling closer to her. "Just say the word and I'll keep you warm."

"Go to hell," she gritted through teeth that had suddenly began to clatter.

"I probably will," he replied. "But not yet. I got me a lot of living to do before then."

"Not if Colter catches up to you," she said coldly.

"Colter?" he questioned. "He your husband?"

She started to deny it, then decided she might fare better if they thought she was married. Perhaps they wouldn't be so quick to misuse her if they thought she'd already been with a man.

"Yes," she said quickly. "He is my husband. And nobody to mess with, either."

"Be that as it may," the gunman said, "nobody can find us in this big thicket. Ain't no man alive knows this place better than me. And even if that husband of yours did come upon our hideout, we'd know he was coming long before he got there." He rose to his feet. "Nope; you might as well make up your mind, honey. There's no way in hell you can count on that man of yours for help."

"You're wrong." She refused to believe him. Colt would come for her. "Colt won't stop until he finds me." Amelia had to believe that for her own peace of mind.

"You better hope he don't," Slade said harshly. "For his own good." The expression on his face told her that he wasn't just trying to intimidate her. If Colt did find her, they would be waiting . . . and no man could beat the odds that would be against him. Not even Colt.

It was then she lost all hope of being rescued. If she were to escape from these men who held her captive, then she must, of necessity, do it alone.

Blake Morgan was weary to the point of exhaustion when he rode into Austin with his prisoner. James Lewis was an innocuous-looking man, one who blended well into a crowd. And he'd depended on that fact to keep one step ahead of the law. Even so, after months of tracking him, Blake had run him to the ground. And now the law would see Lewis punished for his misdeeds.

Reining his mount next to the sheriff's office, Blake dismounted, looped the gelding's reins over the rail, then nodded curtly at his prisoner. "Get down off that horse, Lewis."

Lewis held out his hands, which had been cuffed together in front of him. "Take these cuffs off first, Marshal, and I'll be happy to oblige."

Flattening his lips to show his displeasure, Blake reached out a hand, looped it through the outlaw's arms, and dragged him from his mount.

"Hey, man," Lewis protested, grasping at the saddle to keep his balance. "You didn't have to go and do that!"

"I'm tired, Lewis," Blake grated out, his gaze narrowed on the smaller man. "And I damn well ain't in the mood for your shenanigans."

Boots thudded on the boardwalk, and both men turned to see a heavyset man approaching. He eyed the cuffed man, then turned to Blake. "Who you got there, Morgan?"

"Feller by the name of Lewis, Sheriff. James Lewis."

"Well, I'll be damned!" the sheriff exclaimed. "I recognize him now. That's Gentleman Jim Lewis you got there. He's the feller who always asks real nice when he's robbing a bank at gunpoint."

"That's him," Blake growled. "Now if you'll just take charge of the prisoner, I'll get myself over to the hotel and get a little shut-eye."

"You look like you need it," the sheriff said. "But first I think you'd better come inside."

"What for?" Blake asked, unable to hide his irritation at the delay.

"A couple of telegrams came for you, Morgan. I wondered how I was gonna get them to you. Thought they might be important."

Telegrams? Now, who the hell was sending him a telegram, let alone two? With his lips set in a tight line, Blake followed the sheriff inside and waited impatiently while the prisoner was locked in a jail cell.

Moments later Blake was staring down at the words his brother had written.

Amy's been kidnapped. Need your help. Meet me in Nacogdo-ches.

Colt

"Who the hell is Amy?" Blake muttered.

He opened the other telegram and looked at the signature. It too was from Colt. The words made no more sense than had the first one.

Wait for me. Amy needs an escort home.

"Who the hell is Amy?" he asked again.

The sheriff shrugged his massive shoulders. "No use to ask me," he said gruffly. "I don't know her."

"My brother obviously does. Wonder if he's gone and got married."

"That what he says?"

"No. Just that she's been kidnapped." His brows drew together in a frown. "Wants me to meet him in Nacogdo-ches."

"Better get some rest first, son," the sheriff advised.

"Hell!" exclaimed Blake. "I can't. If Colt says come, then I've got to go. He wouldn't send a wire if it wasn't urgent."

"Then take the stagecoach. At least you can get some rest while you're traveling."

"You're right." Blake rubbed his bloodshot eyes. "But I was sure looking forward to a hot bath and a long sleep in a soft bed . . . among other things."

The sheriff laughed. "I can guess what those other things were, too."

"Yeah. I imagine you can."

"Anyway, you've got time to fill your belly before the stage comes in."

"I guess I should be thankful for that."

Blake hurried across to the hotel, looking forward to the first hot meal his belly had seen for the past two weeks.

But even while he ate, his mind worried over the telegrams he'd received. What had his brother gotten himself into that he needed help? Since Blake had no way of knowing, he decided to send a telegram of his own.

Chapter Eleven

It was late afternoon when Matthew, who had been repairing the corral, heard the sound of hooves and looked up to see a rider approaching.

Seeing it was the sheriff, a longtime friend, he waited silently to see what had brought him out to Morgan's Creek.

"Howdy, Matt," the sheriff greeted, reining his mount up beside the corral.

"Howdy, Skeeter." Matt was the only one who still dared to use the old childhood name given to Jason Crawford because of his diminutive size.

That was not so anymore, though. Crawford's size was more than equal to Matt's, who was taller than most men around. Except Skeeter, he thought with a smile.

"What brings you out here today?" Matt asked, the smile hovering around his lips.

"A telegram," Sheriff Crawford replied. He dismounted and handed Matt a long envelope. "Meant to get out here sooner, Matt," he said. "I figured the telegram might be important, but we had some trouble at the saloon that had to be tended to first."

"Trouble?" Matt asked absently, fingering the telegram, wondering if it contained bad news. Colt had been gone for a long time now, chasing after the men who'd killed their family.

"Yeah," the sheriff replied. "Drifter shot up the place, killed old man Grover. Had to put the drifter under arrest, and he wasn't going to jail easy." Skeeter eyed the envelope, his expression curious. "You gonna open that telegram, Matt?"

Matthew slit the envelope and read the contents. "Hell's bells," he muttered. "Looks like Colt went and got married."

"Well, now, ain't that a fine kettle of fish?" Skeeter said with a laugh. "I never figured him for the marrying kind. Anyways, with him so determined to catch those fellers that killed your ma and pa and little Annie, I never figured he'd stay in one place long enough to get hitched." He eyed Matt. "You don't look too happy about it, Matt. You got something against Colt finding a wife?"

"Not a thing," Matthew replied. "Except it appears Colter might have already lost her."

"Now, how in hell would you lose a wife?"

"Blake says somebody stole her. Says Colter wired him for help."

At the sound of approaching hooves, they turned their heads and Matthew saw his youngest brother, Benjamin, riding in for his weekly visit. "Benjamin's coming," he muttered.

"Must be his day off," Skeeter said, eyeing the approaching horseman.

Everyone around those parts knew that the youngest Morgan brother worked on another ranch. And damn lucky they were to get him, too. Ben was the best horse wrangler around. He had an affinity for animals, as though he could actually speak their language.

"I wondered if he'd show up today," Matt said, his gaze narrowed on his brother.

Ben reined up nearby. "Howdy, Jason," he greeted. "You staying for supper?"

"Hell, no!"

The sheriff's quick reply brought a wide grin to Ben's face. But it was quickly gone. "Can't say as I blame you," he muttered. "Meals around this place could stand a lot of improvement. Don't know why I even bother coming home on my days off." He eyed his eldest brother. "I keep telling you we could do with a woman around here, Matt. You need to get married."

"Colt was bringing us a woman," Matt said shortly. "But somebody stole her."

"Colt was bringing us a woman?" Ben looked confused. "A wife for you, Matt?"

"A wife for himself."

"You're kidding!" A grin pulled at the corners of Ben's mouth. "Hell's fire, Matthew! I can't believe Colter really got himself hitched . . . and without even inviting us to the wedding?"

"Maybe he didn't have time," Matthew suggested with amusement. "Maybe he was so bent on bedding her that he couldn't wait until we got there."

Matthew grinned when his younger brother blushed. It was a fact that Benjamin was afraid of women. But he'd get over it in time, Matt knew. And when he bedded his first woman, he'd wonder why he'd waited so long.

"How much time does it take to send a telegram?" Benjamin asked. "Hell's bells, Matt! He should have brought her home!"

"I guess that was what he was trying to do."

"We gonna go help him get her back?"

"Yeah." Matt's expression was grim. "We damn sure are." He headed for the barn. "Find Charley. Tell him what's going on and that he's in charge of the homestead while we're gone."

"Any way I can help?" the sheriff asked, matching his pace to Matthew's as they entered the barn's shadowy interior.

"Not unless you want to ride along." Matthew picked up his saddle and headed for the last stall, where the sorrel he'd just acquired was stabled.

For some reason he felt a need to hurry. Colter was out there, somewhere around Nacogdoches, trying to deal with God knew what. And Matthew would be damned if he'd leave Colt to face it alone. He'd already lost two brothers and he had no intention of losing another one. Not if he could help it.

"Wish I could go along," the sheriff said. "But I'm afraid the townsfolk wouldn't cotton to their only lawman leaving town." He sighed heavily. "Times like these I wish I'd never run for sheriff."

"Much obliged anyway, Skeeter." Matthew tossed the saddle on the sorrel. She wasn't as large as Thunder, the stallion he'd ridden home from the war, but the mare had stamina that wouldn't quit. He would need such a horse on his journey.

The sheriff took his leave, and as Matthew headed for the house to gather supplies for the trip, Benjamin and Charley hurried toward him.

"You sent for me, boss?" Charley asked when he was near enough to be heard.

"Yeah," Matt replied. "Did young Ben tell you what was needed?"

"He was short on words, as usual. Just said Colt was in trouble. Needed the both of you."

"Yeah. That's right. He does. And I'm putting you in charge while we're gone. You got any questions, you better ask 'em now."

"Won't think of 'em until you're gone, but you don't have to worry none about the homestead. Those two hands you hired on are good workers. Betwixt the three of us we'll handle things around here." The old man worked up a chew and let it fly. A brown stream of tobacco zipped through the air and landed in a huge splat on the ground. "Anybody comes riding in looking for trouble, they'll find they got plenty of it."

"Good!" Matthew knew Charley blamed himself for having been away from the homestead when the raiders attacked. But he'd only been following orders when he'd gone to town for supplies. "If you need anything from town, Charley, send one of the men for it."

"We got all we need here, boss. Ain't none of us leaving this place until you come back."

"Might be awhile."

"It don't make no never mind," Charley growled. "We ain't leaving here, no matter how long it takes you. You can rest easy about this place, son. Just go and help your brother."

"You're a good man, Charley."

The old man turned away, but not quickly enough for Matt to miss the moisture welling in the old-timer's eyes. Like Matt and his brothers, it would take a long time for Charley to recover from the raid. If he ever did. He had always had a soft spot for Annie, from the day she was born. And he hadn't been able to get through the telling of how he'd found her when he'd returned to find the devastation wrought by the raiders.

Having got himself under control again, the old man turned back to meet Matt's gaze. "Wish I could go with you, boss, but these old bones of mine don't—"

"You'll be helping most by staying at the homestead," Matt said. "We'll have an easier mind knowing you're in charge here."

"I appreciate that, Matt. And I won't let you down." *Not this time,* he told himself. The old man cleared his throat, forcing the lump that had lodged there back down. "Guess I might as well get back to work now. Have a nice trip, Matt. And you too, young Ben." The old man strode away then, intent on getting through the work he'd been assigned that morning.

Within the hour the brothers rode away from Morgan's Creek.

Amelia was left alone during the night, and much to her surprise, the outlaws broke camp at daybreak and continued their journey. The forest through which they traveled was thick with trees, some huge. Magnolias grew to great size, as did sugar maples. Amelia recognized buckeyes, beeches, and of course pines, saplings that grew so close together that sometimes there wasn't enough room for a horse and rider to squeeze through. But the outlaws obviously knew where they were going and followed some unseen trail that anyone who was not familiar with the territory would not easily find.

That fact alone made Amelia study the area around her closely as she tried to find something . . . some marker . . . anything that she might use if—no! when—she made her escape.

And she would escape. Some way. Somehow. She would never give in to being victimized by this band of outlaws. Not as long as there was breath in her body. No. She would fight to the death if need be.

Hadn't she already done so? Not her own death, but the death of a man who'd meant to misuse her. And she would not hesitate to do the same thing again . . . if the chance presented itself. And there was the rub. These outlaws were careful. They might not allow her any chance to escape.

A harsh laugh sounded behind her, and Amelia realized that she'd been caught out. She jerked her chin up, ignoring the man who thought her circumstances so humorous.

"Looking for signs, eh?" he asked. "Won't do you no good, missy. There ain't nothing in here that'll show you the way back out. And even if you was to escape, the gators would be sure to get you." He laughed again, tauntingly. "You rather get et by a gator than bedded by old Jude?" Another laugh. "Can't say as I blame you, but I reckon you won't get that choice."

Amelia knew she shouldn't rise to the bait, but the words were out before she could stop them. "Old Jude? Why should I be afraid of him? One man's no different from any other."

"And you'll get all the others before we're done with you," the man said harshly. "But I'm thinking you're gonna be changing your mind about Jude. Yeah, you'll change your mind right enough. The last gal we brought in here only lasted a few days. When Jude finished with her, there wasn't nothing left for the rest of us."

"That's enough, Clint!" the man who apparently was the leader snapped.

Her tormenter fell silent. But his words had already done the damage he'd intended, because Amelia couldn't put them out of her mind. What kind of man were they bringing her to anyway—someone who could misuse a woman so badly that she died at his hands?

She shuddered at the thought and, although she wanted desperately to work at the ropes binding her, to free herself and run through the forest—never mind the alligators or anything else that might be lurking in the swamp—she realized it was impossible. She had tried throughout the long hours of the night to do that very thing, but it had proved useless.

Amelia had discovered that the bindings were too tight to work free. It appeared that her only hope lay in waiting . . . and watching . . . and perhaps there would come a time when she could catch her captors unawares and make good her escape.

Colt wasn't surprised when the sheriff called a halt to the search. "There ain't no use in us going on, son," he said with deep regret in his voice. "We ain't gonna find her. Not alive anyways." He pushed his Stetson back, wiped beads of sweat off his forehead, and studied the tangle of briers that lay ahead of them.

"The ground's getting softer now. This thicket grows on sandy soil, soaks up water like a sponge. We're headed into this bog, son, where the gators are likely to make a meal of our horses, and us as well."

"You're probably right," Colter agreed, eyeing the marshy ground ahead. "A misstep would mire a horse down long enough for the alligators to get to him. That stuff ahead looks too soft to hold man or beast. Must be some way around it, though."

"Might be," the sheriff replied. "I guess there has to be, since the outlaws came this way. But it might take years to find it. And we don't have that much time. Fact is, I'm afraid time might've already run out for that little lady of yours.

"That gang was Jude Tanner's," he continued. "And there ain't no meaner son of a bitch alive. He stole a young girl last year, and when he was done with her he took her to her pa's farm and left her where she'd be sure to be found. What there was left of her anyways. Jude gets a kick out of hurting people. Especially women. But if he don't have one to vent his temper on, he takes it out on his men. That's the reason they keep him supplied with women. To save their own ornery hides."

Colter didn't like what he was hearing. The thought of Amelia being in the hands of such a man was almost unbearable.

The sheriff heaved a sigh. "Come on, boy, let's be headed back."

"No!" Colt said grimly. "There's no way in hell I'm leaving Amelia!"

"Now, son—"

"You go on back, Sheriff." Colt shoved his hat back and studied the area ahead of him. "I'm staying here. There's a way through that swamp, and I aim to find it."

"You can't go in there alone."

"Who's gonna stop me!"

"Nobody, son," the sheriff admitted. "You go and do what you have to. But I doubt we'll ever see you again."

"You've said your piece, Sheriff." Colt's voice was calm enough, but his eyes were cold. "Now leave me alone to find Amy."

As the sheriff turned to leave, Colt stopped him. "My brother will be riding into Nacogdoches one of these days," he said, "and I'd appreciate it if you'd tell him where I've gone."

"I'll do that," the sheriff said, reining his mount around. "You take care, son."

Colt remained silent. He'd said all that was needed. Now he would concentrate on finding Amelia before the outlaws reached their camp.

Chapter Twelve

The cabin was small.

As it was situated in the middle of a clearing, no one could approach without being seen. A good marksman could hold off an attack long enough for reinforcements to arrive. That was the reason Jude Tanner occupied the cabin alone. He had no fear of being caught by anyone who found the place, because his men were posted at strategic spots in the surrounding forest. If anyone tried to approach the cabin, they would be caught in a crossfire.

Jude Tanner appeared almost jovial to Amelia's eyes when he stepped through the open door and paused to look her over. Her fear eased slightly. Perhaps the outlaws had only been taunting her. Perhaps the man who waited quietly on the porch wasn't the evil one they had portrayed. That hope was quickly quashed when he opened the saddlebag and discovered what was inside.

With a roar of rage, he tossed the small bills aside and dug frantically at the strips of newspaper in the bottom of

the sack. Then he became quiet, and the utter silence as
well as the cold look in his eyes made his band of outlaws
retreat to a safer distance. Only one man stood facing him.
The man who'd made Amelia's tormentor hold his tongue.

"Explain yourself," Jude said grimly. "What does this
mean?"

The man faced him steadily. "I reckon they must have
expected us," he said. "Obviously did. They had the bag
ready when we got there."

"And you never thought it might be a trick?"

"We wasn't thinking, Jude. Lem threw that damn knife
of his at the banker. That dude squealed like a stuck pig
before he keeled over dead. I figured the other folks in
the bank wouldn't stay quiet much longer. That was the
reason I didn't take the time to look in the bag, just figured
we'd best make tracks out of there."

Jude turned to the man called Lem. "Just had to kill
somebody, eh, Lem?"

"Hell, Jude," Lem said. "You don't usually mind killing
people. I didn't think—"

"You're damned right!" Jude said, his fist lashing out
and knocking Lem down with a hard thud. "You didn't
think!" He hooked his fingers into the man's shirt and
pulled him upright. "Now we're gonna have to go somewheres else for our money. And that's gonna make it more
dangerous."

"Why do we have to go somewheres else?" Lem whined.

"You killed the banker, you fool! He was the reason the
bank stayed open. Now they'll have to find somebody else
to take it over, and that probably won't be easy. If it can
even be done at all."

"I never thought—"

"No! You never do!"

"It wasn't a total loss, boss. We brung you a girl."

Jude turned to Amelia, seeming to notice her for the

first time. "I guess that's something," he admitted slowly. "At least I'll have something to occupy my time while I'm making my plans." He crooked a finger at Amelia. "Come here, girl. Let me have a look at you."

Amelia stayed where she was. One of Jude's henchmen shoved her forward, and Jude curled his fingers around her upper arm and yanked her toward him. She tried to jerk away and heard the rip of fabric as her sleeve tore off.

Smiling, Jude caressed her bare flesh. "Now ain't she soft . . . like silk. We're gonna have us a real good time together, missy. At least I will."

She shivered beneath his touch. "Release me," she said sharply. "If you don't . . . well, there are people looking for me and . . ."

He laughed harshly. "There could be a hundred people looking for you, missy, and it wouldn't do you no good. Nobody comes in this thicket after us. Not and lives to tell about it."

"My husband—"

"Can't do a damn thing for you. All you got left now is me. And you'd better be thinking on how to make me happy . . . it's the only way you're gonna stay alive."

Jude Tanner cupped Amelia's chin in his palm and studied her closely; then he looked at his henchmen. "Maybe you boys didn't do so bad after all," he said. "Yeah. Maybe it wasn't a total washout. I'm gonna really enjoy this one. Maybe she'll stay alive a little longer than the last one did."

Amelia controlled a shiver of fear mingled with revulsion. She recognized evil when she saw it. And the man standing before her was evil incarnate. The devil himself. And she was afraid there would be no escaping the devil this time.

Oh, Colt, she cried inwardly. *Where are you? I need you so much.*

But Colt wouldn't come this time. These men were right.

He'd never find his way through the forest. And even if he did, he would never get through the marshy bog.

"Come on, girlie," Jude said. "I got a room just waiting for you." He dragged her into the other room and closed the door behind them.

The room couldn't have been much bigger than eight feet by eight feet and was dense with shadows. There was only one small window, high in the wall. But the light filtering through that window was enough to show her there were no furnishings except for a four-poster bed and one ladder-back, cane-bottomed chair.

Amelia's narrowed gaze became riveted on the bed . . . on the ropes with dark stains that were fastened around each post. She stared at the ropes in horror as her stomach suddenly threatened to erupt. The stains looked like blood. Dried blood.

Oh, Lord! What had happened there?

Amelia looked away quickly, unwilling to contemplate what might have taken place on that bed. Her frantic gaze swept the room again and again, searching for something . . . some way out of the room.

But there was none. No escape. Only that window, that high window that appeared way too small to crawl through, even if she could reach it.

Jude Tanner laughed, but there was no humor in the sound. "How do you like my house, missy? Everything has been prepared for your pleasure . . . if you like that sort of thing. And some women do, you know. Some women like a little pain with their pleasure. Others"—he shrugged— "well, they don't seem to enjoy it very much." He came toward her. "Now you. I wonder how you'll be."

He curled his fingers around her upper arm and unsheathed his knife. Amelia stared at the long, thin blade that appeared to be as sharp as a razor.

She swallowed around the lump of fear that had lodged

in her throat. "What are you going to do?" she whispered hoarsely.

He laughed again. "Don't worry. I'm just cutting you free," he said.

Amelia felt a burst of hope blossom within her breast. "Are you really going to let me go?"

He threw back his head and laughed, and the sound sent cold chills racing down her back. "Now, wouldn't that make a lot of sense?" he asked. "I ain't gonna turn you loose, girlie. Not when we're just getting aquainted." He grinned at her as his blade sliced through her bonds.

Pain stabbed through her wrists, and Amelia rubbed the rope-burned flesh, trying to get the blood to start flowing again. But she was allowed no time. Jude snagged her right wrist and pulled her toward the bed.

Amelia's eyes opened wider as the outlaw reached for the rope attached to the nearest post and looped it around her left wrist before she had time to gather her wits enough to struggle.

As he began to tighten the rope, a knock sounded at the door. "What?" he shouted, his anger evident in his voice.

The door opened to a narrow crack, and the man they'd called Slade stuck his head through. For a moment his eyes met Amelia's, and there was something in his gaze that suggested he might be feeling sorry for her. It was only a momentary perception, though, gone as quickly as it had appeared. He turned to the man who was waiting beside his prisoner, his gaze hard and angry.

"Carla's coming, boss."

"Dammit!" Jude said harshly. "She would show up right now." He pinned his henchman with a dark look. "Stall her! I'll be right out."

Yanking Amelia's wrists together, Jude bound them quickly. "That oughta hold you until I get through with

Carla," he said grimly. Then he strode across the room and through the doorway and slammed the door behind him, leaving Amelia alone to contemplate her fate.

Amelia uncurled her fingers and flexed her wrists, and the rope loosened slightly. Jude had been too impatient to notice that her hands had not been pressed together when he'd bound them.

It was only moments before Amelia had freed herself from her bonds. For all the good it did her, she quickly realized, since there was no way to escape from the room.

Her gaze scanned the room for something to use for a weapon. The chair. Perhaps she could defend herself with that. But even if she managed to subdue Jude, the odds were still against her.

Crossing quietly to the window, Amelia looked up at the patch of blue sky that could be seen through the small opening.

A slight breeze drifted into the room, not enough to take away the horrible smells that teased her nostrils. It was a musky smell overlaid by an acrid scent reminiscent of rusty nails.

And even though Amelia hadn't had occasion to smell it before, she recognized it for what it was. Blood. Old blood. And soon, if she didn't find a way out of this mess, those smells would mingle with that of fresh blood. Her blood.

Oh, God, she had to get out of here!

As quietly as possible, she picked up the chair and placed it carefully beneath the window. Grasping the ladder back to steady herself, she stood on the cane seat and stretched until she could reach the opening. Then, gripping the sill tightly, she pulled herself upward until she could peer outside.

But there was nothing there to see. Nothing but a wide stretch of meadow between herself and the piney woods.

No guards. But why should guards be posted there when there was no way out of this room?

"Oh, God," she murmured, weak tears welling in her eyes. "Please help me."

Defeat settled over her as she lowered herself and slumped in the chair. It appeared she had no alternative but to remain captive and submit to whatever Jude Tanner had in mind for her. A quick look at the bed was all she needed to tell her that, if she remained his prisoner, her future would not be a pleasant one.

Colter lay on his stomach, hidden by a large rock, looking down at the cabin below. An armed guard stood outside the cabin, and several more had been posted in the forest where they could watch the front of the house.

As he watched, a woman left the cabin, and his heart skipped a beat. But it wasn't the woman he was searching for. Even at this distance, he could see that her hair was dark and she was taller than Amelia.

Was Amy inside the cabin?

Knowing he could do nothing at the moment, he forced himself to remain motionless, except for his eyes, which skittered back and forth as he studied the situation and learned the positions of the guards, counted the outlaws, and made his plans.

At dusk the guards were changed and several men lingered on the porch, talking together while the woman cooked their food over a campfire. And still he waited, his gaze fixed on the cabin. It would be dark soon. And then he would set his plan in motion.

Inside the cabin, Amelia crouched in a corner of the room, her hands gripping the ladder-back chair, her gaze never wavering from the door lest she miss the moment when Jude returned.

But, strangely, it had been hours since he'd left the room.

During that time Amelia had heard people speaking in the other room, although she'd been unable to hear what they were saying. But the voices had become louder in the past few minutes, as though they were arguing.

Amelia knew the woman was still around. She'd heard her voice several times during the day and wondered if the woman had been told about their prisoner. Should she make her presence known? If the woman already knew and didn't care, then all Amelia would accomplish by doing so would be to remind Jude of his prisoner.

No, she decided. It would be best if she remained absolutely quiet.

Amelia looked at the window again, wishing it were larger. Or that her body were smaller. She was almost certain her waist would fit through the opening. And her hips might. But her shoulders were certainly too wide to go through.

Sighing with despair, Amelia slumped on the bed. But even as she did so, her eyes returned to the window. It was her only hope, slim though it was.

Amelia climbed on the chair again and gripped the windowsill tightly. Then, with her arms taking most of her weight, she climbed the ladder back, standing at the uppermost rung while visually measuring her shoulders against the window.

Yes, she decided, her shoulders were definitely too wide, but perhaps if she slanted them just so, she could work her way through.

It might work, she told herself. She just might fit through that space. She looked down at herself. Although her shirtwaist was cotton, her riding skirt was of heavy linen that only added to her bulk.

Without a second thought, Amelia stripped down to her camisole and bloomers, then hoisted herself upward again. She could easily get stuck in the opening, she knew, but her predicament would be no worse than it was now, and at least she would know she'd tried everything possible to free herself.

She stuck her head through the window, then slanted her shoulders and began to wiggle her body, trying to force it through the small opening, never allowing herself to wonder how she would reach the ground even if she made it through the window.

Colt continued to wait as the shadows lengthened. It was the hardest thing he'd ever done, yet he knew that if he went down there in the light of day, he would surely be seen and gunned down. Then he would be of no help to Amelia.

His gaze skittered back and forth continually, sweeping across the area all around the cabin, even though he'd already ascertained there was only one small window in the back . . . too small for entry or exit.

Since most of his attention was on the front of the cabin, where the men were, he almost missed the action taking place behind the cabin.

As Colt's narrowed gaze swept over that area again, a flicker of movement, barely perceptible, caught his eye. He looked again and saw a brief flash of gold, gone as quickly as it had appeared.

Probably a leaf blowing in the wind, he thought. Then he frowned and turned his attention there again. Leaf? Wind? There was no wind. Only a slight breeze. Not nearly enough to carry leaves.

Colt waited a long moment; then he saw the glint of gold again. It was a mere flicker of color, as before.

He turned his attention to the front of the cabin. The men were still there, lounging around on the porch. And the woman was there too, appearing deep in conversation with one of the men. Nothing had changed. Yet something had. He was positive of that.

Moving quietly, he changed his position, making no sound as he did so. He had learned during the war that even the snap of a twig could mean instant death. And he was taking no chances that the men below might hear. It was only a matter of moments before he was in a position to see the whole area in back of the cabin.

And there, apparently stuck in that window, was the woman he'd been searching for. Amelia. It had been her frantic movements to free herself that had caused her hair to flow wildly around her head.

Beads of perspiration dotted Amelia's forehead as she struggled to push herself through the window. Although she had managed to get her upper body through the opening, her hips would not budge.

Caught in the grip of panic, she had abraded her skin in several places in her attempt to escape, yet she ignored the pain. It was nothing compared to what would happen if she were caught.

She was despairing when she heard a whisper of sound, followed by a husky voice, barely distinguishable to her ears.

"Amelia."

Stifling a scream that would surely have brought the outlaws running, Amelia twisted her head around until she could see the man who'd spoken her name. "Colt?"

Her eyes widened and she stared at him as though he were a ghost.

"Shhhhh," he whispered. "We can't let them hear. Are you stuck?"

Blinking away tears, she nodded her head.

"You have to try harder, honey," he said gruffly. "Put your hands against the wall and use them for leverage."

Drawing courage from his presence, Amelia did as he asked and felt her body slide forward a few inches.

"Again," he said.

She tried again, feeling the rough boards digging into her flesh as her body moved again. Stuck. Then slid farther out the window.

"Come on," Colt whispered. "You're doing it."

It happened so suddenly that it was totally unexpected. Amelia's hips cleared the window, and only her thighs and legs remained inside. And as she gripped the upper sill while she wriggled her legs, she looked down to where Colt waited, his arms held high to catch her.

Without a moment's hesitation, she let go of the window-sill.

Amelia was a small woman, and Colt would have been able to take her weight easily if she had simply fallen into his arms. But when she released her hold on the windowsill, her foot caught on the shutter and she twisted frantically to wrench it free. The action caused her to fall head downward.

Fearing she would break her neck if she landed head first, Amelia cartwheeled her arms, trying to right herself.

Whump!

Her body struck solid flesh. Strong arms tightened around her, breaking her fall. Colter stumbled backward; then his knees buckled, and he and Amelia struck the ground. Hard.

Amelia lay beside him, breathless, her heart thumping

at the near miss. And then she turned to look at the man who had most likely saved her life.

"Colt . . ." Her eyes widened.

He lay beside her, his eyes closed, a knot already forming on his temple.

My God, I've knocked him out!

She crawled to her knees. "Colt," she whispered, patting his cheeks lightly. "Wake up, Colt. We have to get out of here."

He groaned, and her heart skipped a beat.

"Shhhh," she whispered. "They'll hear us, Colt. We have to be real quiet. And we have to get away from here before they find us."

He groaned again, then opened dazed eyes and looked up at her. "What happened?" he asked.

Chapter Thirteen

Amelia swallowed hard. "I knocked you out," she whispered unsteadily.

"Why did you do that?" he complained, obviously forgetting how desperate their circumstances were. He pushed himself to a sitting position, using the wall of the cabin to support himself.

Amelia tugged at his arm, trying to make him understand the urgency of their situation. "We don't have much time, Colt," she said, unable to keep the fear out of her voice. "If we don't leave right now we stand a good chance of losing our lives."

But she didn't have to explain further as she saw comprehension dawn in his dark eyes. "Dammit! We've got to get out of here," he muttered.

His gaze flickered to the wide area between them and the heavily wooded area. "There's much open space between us and those woods, Amelia. We're gonna have to cross it as fast as we can. Are you able to run?"

"Just try and stop me."

She helped him to his feet, noticing how he swayed unsteadily. But it was only momentary. Locking his knees in place, he curled his big hand around hers.

Then, nodding toward the forest, he urged her toward the thick growth of trees that would cover their escape.

Although Amelia expected to hear an alarm given at any moment, the only sound she heard was the beating of her heart as it thundered in her chest.

But their luck was about to change.

With the verdant forest only yards away, she heard a hoarse yell, followed by a loud noise, then the whine of a bullet displacing the air beside her face.

"Don't let them get away!" a voice yelled.

And then Amelia and Colt plunged into the forest, but even so they dared not slow down, lest they be caught.

Colter's grip was tight as he pulled her along through the trees and underbrush, racing along the worn path made by animals on their way to water.

They leaped over fallen logs and rotted limbs, but Amelia realized that neither of them could keep up the pace very long. And when they slowed down, their pursuers were bound to catch up.

The sounds of pursuit grew louder. Underbrush cracked beneath heavy boots. The outlaws seemed to be closing in on them.

Amelia's breath came in quick gasps, and her legs were on the point of buckling.

As though he realized it, Colter tugged her off the path, pushing his way into a tangle of vines beside a ravine. They clambered down the slope, losing their balance halfway down and landing in an ungainly heap at the bottom.

The voices were louder now as their pursuers closed the distance between their quarry.

Realizing they were not safe yet, Colter pushed Amelia

toward a moss-covered rock that, at some time in the past, had slid down the slope and become wedged near the bottom, leaving a space about two feet high beneath.

Dropping to his knees, Colter entered the shadows beneath the rock, pulling Amelia behind him.

The men were directly above them now, their voices clear enough to make out the words.

"How in hell did she get out of that room?" one of the men asked.

"Beats me," said another. "But it'll be our heads if we don't find her."

"Who was that with her?"

"How in hell should I know?"

"What I want to know is how he got by the guards?"

"Hell! I don't know. I'm just damn glad I wasn't one of 'em,"

"Me too. They're gonna have a lot of explaining to do."

"Or dying."

"Shut up back there!" growled another man. "And beat them bushes as you go. They might be hiding alongside the trail."

Amelia was tense, her body trembling with fear. It wouldn't be long before the men decided to search the gully where they were hiding.

Apparently Colter was of the same mind. The voices had barely faded before he crawled out from beneath the rock and helped her stand upright.

"We'll have to take our chances in the swamp, Amelia," he said gruffly.

"The swamp?" she repeated. "But there are alligators there, Colt. And water moccasins."

"I'd rather face them than what those men have in mind for us. At least with the alligators we have a chance."

"Do you know how to get there?'

He nodded. "I had plenty of chances to look this place

over while I was looking for you. Nearly got lost several times. Until I came across that animal trail that led straight to the cabin."

"What about your horse?"

"Had to leave him several miles back," he told her, trying to keep his eyes away from the flesh that was barely covered by her thin camisole. He didn't like to think about why she was half undressed, but the thought of another man touching her caused a curious rage to coil deep inside him.

The area they traveled through was so green that it was hard to separate the colors. Moss hung from cypress limbs, looking almost ghostly in the twilight.

"We need to find a place to hole up for the night," Colt said. "It will be dangerous traveling through here in the dark."

"Do we dare stop, though?"

"They won't be able to search at night."

The ground beneath their feet had become soft and damp. The swamp couldn't be far away, Amelia realized. She became certain of it when she heard the croaking of frogs in the distance.

"The swamp is just ahead," she said. "But we can't go in there at night, Colt. The alligators will be foraging for food."

Colt remained silent, stopping at the base of an enormous tree that grew alongside a drop-off. He parted a tangle of vines and moss that draped the branches and peered below. A narrow stream wound through the forest, the water green and murky, mysterious-looking.

"We're going down," he said, grasping her hand in a hard grip.

Fearing they were leaping from the frying pan into the fire, she followed him down the mossy slope to the banks of the stream.

Then he began to search along the creek, separating the bushes as though looking for something.

"What are we looking for?" she asked.

"A canoe."

"A canoe?"

"Yes. I saw it on my way to the cabin."

"Don't you remember where you saw it?"

"Thought I did, but these bushes all look alike."

Moments later they found the canoe, and after Colter put the oars into the boat, Amelia helped him drag it to the water. "There might be holes in the bottom," she whispered as they shoved the craft into the stream.

"Let's hope not," he replied.

Holding the canoe steady, he waited while she stepped into it, and moments later they were shoving off into the slow-moving stream.

Time passed as Colt paddled steadily, trying to put as much distance as possible between themselves and the outlaw band while they were cloaked in darkness. But, as Amelia had told him, the night held many dangers for them.

Colt was weary beyond belief. He stopped paddling and looked at Amelia, who had finally succumbed to exhaustion. She was fast asleep. He sighed deeply and surveyed his surroundings.

Nothing looked familiar. He was afraid they had become hopelessly lost.

He remembered the sheriff's words just before they'd parted. "You be careful in there, son," he'd said. "There's quicksand in those bogs. A man could get caught in it and be sucked down sure as anything. And there's places in that swamp that no man's ever seen before. Some folks have gone in there and never been heard of again."

But that wouldn't happen to them, Colt told himself.

He had no doubt they would survive, if they kept ahead of the outlaws. And to do that, he had to keep moving.

The moonlight helped some, since the cypress trees that grew in the water didn't have leaves to stop the silvery beams from lighting their way. But the twists and turns in the stream might prove deadly in the end.

Colter looked at Amelia again, sleeping so peacefully in the prow of the boat, and sighed heavily. God, he was tired. If only he could rest for a while, but the ground on each side of the stream looked marshy, completely unstable, and he dared not beach the canoe yet.

Perhaps, though, he could rest without beaching the canoe. He eyed a moss-covered cypress ahead in the middle of the stream. Perhaps he could stop the canoe there, rest his weary arms, and close his stinging eyes for a little while.

Just a few short minutes. That was all he needed. A little rest and they could go on.''

Suiting thought to action, Colter paddled to the cypress tree and looped the rope over a broken branch. It looked strong enough to keep the canoe where it was for a while.

With a weary sigh, he shoved the paddle into the bottom of the canoe, then stretched his long frame on the bottom and closed his bloodshot eyes. Moments later he was sound asleep.

Water lapped softly against the canoe, and the night creatures that had been silent since the intruders came among them began to prowl again. An alligator that had been submerged except for its eyes rose in the water, looked at the canoe, and glided toward it, creating a slight current that hadn't been there before.

The rope loosened as the alligator swept by, then turned toward the boat again, almost playfully. Then, making another sweep at the canoe, the alligator lashed its tail beneath the water, loosening the coil of rope even further.

Splash. The sound was a gentle one, merely a whisper really as the rope dropped into the water, then rose again.

The alligator nudged the rope curiously, but found nothing of interest there. With a soft swish, the alligator moved away, and the canoe, pushed by the artificial current created by its passing, bobbed gently on its way. It stopped momentarily when it reached a fallen branch, then floated free into the stream, leaving the people asleep in the canoe unaware of its movement.

Amelia awoke with a start. Something had disturbed her. She stared up at the trees overhead in the early light of dawn.

She sat up, her gaze going to the sleeping Colt.

"Colt?" she whispered.

He woke immediately, sitting up and reaching for her. "What is it, Amelia?"

"Where are we?"

He sighed heavily and raked a hand through his dark hair. "In the middle of the creek," he replied. "God, I'm tired. I had to rest for a while so I tied the—"

He broke off and frowned, taking in his surroundings. "Did you untie us, Amelia?"

"No."

"Damn it!" he swore. "I guess the rope didn't hold." He studied the densely wooded forest around them, taking note of the rocks that covered the mossy ground. "I suppose it doesn't really matter, though. We've reached stable ground. Maybe we'll be out of here soon."

"Let's hope so." Amelia studied the moss-covered ground. "Do you really think it's stable enough to walk on?"

"Yeah. But to make sure, we'll use the paddle to test the ground. Here." He handed it across to her.

Amelia stood in the canoe and shoved the paddle hard

against the ground. "It seems firm enough," she said doubtfully. "But I'm not really sure I want to get out."

"Then sit down and let me check it first."

She sat, leaning back so he could pass her, watching as he stepped out of the canoe and tested the ground. "Yeah," he said. "It's firm enough. Hop out so I can drag the canoe ashore."

Moments later they were hiding the canoe beneath the heavy growth of bushes growing along the edge of the bayou.

Taking their direction from the sun that was topping the trees with gold, they began the long trek that would take them out of the forest. Although they walked for hours, they appeared to make little progress. The trees were just as thick, the saplings so close together it appeared the forest was closing in around them. And by the time the sun hung directly overhead, Colt finally admitted what he'd been suspecting for some time.

They were lost.

Hopelessly, irrevocably lost.

"What are we going to do?" Amelia asked, licking dry lips.

"Keep moving," he replied.

Sighing heavily, she did just that, but as the day progressed, Amelia's thirst deepened and became almost overpowering. When they heard the sound of running water, she thought she must be imagining things. And then they saw it. A narrow, spring-fed creek, bubbling merrily along as it flowed toward some unknown destination.

With an exclamation of delight, Amelia hurried forward and dropped down on her stomach to quench her thirst.

Colt stopped her with a hand on her shoulder. "Just a little," he said gruffly. "Let your stomach get used to it first, Amelia."

After cooling herself with the sweet water, Amelia sat

back on her heels and looked up at Colt. "I was beginning to worry," she said. "I thought we'd never find water we could drink, and this tastes so good."

"You're not the only one who was worrying," he replied.

They stayed awhile at the creek, neither of them in a hurry to resume their journey. They were both too weary, too tired to continue, and while they rested, each of them was occupied with their own thoughts.

Amelia was thinking about what she'd do when she reached town, about the huge steak she would order from the nearest eating place.

But Colt's thoughts were on their immediate circumstances. He knew they were a long way from reaching civilization.

Finally, his worry took precedence over his weary state. He rose to his feet and said, "Stay here, Amelia, while I look around."

"You won't go far?" she asked anxiously.

"No. I won't go far."

She leaned back and closed her eyes and sighed deeply. She could rest easily now. Colt was with her. He would see them safely home.

Chapter Fourteen

It was high noon when the Morgan brothers rode into Nacogdoches. The town had nothing to distinguish it from the others they'd passed through. Wooden buildings, connected by boardwalks, lined the street. It was easy to recognize the stores since the merchants had fronted their businesses with hitching posts to accommodate their customers.

Matthew's gaze flickered back and forth as he rode down the street. He saw two old men seated on a bench in front of the mercantile. A ladder-back rocking chair stood nearby, empty, looking almost forlorn. A gust of wind set the rocker to moving. The nearest old-timer gave a start of surprise, then laughed and turned back to his companion.

A woman wearing a calico dress made her way down the boardwalk, and as she passed the old-timers, she lifted the hem of her skirt and circled around them.

Matthew smiled at the woman and tipped his hat, but before she could respond, his searching gaze had already left her. The bars on the windows clearly identified the building he was looking for. He knew the sheriff's office would be there.

At the precise moment he spotted the building, the door opened and two men stepped out onto the boardwalk. They stood there talking together. The six-sided stars both men wore pinned to their vests identified them as lawmen.

Although both men were broad, one was a good head taller than the other. It was to that man Matthew directed his attention, because he'd already recognized him as his brother Blake.

Matt and Benjamin reined their mounts up in front of the jail and waited silently for the lawmen to end their conversation.

Blake was the first to become aware of their scrutiny. He looked up with a frown that quickly dissolved into a wide smile. "It's about time you two got here," he said. As the two brothers dismounted, Blake went on, "What in hell took you so long anyway?"

"We left as soon as we got your telegram," Matt said, clasping his younger brother's hand.

Benjamin threw an arm across Blake's shoulder. "Where's Colt?" Although his voice was gruff, it didn't hide his anxiety.

"I don't know." Blake was as worried as his brothers were. "The sheriff here told me Colter went into the big thicket to look for his wife. Sheriff has a man posted there to keep watch, but Colt hasn't come out of there."

Benjamin turned to the sheriff. "Colt went in there alone?"

"Yeah," the sheriff replied. "He did. I tried to convince him to wait, but he wouldn't listen. He was determined to find his wife . . . can't say as I blame him, neither."

"Why didn't you send a posse with him?" Matthew asked grimly.

"I've had one in there before." The sheriff looked away from Matt's cold gaze. "We couldn't go very far, though. It ain't no place for man nor beast, that's the reason the outlaws go in there. It's an easy enough place to hide. Horses get mired in the bogs . . . if they don't get et up by alligators. A man who knows the thicket could hide in there for the rest of his life and never be found."

"So you're saying Colt is as good as dead?" Matthew's voice was cold enough to freeze hot coals.

"No," the sheriff replied. "I'm just saying he's gonna be damned lucky if he finds his wife. And luckier still if the two of 'em find their way back out of there."

"So what are we gonna do?" Benjamin asked, his gaze flickering between his two brothers. "We're not just gonna leave 'em in there, are we?"

"Damned right we're not!" Matthew said emphatically. "Even if we were willing to leave Colt—which we're not— we couldn't leave his wife. Hell! We need a woman on the ranch too bad to let one escape."

Neither of his brothers took exception to his words. They knew how loyal he was to family, knew how much he cared about each of them. He would never say the words aloud, though. But they knew.

"What are we waiting for then?" Benjamin said, his gaze dwelling wistfully on the eatery across the street. "Let's go after them."

"Don't get so impatient, little brother," Blake growled. "I just rode into town myself and I've been a mighty long time without grub. The sheriff was just telling me the hotel restaurant has a way of cooking steak that makes it almost melt in your mouth. We were on our way over there when the two of you rode in."

Benjamin's stomach growled at the mention of food. And, although he was eager to start the search for his brother, he figured another hour probably wouldn't make that much difference to Colter's circumstances. It was a certainty that Ben himself would function much better if he filled his stomach with food before taking on a band of outlaws.

"Just lead the way," he said.

The four men headed toward the hotel.

A hand on Amelia's shoulder woke her.

With a gasp of fear, she jerked upright, her eyes snapping open and her heart fluttering wildly as she stared up at the huge figure towering over her.

Colt.

"Oh, Lord, Colt," she exclaimed, putting a hand over her heart. "You frightened me half to death."

"I'm sorry," he said gently. "I didn't mean to." He smiled down at her. "Are you hungry, Amelia?"

"Oh, God, yes." As if on cue, her stomach rumbled.

Laughing, Colter curled his fingers around hers and pulled her to her feet. "Come with me then," he said. "I have a surprise for you."

"I hope it's a six-course dinner," she said dryly. "Or even a five-course dinner." She met his laughing eyes. "I guess it's too much to hope for."

"I'm afraid so."

"I'd settle for a big, juicy steak," she told him mournfully. "Or if you can't manage that, a handful of berries would do." She gave him a long look. "Is that what you found, Colt? Did you find a berry bush?"

"You'll see."

He led her toward a thick tangle of vines and held them aside while she went through. She paused on the other side, wondering why he was being so mysterious. As he stepped around her, she realized that a huge moss-covered boulder draped with vines and briers loomed before them, blocking their way.

She met his eyes in silent question.

"Just a little farther now," he said, snaring her wrist in a hard grasp.

"We can't go any farther," she protested.

"Yes, we can."

He followed the circle of vines and briers a short way and then stopped, reaching out to push aside a dense growth of leaf-covered vines.

Amelia's eyes widened as she stared at the opening Colt had exposed. "A cave, Colt?"

He nodded his dark head. "Yeah, it's a cave. And it's a perfect place to hide."

Hide? Her face blanched, the color leaching out of her cheeks. "Are we going to stay here?"

He circled her shoulders with his arm and pulled her hard against him. "Just for a little while, Amy," he said gently. "We need to give them time to stop searching for us."

"But what if they find us?"

"They won't while we're in there." He nodded his head at the hole in the rock.

"How long will we have to stay here?"

"Just a few days."

Amelia's heart beat fast with trepidation as she followed Colt into the hole. The small cave had a narrow entrance that widened several feet inside. The ceiling was too low for Colt to stand upright, but Amelia had no problem doing so. On the far side of the cave was a narrow tunnel. Despite her misgivings, Amelia followed Colt into the dark passageway. It was only twenty feet or so before the passage opened into a large cavern at least forty feet in circumference.

Amelia's eyes widened in amazement. The cavern was

remarkable enough in itself, but the rays of sunshine that glimmered on the rock walls almost took her breath away.

She looked up to find the source of the sunshine, and there, high above her head, was a large hole in the roof of the cavern.

"I never would have believed it, Colt," she exclaimed. "How on earth did you find this wonderful place?"

He laughed at her pleasure. "I literally stumbled over it."

"What a perfect hiding place," she whispered in awe. "Do you suppose the outlaws know it's here?"

"I doubt that anyone has ever found it before," he replied. "It was just by luck I stumbled across it. If the rabbit I was pursuing hadn't dashed in here, I would have passed it by."

"A rabbit? Did it get away?" Even as she asked the question, her nostrils twitched, assailed by a delicious aroma, that of roasting meat.

"No," he replied with amusement. "The rabbit didn't get away. It's cooking right now."

"I can smell it," Amelia said, her mouth watering at the thought of roasted meat. She followed her nose through another narrow passage, searching out the source of the wonderful aroma. She had only gone a few feet when it began to widen. Moments later she stepped into a small chamber where a fire, ringed by rocks, blazed cheerfully.

"You've certainly been busy," she said. "I must have slept for a long time for you to do all this."

"No. Not long," he said. "I gathered the mushrooms on the way here, and the rabbit almost leaped into my arms." He laughed, and the sound sent shivers up and down her spine.

Amelia lowered her eyes, unwilling for Colt to read her expressive eyes. Then suddenly she realized what he'd just said. "Mushrooms, Colt?" she asked hopefully. "Are they edible?"

"Yeah." He bent over and pulled one off the roasting stick that nestled over a bed of coals. "Want to try one?"

Amelia took it eagerly and popped the golden brown mushroom into her mouth. "Hot," she mumbled, snatching it out again.

"You'll burn yourself," he warned. "You should have cooled it first."

"I'm too hungry," she complained.

Even so, she blew on the mushroom several times, then took a bite. "Oh, Colt," she sighed. "This is absolutely wonderful." She eyed the roasting rabbit. "That meat looks done. I wouldn't cook it any longer."

"Let's give it a few more minutes," Colt said. "You can have some more mushrooms, though. And if you want to wash up, there's a spring at the far side of the cavern. The water's cold but—"

"You've thought of everything, haven't you?"

A feeling of pleasure washed over Colt as he watched her hurry toward the spring. He was glad she liked his surprise. He'd never seen a woman before that was so easy to please. She had yet to complain about their circumstances. Most women he knew would be crying, moaning every minute, and insisting they be taken home immediately.

It was a good thing Amelia wasn't like that, he knew, because he had no idea how to get out of the thicket. He was completely and utterly lost. But at least they had a good hiding place for the time being. They could remain in hiding while he regained his strength.

That thought comforted him. And the knowledge that food should be no problem. There was plenty to be found in the thicket. He'd gathered berries for Amelia and was saving them for a surprise, after she'd eaten her fill of the rabbit and mushrooms. No, food would most certainly be no problem. A good thing too. Because they might be here for a long, long time.

He watched Amelia bend over the spring and scoop water into her hands. As she did so, her chemise dipped low, exposing the creamy swell of her breasts. He would have to find her something to wear, he decided. She looked far too luscious in her scanty undergarments, and since they were no longer running for their lives, his body was reacting to that fact.

Colter didn't like to think about how she had come to be wearing nothing else. But he imagined he knew. And the thought of other hands on her, other lips on hers, was almost unbearable.

As though sensing his thoughts, Amelia looked up and saw the direction of his gaze. Her cheeks flushed with color and she lowered her lashes, hiding her expressive eyes from him as she covered her bosom with one outspread palm.

Amelia knew that there was no reason for her to feel shame. She had done nothing wrong. Yet the speculation she'd seen in Colter's eyes had chilled her to the bone. She realized it was past time she explained how she had come to be wearing nothing but her undergarments.

Chapter Fifteen

Colter frowned at Amelia, who was so embarrassed she could no longer hold his gaze. Her eyelashes brushed her soft cheeks, the dark, half-moon fringes in sharp contrast to the rosy flush that stained her pale skin. "Amelia." He covered the distance between them. "You have no need to be embarrassed."

"I know." She met his gaze. "But do you?"

He brushed the back of his hand against her cheek. "Whatever happened in that cabin was not your fault."

"I know." Her voice was husky with emotion. "But there was . . . I don't want you to think . . . to think that—"

"You don't have to explain."

"Yes," she insisted. "I do." The rest of her words were spoken in a rush. "I know what you've been thinking. What it must look, like since I'm wearing nothing but my . . . unmentionables. But . . . nothing happened."

Colter's eyebrows drew together in a frown. Amelia could see he didn't believe her.

"Nothing?"

"Nothing like you're imagining anyway. Oh, he—that man, Jude Tanner, was going to do something. I'm not sure just what he had in mind, but we were in the bedroom and he was going to tie me to the bedposts." She explained about the ropes hanging from the posts. "And then Slade knocked on the door and told him somebody was coming, so Tanner tied my wrists together again and left the room."

"A woman," Colt said.

"What?"

"It was a woman who rode in." He frowned at her, his gaze skimming lightly over the rounded curves left exposed by her chemise, then returning to her eyes. "How did you come to be undressed, then?"

"Because of the window." She tightened her lips and glared at him. "Don't you see? The window was too small for me to fit through." She frowned and tugged at her pantaloons, exposing a long tear that he hadn't noticed before. There was a streak of blood edging the tear. "I got stuck anyway," she added ironically. "And the window-sill took some skin off when it tore my bloomers."

The thought of her tender flesh being torn was like a pain stabbing through him. Colter eyed the bloomers. "Maybe you'd better let me have a look—"

Her eyes widened, and she dropped the fabric she'd been holding so fast it might have been greased with hot butter. "No!" she said. "That's all right, Colt. I can deal with it alone."

"Make sure you do, then," he said gruffly. "The wound will need cleaning good to keep it from getting infected."

She laughed uneasily. "I sure wouldn't want that to happen. I'll take care of it right now."

Although Colter turned away to allow her privacy, Amelia was conscious of his presence when she pulled her bloomers down on one side to examine the wound. It was only a long scratch, but it was wide, telling her that she'd left a goodly amount of flesh on the window. Nevertheless, it should heal with no problem if she kept it clean.

As Amelia returned to the fireside, she was aware that something had changed between them. Colter had removed his shirt, leaving only his undershirt to cover his upper body, and the sight of his muscled torso almost took her breath away.

Her heart began to race and her breath came in short bursts as though she'd been running at top speed for several minutes. Darn it! He was too handsome for her peace of mind.

As though he'd guessed her thoughts, Colter held out his shirt to her. She looked at him in confusion, then realized his gaze was riveted to the creamy swell of her bosom.

She flushed hotly and took the shirt, sliding her arms into the sleeves and fastening it with trembling fingers.

Amelia hadn't even thought about refusing the offering. Not when Colter appeared as affected by her feminine form as she was by his masculinity. To continue wearing only her underclothing was unthinkable.

She looked down at her shirt-clad body, and a grin curled her lips. "It's a mite large," she said.

The shirt that had fit his body so well just about covered hers, falling almost to her knees.

"A mite," he agreed, a twinkle in his dark eyes.

The tension that had gripped the two of them for those long moments had completely dissipated now. Amelia seated herself beside the fire and accepted the meat he offered, biting into it with an eagerness that at any other time would have embarrassed her.

"Oh, this is so delicious, Colter," she said after swallowing the first bite.

"There's watercress and wild onions and some berries

to go with it," he told her. "And, of course, the roasted mushrooms."

"Heavenly. Who could ask for more?"

"Most women would," he replied.

"Well, considering our circumstances . . ."

"Even in our circumstances." Colt handed over a handful of watercress and some wild onions that he'd already cleaned.

"There's a creek on our farm where we used to gather watercress," Amelia said. "And wild onions grew nearby. Poke salad too. Mama used to send us down there when she wanted to cook up a mess of greens. And . . ." She frowned at the greens in her hand. "I can remember that, but it's almost all of what I remember about my sister."

"You must have been very young when she died."

"I guess so." She looked across at him, her gaze wistful. "I imagine you had a wonderful time growing up with your brothers."

"You bet." He chuckled. "There's no place better than Morgan's Creek to raise a family."

"Morgan's Creek." She closed her eyes and tried to imagine the place. "Describe it to me, Colt. Let me see it in my mind."

He laughed huskily. "Morgan's Creek is wide. And shallow in most places. It's fed by hundreds of springs that bubble out of the surrounding hills. The water is cool and sweet. The bottom of the creek is mostly marble rock, and along its banks sycamore trees grow to incredible heights."

Her eyes flew open. "Sycamores? That's the tree with the huge, bright green leaves."

"Uh-huh." His voice was gruff with memory. "My grandfather built the house and homesteaded the land. He was one of the original settlers in Texas. Had to become a Mexican citizen to live there." He told her about the land grants Spain had allowed the settlers. "Things changed, though, when Texans decided they wanted independence, so the old man fought with Austin to keep what he owned."

"It's obvious you're proud of your home."

"I am." He laughed huskily. "I wish you could see Morgan's Creek right after a rain. The sycamore leaves are vibrant with color. The land is regenerated. Birds sing their sweetest then. And us boys, why, as soon as the rain would stop falling, we would be outside. We'd head straight for the creek and we'd splash and play in the water that is so clear you can see the fish swimming around. Of course it works both ways; they could see us too. But Matthew—he was the brains of the outfit—"

"Matthew couldn't possibly be any smarter than you are, Colt," she interrupted.

"Maybe not," he said with a grin. "But being older, he knew more. Anyway, Matthew made a seine and we sometimes took it down to the creek and pulled it through the water to trap the fish."

"But—is that fair to the fish?"

"We weren't too concerned about being fair," he said, humor lighting his dark eyes. "We were mostly concerned with eating them."

"You didn't have beef?"

"Plenty of beeves," he replied. "But we didn't eat them much. Pa was dead set on raising a big herd. We mostly ate deer and ducks, geese and pork."

"Pork? On a cattle ranch?"

"Javelinas. Wild hogs with razor-sharp tusks."

"Oh." Amelia shuddered at the thought. "Tell me some more about your brothers, Colt. You said Matthew was the smartest."

He looked at her with a pained expression. "Yeah. But I thought we'd already settled who the smart one was."

She laughed, a tinkling, bell-like sound that made Colter smile at her. "Yes. We did," she replied, giving him a honey-sweet smile. "I guess I forgot. Matthew was just the oldest."

"Yeah. And he was bigger. I remember ... there was this boulder in the middle of the creek down by the old swimming hole. And for some reason it was always our goal to reach that boulder. Especially when the creek would flood. We liked to stand on it and pretend we were king of an island. But to get there we had to cross deep water that was over our heads. Anyway, Matt would set us on his shoulders and carry us over there. One at a time, of course."

"So it wasn't too deep for Matthew to cross?"

"Yeah. It was too deep for him too. But he carried us anyway."

"He could swim?"

"No. He couldn't swim either."

"Then how did he get you there?"

"Simple. He merely held his breath and walked on the bottom across the deepest parts."

"Couldn't you boys have done the same?"

"Hell, I don't know!" he said, suddenly exasperated with her questions. "We never tried. We liked to have Matt carry us across."

"Oh." A small smile twitched her lips. "I see. He sounds like a good brother."

"He is." Colt was silent for a long moment, thinking about what she'd said. "Matt's always been ... Matt. He's always been there for us. Even now."

"Even now?"

"Yeah. He's the one that stayed home to rebuild Morgan's Creek. While the rest of us went on our way to other things ... other lives."

"But you're all doing what you can to help him ... in your own way," she said.

"I'm not," he replied. "I'm off chasing the Kincaid gang, for all the good it's done me."

"It's for all of you, though," she told him. "You're not chasing them for your own satisfaction, Colt. I believe that you and all of your brothers need to see the Kincaid bunch brought to justice."

"Yeah," he agreed. "But not just any justice, Amelia. That won't be enough. We want them wiped off the face of the earth. Dead. Finished. Forgotten."

"You may never forget," she said softly. "Fate has a way of taking a hand no matter how the cards are dealt."

"You sound as if you know something about cards," he said, needing a change of subject.

"Oh, I've played a hand now and then. When Pa felt like gambling but had no money for doing so, he taught me how to handle cards, how to deal and so on. But he had a tendency to get angry when he wasn't winning. So I learned how to let him win without him knowing it."

"He never discovered what you were doing?"

"No. He never knew."

"Then I'd say you're mighty good at cards."

"I'm not bad."

"Too bad we don't have a deck here. It would help pass the time."

She frowned at him. "Are we going to be here long, Colt?"

"It's hard to say."

"There's a posse looking for us, isn't there?"

"No," he replied. "The posse went back to town."

"Then we have to get ourselves out of here, don't we?"

"Yeah," he replied. "It's for sure nobody will come looking for us . . . unless it's my brothers."

"Your brothers? But how would they know to come look for us?"

"I sent Blake a telegram. He'll ride to Nacogdoches to

find out what's going on. And I imagine he'll let Matt know, too."

"Then there is hope," she said quietly. "Matthew won't just leave us in here, Colt. He'll find a way to get us out."

Colt felt a sudden stab of jealousy that she was depending on his brother to save them. He quelled it quickly, knowing how ridiculous such a feeling was.

"You have a lot of faith in a man you've never met," he said quietly.

"You have so much faith in him yourself," she replied. "How could I not have faith, too?"

Colter smiled at her. "You're right, of course. There's no way in hell that Matt's going to leave us here. He'll be looking for us, and so will Blake and Benjamin. Problem is, though," he mused, "the thicket is mighty big. You saw how easy it was to get lost."

"But Matt won't give up," she replied. "He'll keep looking until he finds us."

Colt wished he could believe that, too. Yeah. Matt would look, but Amy didn't seem to realize the enormity of what he'd be taking on.

Chapter Sixteen

Although Matthew chafed at the delay in beginning the search for Colt and his bride, he realized nothing would be accomplished by starving themselves. It would only serve to weaken them at a time when they most needed to keep up their strength.

According to the sheriff, Colter had entered an area where it would be hard to follow. Matthew consoled himself with the fact that more information might be forthcoming if they lingered awhile in Nacogdoches.

The four men entered the hotel and crossed the lobby to the dining room. There were a few patrons there—a couple of men who looked like cowboys and two women at a table near a side window.

The sheriff pointed to a corner table beyond the women. "I always sit there," he said. "That way my back's always covered."

As Matthew and his brothers followed the sheriff, Matt noticed one of the ladies—the younger of the two, who couldn't have been more than eighteen or nineteen—drop her handkerchief just as Benjamin was approaching their table.

A grin curled Matthew's lips. It was an obvious bid for attention, but the young lady, although pretty enough, wouldn't get it from Benjamin.

True to form, Ben stopped short, looking at the handkerchief on the floor as though it were a coiled rattler on the verge of striking.

Matthew nudged his younger brother's shoulder, reminding Benjamin of his manners. Ben pretended not to notice the handkerchief, so Blake, who stood behind their youngest brother, gave him another nudge.

A flush crept up Benjamin's cheeks, and his eyes flickered back and forth as though measuring the distance between himself and the door.

Matt knew Benjamin had the urge to run, but good manners had been their mother's creed. Matthew wasn't really surprised when Ben bent over and retrieved the delicate scrap of cloth, holding it between his thumb and forefinger toward the young lady.

"Uh . . . you dropped your handkerchief, miss." His voice was almost harsh, his words jerky as he stood there, waiting for her to take it from him.

The young woman looked up at Benjamin and offered a brilliant smile that lit up her whole face. "Why, thank you," she trilled. "I'm afraid I didn't notice. You're such a gentleman to be . . ." Her voice trailed away, and she looked wistfully at the young man who was already halfway across the room.

Matthew stifled a grin as he followed his younger brother. Benjamin hadn't yet learned how to deal with the feminine variety of humanity. But he would learn in time.

Benjamin had a habit of avoiding women, though. He preferred to spend time with his horses. He had a way

Take advantage of this offer to enjoy Zebra's newest line of historical romance novels....Splendor Romances (formerly Lovegrams Historical Romances)- Take our introductory shipment of 4 romance novels -**Absolutely Free!** (a $19.96 value)

Now you'll be able to savor today's best romance novels without ever leaving your home with our convenient and inexpensive home subscription service. Here's what you get for joining:

- 4 BRAND NEW bestselling Splendor Romances delivered to your doorstep every month
- 20% off every title (or almost $4.00 off) with your home subscription
- A FREE monthly newsletter, *Zebra/Pinnacle Romance News* filled with author interviews, member benefits, book previews and more!
- No risks or obligations...you're free to cancel whenever you wish...no questions asked

To get started with your own home subscription, simply complete and return the card provided. You'll receive your FREE introductory shipment of 4 Splendor Romances and then you'll begin to receive monthly shipments of new Zebra Splendor titles. Each shipment will be yours to examine for 10 days. If you decide to keep the books, you'll pay the preferred home subscriber's price of just $4.00 per title plus $1.50 shipping and handling. That's $16 for all 4 books plus $1.50 for home delivery! And if you want us to stop sending books, just say the word...it's that simple.

4 FREE books are waiting for you!
Just mail in the certificate below!

If the certificate is missing below, write to:
Splendor Romances, Zebra Home Subscription Service, Inc.,
P.O. Box 5214, Clifton, New Jersey 07015-5214
or call TOLL-FREE 1-888-345-BOOK
Visit our website at www.kensingtonbooks.com.

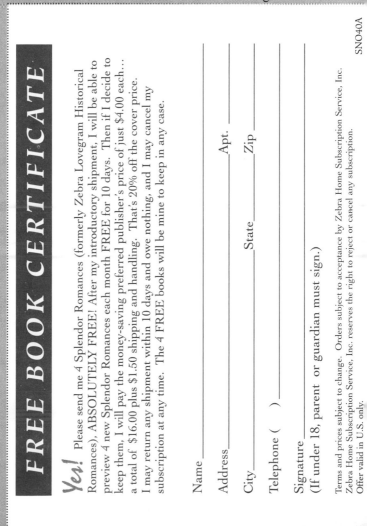

FREE BOOK CERTIFICATE

Yes! Please send me 4 Splendor Romances (formerly Zebra Lovegram Historical Romances), ABSOLUTELY FREE! After my introductory shipment, I will be able to preview 4 new Splendor Romances each month FREE for 10 days. Then if I decide to keep them, I will pay the money-saving preferred publisher's price of just $4.00 each... a total of $16.00 plus $1.50 shipping and handling. That's 20% off the cover price. I may return any shipment within 10 days and owe nothing, and I may cancel my subscription at any time. The 4 FREE books will be mine to keep in any case.

Name _____

Address _____ Apt. _____

City _____ State _____ Zip _____

Telephone ( ) _____

Signature _____
(If under 18, parent or guardian must sign.)

Terms and prices subject to change. Orders subject to acceptance by Zebra Home Subscription Service, Inc.
Zebra Home Subscription Service, Inc. reserves the right to reject or cancel any subscription.
Offer valid in U.S. only.

SNO40A

PLACE
STAMP
HERE

lll..l...lll....lll.l.l..l.l..l.l..l.l.l.l.lll..l

SPLENDOR ROMANCES
Zebra Home Subscription Service, Inc.
P.O. Box 5214
Clifton NJ 07015-5214

with them, as well as other animals, that was a part of his personality. And if he ever learned to use that knowledge on women, he would surely be a heartbreaker.

A blush still stained his cheeks as Benjamin took a chair that would put his back to the women. He ordered steak and potatoes and had already eaten a hefty portion of it when suddenly there was a flurry of movement across the room.

Benjamin paused in the act of spooning mashed potatoes in his mouth, afraid that, for some reason or other, the young woman was headed his way, even though the door was on the other side of the room.

He expelled a breath of relief when, instead of the young woman, a squatty, skinny-legged man of indeterminate age stopped beside the table. Although Ben gave the man his attention, it was obviously the sheriff whom Skinny Legs had come to see.

"You better come quick, Sheriff," the newcomer said, "All hell's about to break loose."

The sheriff appeared unaffected by the news. He forked another piece of steak into his mouth and eyed the man. "You know better than to interrupt me when I'm eating, Curtis," he growled, looking down at the steak as though it would explain the man's reasons. "What kind of hell are you talking about anyway?"

"I know you don't like being interrupted, Sheriff," Curtis whined. "But I knew just as soon as I saw him that you'd want to know."

The sheriff uttered a long-suffering sigh, then asked, "Just as soon as you saw who, Curtis? Get it told, man, so I can get back to my dinner."

"Well, hell, Sheriff!" the other man exclaimed. "I thought you'd want to know right away."

"Dammit, Curtis!" the sheriff roared. "Spit it out, man! Who the hell did you see?"

Curtis looked pained . . . and slightly fearful. "The bank robber. He's the one I've been talking about. One of them fellers that robbed the bank just rode into town."

Although the sheriff appeared to take the news calmly enough, even taking a long swallow of coffee before he replied, a heavy frown wrinkled his forehead. "You reckon he's gonna rob the bank again, Curtis?"

"He can't do that!" Curtis grumbled. "The bank's been closed ever since they shot the banker."

"That's right, Curtis. The bank is closed. So what do you think he's here for?"

"How should I know?" Curtis whined. "You're the one that should find out, Sheriff. Not me. Nobody's paying me to do the job."

"Well, they sure as hell don't pay me enough!"

"Maybe you could tell—"

Matthew was on the verge of interrupting the two men when the sheriff asked the question for him. "Where did he go, Curtis?"

"He stopped in front of the mercantile."

"Might be here for supplies," the sheriff said.

Curtis shifted his weight from one leg to the other, watching the sheriff with avid eyes. And when the sheriff turned his attention to his food again, his eyes widened with amazement. "Hell's fire, Sheriff!" he exclaimed. "Ain't 'cha gonna do anything about it?"

"Describe him!"

It was Benjamin who spoke, and the sheriff sent an appraising glance over him. Gone was the young man who blushed at a woman's attention. Instead, he was replaced by a man whose harsh expression made him appear older than his years.

"Who's he?" Curtis asked gruffly.

"Never mind," the sheriff said. "Just do like he says, Curtis. Describe the man."

"Well, hell's bells! There ain't nothing much to describe. He looks like most any other drifter that rides through these parts."

"What's he wearing?" Benjamin asked.

"Uh . . . homespun shirt and britches. Mud color. Black slouch hat." Curtis scratched his grizzled head. "Fancy boots, though. Looked Mexican."

"The man?" Ben interrupted.

"No. The boots. They was black, with fancy carvings in the leather."

"Hand-tooled?" Matthew asked.

"Yeah," Curtis answered. "That's what they call them. And he wore fancy silver spurs. And some of those blue rocks the Indians like so much on his hat."

"You said he went in the mercantile?" Benjamin asked softly.

"Yeah."

Curtis's gaze flickered across the table. "If you fellers is gonna be leaving all that food, then I 'spect you won't mind if I eat it."

"Dammit!" The sheriff looked down at his laden plate. "Seems like it always happens this way. Just set myself down to a meal and somebody runs in to tell me I'm needed elsewhere."

"You've got plenty of time to eat," Matthew replied mildly, concentrating on his own plate. "Benjamin's gone to handle it."

The sheriff's eyes flicked to Benjamin's empty chair, widening slightly when he realized the younger brother was no longer with them. "Now, how'd he get out of here without me noticing?"

"It's his way." Matthew pointed his fork at the empty chair. "You can eat Ben's portion," he told the man who was hovering at his elbow. "He won't be eating it."

The sheriff scraped back his chair and rose swiftly to his

feet, his hand on his six-gun. "I'm the sheriff here," he protested. "It's my job to arrest people in this town."

"Nobody's going to be arrested," Matt said calmly.

"The hell you say!"

"He's right." Blake, who'd been calmly eating his food, met the sheriff's belligerent gaze. "Ben's the best tracker in the South. Bar none. When that outlaw leaves town, Benjamin will be following along behind."

"Not into the Big Thicket, he won't."

"Benjamin would follow him to hell and back if it meant helping his brother."

"He don't know them woods. They got bogs, swamps, quicksand, alligators, and more ways to kill a man than you could imagine."

"Benjamin went through the war, Sheriff. He fought in the swamps. He's used to marshy land, alligators too." As though that was explanation enough, Blake pointed at the sheriff's plate of food. "Better eat that stuff before it gets cold."

The sheriff dropped heavily to his chair again. Picking up his fork, he grumbled, "Well, he's your brother. I guess you know what you're doing."

It was a statement, needing no answer, so the men returned to the business at hand, which was filling their bellies with food.

As the day passed, the air in the cavern became cooler and there was the scent of rain in the air, mingling with the ever-present one of mildew.

The sky, seen through the hole in the ceiling, darkened, and a fine mist drifted into the cavern.

Colter, who had been sharpening his knife beside the fire, felt the mist and narrowed his gaze on the angry-looking clouds overhead. "I don't like the looks of that sky." He rose to his feet. "Can't tell how long or hard it'll rain. Guess I'd better gather some more wood while there's some dry stuff left out there."

"I'll come with you," Amelia offered.

"No." Colter had been feeling a need to put some distance between them. "You'd only get wet."

He was grateful that he had an excuse to leave her. Even though she wore his shirt, he couldn't forget the way she'd looked in her chemise, remembered every inch of the silken flesh that had been left exposed, every luscious curve. And if the shirt she was wearing now should get wet, it would cling to her like a second skin, and if he saw her that way, he would probably lose control and take her where she stood.

Even now, the knowledge that she wore nothing except her bloomers and chemise beneath his shirt was driving him crazy. No! He couldn't let her go with him, dared not.

But Amelia was unaware of his aching body and proved determined to accompany him. "I won't get any wetter than you will," she argued. "Anyway, a little rain won't hurt me."

No, he silently agreed. *But if you get wet, you'll damn well drive me crazy!*

Aloud he said, "No, Amelia. You're not going. And that's my final word on the subject."

Amelia felt hurt by his attitude, but she held her tongue. It was obvious he didn't want her company.

Colter felt like a dog for being so short with her. It wasn't her fault that he was having a hard time controlling his body.

"I didn't mean to sound so harsh," he said gently. "But it won't hurt me to get wet. My britches will dry soon enough when I come back."

Amelia nodded her head, but she couldn't look at him for a long moment, afraid he would see the hurt in her eyes. He was probably tired of being alone with her and needed some time to himself. She could understand that. Hadn't there been times in the past when she would have given anything for solitude?

He brushed his palm across her cheek just before he left, and Amelia found comfort in his quiet touch. She concentrated on stacking the wood he'd gathered in a neat pile away from the hole above them so it would keep dry. And when he returned with an armload of thick branches, she added the wood to the growing pile.

Smiling at her, Colter left the cavern again and a short time later returned with an armload of mushrooms, several bunches of fresh greens, and some roots that resembled turnips.

That evening Colt searched the cavern floor until he found a patch of brown dirt. He dug a good-sized hole and dropped in some live coals, then shoved in several inches of dirt. After dropping in two of the roots he'd gathered, Colt covered them with dirt and placed more live coals over the top.

Several hours later, Colter dug up the roots, slit one open, and handed it to Amelia, along with a leg from the rabbit he'd just roasted.

Amelia peeled away the outer shell of the root and took a bite. "It tastes something like a turnip," she said.

"It is," he replied. "A swamp variety of turnip."

They relaxed over their meal and spoke of nonsensical things that held no importance to either of them. And when the meal was over and darkness settled around them, Amelia stretched out near the cavern wall farthest away from the open hole that gaped high above them.

"Are you cold, Amelia?" Colter asked gruffly.

"No," she lied, curling her knees against her chest and wrapping her arms around them.

She closed her eyes, intent on courting sleep, but she couldn't get comfortable on the rocky floor. She felt every bruise on her body, and the night air was so cold that it made her teeth chatter, despite every attempt she made to keep them together.

Colter had been sitting beside the fire, swearing beneath his breath, trying to make himself stop thinking about how she'd feel beneath his naked body, when he heard the clatter of her teeth.

"Dammit," he swore softly.

Quickly crossing the distance to her, Colter knelt beside her, noticing as he did her goose-pimpled flesh. "You're cold," he said.

"No," she lied again. But her chattering teeth gave proof of the lie.

"Come here," he said gently, stretching his long length out beside her.

"Colt—"

"Hush." Although his voice was soft, it was also determined. He pulled her against him spoon-fashion, his front to her back. "I'm not going to ravish you, Amy. I'm just doing this to keep you warm."

Ha! an inner voice said. *That's a good excuse if I ever heard one.*

"Shut up," Colt growled.

"What?" Amelia asked, startled.

"Never mind," Colt said gruffly. "Just keep still and you'll get warm soon."

Realizing he was right, Amelia allowed herself to relax. She could feel the heat of his body and took pleasure in his strength. Sighing, she nestled closer to his warmth. Whatever happened, Colt would protect her. She knew that with absolute certainty. He had risked his life for her, and would do so again if he found it necessary.

Yes. She could trust him.

Snuggling even closer, she closed her weary eyes and was soon fast asleep.

* * *

Colter lay on the cavern floor with Amelia's sweet form held tightly against him, trying desperately to control his desire, as he'd been doing for most of the day.

Dammit! he silently cursed himself. What was wrong with him anyway? How could he even think such thoughts when he knew Amelia was an innocent, unused to the passions that controlled a man's life. But no matter how much he chastised himself, he couldn't stop wanting her. Nevertheless, he *would* control his lust! She had already suffered the advances of one man . . . he'd be a pig to make her go through that again.

Even as he silently lectured himself, his desire for the woman in his arms grew stronger. His body was mindless, refused to listen to his conscience. His breeches that had fit so perfectly only a couple of hours ago had suddenly become too tight.

And as if that weren't enough, his nerves were frazzled just from being so close to her. And the sweet fragrance that surrounded her, like the scent of wildflowers in bloom, didn't help one bit to calm him, either.

Colter knew he needed to put some distance between them, as he had done earlier that day. But how in hell could he when she needed his warmth so badly?

His desire became all-consuming. He needed desperately to ease it, and yet he could not. No matter how much it pained him.

Amelia murmured in her sleep and her mouth opened against his neck. His manhood immediately stood up and saluted, stretching his breeches even tighter across his hips. She was unaware of his struggle as she cuddled against him, looking to him for safety.

God! She was like a drug to his senses, something he needed, wanted almost to the point of desperation. And yet he would not release her, not as long as she was willing to remain where she was.

What was happening to him? he wondered. He'd never felt this way before. And he didn't particularly like the feeling. To need someone so badly, to want them so painfully, made a man too vulnerable.

Vulnerable.

Yes, that described him perfectly, Colter realized. He was vulnerable to this woman. And he might as well face that fact.

Somehow, some way, Amelia had wormed her way into his heart and laid claim to it.

His arms tightened around her, and she sighed deeply, then tried to roll away from him, making him wonder if he was holding her too tightly.

Colt loosened his hold, and she sighed again and turned over, bending her knee and throwing her leg across his thigh as though she craved that closeness.

Colt's breath caught in his throat. He lay there, utterly motionless, his heart beating furiously. He was too aware of the rounded curves of her breast, pressing so firmly against his chest. Yet he knew Amelia was totally unaware of that intimate contact.

Then suddenly she spoke. "Colt," she mumbled.

"Yes?"

She patted his unshaven cheek. "I just wanted to make sure you were here." The last word was a mere sigh, uttered as sleep claimed her again.

Colt remained absolutely rigid, his body flushed with heat, raging with a passion that he knew he dared not unleash. To do so would surely wake her fully, and she would most certainly put as much distance between the two of them as quickly as possible.

And the thought of releasing her was almost as unbearable as her touch.

Chapter Seventeen

At the first light of dawn Colter eased away from Amelia, and when he was free of her womanly curves, he uttered a sigh of relief and set about building a fire to warm the cavern.

He'd spent a miserable night. Had barely slept a wink, fearing that if he did, in that twilight state of mind, he might lose control and wake to find himself making passionate love to her.

And much as he desired to do exactly that, he was determined that it would not happen. No! He would control his baser instincts. When they made love, he wanted Amelia fully aware of what they were doing.

Colter gathered kindling and set it aflame, and when the fire was blazing to his satisfaction, he allowed himself to look at Amelia again. She had pulled her knees up in a fetal position after he left her, apparently missing the warmth he had provided.

He was tempted to stretch out beside her again, to wrap

his arms around her and warm her with the heat of his body until the flames had gathered enough strength to heat their shelter. Yet he knew for a certainty that if he returned to her on that rocky bed now, nothing would stop him from making love to her.

It took every ounce of strength Colt possessed to remain motionless, when he wanted so badly to go to her, to love her until she was senseless. But to do so would be unconscionable.

He knew he should leave the cavern while he could, yet he was hypnotized by the sight of her. Her tousled curls were spread out around her in a tangle of copper, and the flickering flames of the fire sent shadows dancing across her translucent skin. She'd left several buttons on the shirt unfastened and another one had come undone to expose the creamy swell of her breast. It was an enticing sight, and he fought against the urge to join her there, to take what her body seemed to be offering.

Fool! an inner voice said. *She's asleep. She has no idea how you're feeling. Get out of here before you do something you'll always regret.*

Colter's breathing was ragged as he cursed himself for a fool and almost ran out of the cavern to get away from the woman who would surely destroy his sanity if he remained in her presence.

He would go back to the spring he'd found and immerse his heated body in the cold water there. And if that wasn't enough to cool his passion, then he would hunt the entire morning, because he dared not return to Amelia until he had himself . . . and his lust . . . under complete control again.

It was midmorning when Benjamin walked into his oldest brother's campsite on the northern edge of the Big

Thicket. Ben's clothes were dirty, torn, as though he'd been crawling through briers and mud. His eyes, shot with red streaks, were sunken, rimmed with dark shadows that attested to his apparent lack of rest.

Matthew had been sitting beside the campfire sipping a cup of coffee when Ben loped into the camp. He looked over the rim and watched his youngest brother approach.

A moment later Ben slumped down beside Matt and mumbled, " 'Lo, Matt." Drawing his knees up beneath his chin, he rested his head against them and closed his eyes. A moment later he was snoring softly.

"Damned if he ain't something," Blake said, stepping out of the shadows cast by the branches of a towering oak. He slid the six-gun he'd drawn into the holster buckled around his hips and muttered, "I don't think young Ben even saw me before he went to sleep."

"He saw you before he entered camp," Matthew said calmly. "And if you'd have been somebody else, he wouldn't have come in."

"I ain't so sure about that," Blake replied. "He looks too damn tired to have any sense left. You think we oughta wake him and find out what he knows?"

Matthew frowned at his little brother. Ben's right forearm had a cut running the length of it, as though he'd been in a knife fight since he entered the thicket, but the wound didn't look deep enough to require stitches.

"No," Matt replied. "If Colter was in immediate danger, Ben wouldn't be sleeping like a baby now. The boy looks like he's been to hell and back, so we'd best just leave him be for a while. He'll come around soon enough when he's rested."

And Benjamin did. About an hour later he raised his head and looked at Matthew. Then his gaze turned to Blake, who was pouring himself another cup of coffee.

"If that's the last of the coffee in that pot, then you

damned well better not drink it," Benjamin said belligerently.

"Settle down, Ben," Blake said mildly. "I just made a fresh pot."

"Pour yourself another cup then and give me that one since it's already poured." Benjamin wiped a hand across his brow, then rubbed his temples with his thumbs and forefingers. "God," he groaned. "I don't think I've ever been so damned tired in my life."

"Feeling like you broke a dozen wild mustangs already this morning?" Blake asked, handing over the steaming cup to his brother. Ordinarily he would have taken offense at his brother's tone of voice, but he knew Ben needed the coffee more than he did right now. The stimulant should help clear away the cobwebs that clouded his mind.

"Hell, no!" Ben replied. "Breaking a hundred mustangs wouldn't have left me feeling like this. Mustangs I can handle. Alligators are another thing."

Matt's eyebrows raised. "You taking on alligators now, little brother?"

"Not on purpose," Ben replied. "But they're just naturally ornery creatures. They take offense at being stepped on."

"You stepped on an alligator?" Blake asked, raising a dark brow. "How in hell did that happen, Ben?"

"Don't even ask," Benjamin growled, taking a long swallow from the steaming cup. "Damn!" he exclaimed. "That's hot!"

"Just came off the fire," Blake reminded him.

Benjamin blew on the steaming liquid for a moment, then raised the cup again and took a cautious sip. Although it was still hot, it had cooled enough so he could drink it without burning his mouth in the process. When half the coffee was gone, he looked up to find his brothers watching him. "What?" he demanded.

"Colter," Matt reminded gently. "You went to find Colt, Benjamin."

"Yeah," Ben replied heavily. "I did."

Fear slithered through Matthew at his brother's reply. Was Colt dead? Was that the reason he had to drag every word out of Benjamin?

"Well?" Matt's voice was harsh. "Where is he?"

"I don't know."

"You don't know?" Matt growled. "Then what are you doing here if you didn't find the outlaws?"

"Didn't say I didn't find the outlaws," Ben rejoined. "Said I don't know where Colt was."

"Then Colt didn't find the outlaws."

"Didn't say that neither."

Blake scowled at his brother. "You're not saying much of anything, Ben."

Matthew expelled a long breath and tried to relax his taut muscles. "So what exactly *did* you find, little brother?"

"I found the cabin where the outlaws hide out."

"And the girl?"

"They don't have her."

"Are you sure of that?"

"Hell, yes!" Benjamin looked pained, as though he'd been accused of lying.

"Okay, Ben," Matt said, "Tell it your way."

So Benjamin did exactly that. He told how he'd trailed an outlaw into the Big Thicket, how he'd followed him to the cabin and listened long enough to know that the girl had escaped by crawling through an impossibly small window near the ceiling.

"She's got plenty of spunk," Benjamin said with a laugh. "That window was so small she couldn't get through it with her clothes on, so she just shucked 'em off and left 'em behind on the floor."

"She's running around naked?" Blake asked, a grin curling the edges of his mouth.

"I reckon. Or wearing something of Colt's."

"You're sure they're together?"

"Yeah. The outlaws know she's with a man, saw him with her as the two of 'em ran across the clearing . . . just before they reached the wooded area that completely surrounds the cabin."

"How do you know it was Colt with her?"

Benjamin grinned. "He left his calling card scratched in the dirt beside the big rock where he hid and watched the cabin."

All of the brothers were aware of the sign Colter had devised to let them know he'd been somewhere. It was a simple mark that could have been made by any raccoon, if it happened to have seven toes.

"So they're all right," Matt said, his relief heard clearly in his voice.

"They were when they left the cabin," Benjamin replied. "And the outlaws haven't caught 'em yet. But as for being all right . . . well, only God knows that, and He ain't telling."

"You couldn't track them down?" Matt asked, knowing that his brother wouldn't have returned unless he had at least tried to do that.

"Not through water. They found a canoe and headed downstream, but they never beached it anywhere on my side. I went for miles in both directions. Found where Colt left Thunder, though."

"He all right?"

"Yeah. Colt left him close to water and forage. Figured I better leave him there until we know for sure that Colt won't need him anymore."

Matt was silent for a long moment, then said, "You think you'll be able to lead a posse to that cabin?"

"Yeah," Ben replied. "I can lead them."

"Good. At least we can eliminate that nest of vipers so Colt won't have any more trouble with them."

Benjamin sighed and stood up. "Guess we'd better go after that posse, Matt. Those outlaws are still looking for Colt and his wife, and I don't like to think what will happen if they find them."

"You rest some more, little brother," Blake said. "I'll go round up the posse."

Benjamin wasn't about to argue. He crawled into the shelter his brothers had erected beneath the centuries-old oak tree and dropped to the bedroll stretched out on the ground. Moments later he was sound asleep.

Matt watched Blake saddle his mount. "I'll wait here with Ben," he said. "He's so tired, somebody could murder him in his sleep without him ever waking up."

"Yeah," Blake agreed. "And we're going to need him fresh when that posse gets here." He shoved his hat back on his head. "You keep a sharp eye out, Matt," he said grimly. "We can't be sure that band of outlaws won't ride out of there anytime. And if they do, you sure as hell don't want to be in their way."

"You don't have to worry about anything that goes on here," Matt said gruffly. "I'll be ready to deal with anything that comes around. Just see that the sheriff rounds that posse up again and gets them here as soon as possible. We have to deal with the outlaws before they catch up with Colt and that new wife of his."

"Don't worry," Blake said. "My U.S. marshal's badge gives me jurisdiction over a local sheriff anytime. It shouldn't be long before I'm back with that posse."

But it was. In fact, Blake didn't return at all that day. And there was no sign of the posse he'd gone after, either. Or the sheriff. Matthew chafed at the delay, pacing back and forth as he wondered what could have gone wrong.

Something obviously had or his brother would have returned with help.

It was a chain of mishaps that rendered Blake Morgan unconscious only moments after he rode into town. He was so deep in thought as he guided his mount toward the sheriff's office that he didn't see the child until it was almost too late.

The boy couldn't have been more than five or six years old and his bright hair glinted beneath the afternoon sun. It was the only thing that saved the youngster, who had dashed out of an alley to chase a black and white puppy into the road.

"Dammit," Blake muttered, tightening the reins as he tried to control his startled mount. The horse reared back, pawing at the air with his forelegs and threatening to unseat the man who fought so desperately to control him. In his fear the animal jerked sideways, right into the path of an oncoming rider.

The terrified horse struck the paint a heavy blow on the flank, then began to buck, determined to dislodge his rider.

The animal was too frightened to control. Blake knew that, knew also that he'd have to allow the animal to run off his terror. He'd seen the boy reach the sidewalk, knew he was unharmed, so his only worry now was to keep from being thrown.

Even as that thought occurred, Blake became aware of another sound that covered the noise his mount was making. It was the sound of thunder, yet there wasn't a cloud in the sky, or at least there hadn't been only moments ago, the last time he'd looked.

It happened so quickly that, later, when he'd regained

his senses, Blake was unable to remember the exact
sequence in which it happened.

The thundering sound had nothing to do with the
weather. The stagecoach had reached town. And just as
he became aware of that fact, Blake's terrified mount
bunched his muscles and leaped high into the air, coming
down with a resounding thud that jarred his rider to the
bone. Stunned, Blake lost his grip and went flying through
the air, landing directly in the path of the stagecoach. He
was vaguely aware of the team of horses, realized they'd
swerved to keep from trampling him. But the wheels struck
him a hard blow, and pain lashed through him.

And then Blake knew no more.

Despite their circumstances, Amelia was enjoying herself. It had drizzled throughout the day, making travel
impossible without the proper clothing—which they didn't
have—so she was bent on enjoying her time with the man
who was becoming so necessary to her well-being.

Something about their relationship had changed during
the dark hours of the night. When she'd awakened from
a deep sleep alone in the cavern, she'd felt more rested
than she had in years. And it was because of him, she knew,
and the way he'd held her in his arms during what could
have been a long, miserably cold night.

She tried to analyze her feelings, tried to explain them
to herself, but they could not be broken down and cata-
logued. The sum of it all, though, was that she cared for
him. Deeply. And with each passing day she was coming
to depend on him more and more.

Amelia was adding wood to the fire when Colter
returned to the cavern. She smiled up at him, then looked
at the brace of rabbits—already skinned and cleaned—

that he was carrying. "I see you brought my breakfast," she said. "You're going to spoil me, Colt."

"Spoil you?" He skewered the rabbits and slanted the sticks over the fire to roast, then sat down beside her. "You're easy to please," he said, studying her closely. "Is that all it takes, Amelia? Just food and a warm place to sleep?"

"And you beside me?" She blushed as she realized what she had revealed.

Colt, although startled at her words, gave no indication that he'd heard. But he wouldn't soon forget them. He watched her in silence, wondering if she knew how much of her feelings she'd revealed. He wanted to take her in his arms and hold her close, but he dared not do so. Not if she was to remain innocent. But there would come a time, he knew, when he'd not be able to keep his hands to himself. And since she'd spoken aloud her feelings, he realized she would not resist his advances.

For now, though, he must keep silent, and take what pleasure he could from just looking at her. But when they left this damned place, when she was no longer vulnerable, he would teach her how to love a man. They would have to leave soon, he knew, before he did something he might regret. Amelia wasn't a woman he'd soon forget. It would be hard to walk away from her, yet he must when this was over.

The day passed slowly, with Colt's hunger for Amelia burning hotter and hotter with each passing hour. And when night was upon them again and they sought their rest, he was afraid the devil that had been riding him all day would no longer be denied.

It was with a sense of fatality that he stretched out on the ground and pulled Amelia against him. Her fragrance, the sheer femininity of her as well as her womanly curves overwhelmed him almost immediately.

Was Amelia feeling that same attraction toward him?

She curled against him like a child, her head resting on his shoulder, seeming to be completely at peace, unlike Colt, whose body was taut with tension.

Leaning forward, he brushed aside a tangle of copper curls. "Amelia," he said softly.

But Amelia did not answer. Colt was doomed to disappointment, for, strange as it seemed, she'd already descended into the arms of Morpheus.

Chapter Eighteen

Amelia didn't know how long she slept. She just knew that she woke to incredible heat, centered mostly in that secret place between her legs.

She moaned softly, moving restlessly, wanting, needing something that remained just beyond her reach. Her nipples ached, and she realized they were taut, hard, aching.

What was wrong with her? She was on fire, burning as though with fever, and yet the fire appeared to be localized in two places: her breasts and that place between her thighs.

Lifting heavy eyelids, Amelia stared up at Colter, who was watching her with dark, passionate eyes. "Colt?" she whispered. "What's happening to me?" His hands cupped her breasts through the fabric of her chemise, teasing her nipples until they were as tight as rosebuds too new to blossom. "Colt. What are you doing?"

"I'm loving you," he muttered. "Let me have your mouth, Amy. I have to know its taste."

Amelia lifted her face, and his mouth covered hers in a kiss so exquisitely sweet it rendered her almost mindless.

When he had kissed her almost breathless, Colter lifted his head and met her eyes. "I shouldn't be doing this, Amy," he muttered. "You need to stop me now."

"Stop you? Why?"

"Because you're an innocent. I'm supposed to be protecting you." His dark eyes were tormented, his voice harsh. "Tell me to stop or give me your mouth again."

She slid her arms around his neck and pressed her lips to his, wishing she knew more about kissing.

He groaned. "Open your mouth," he said hoarsely.

She had no thought of ignoring his command. Her mouth opened, and his tongue slid inside, sweeping that inner moistness so thoroughly that it was like setting fuel to the spark he'd already created. She whimpered low in her throat, and, as though he'd just been waiting for the sound, Colt lifted his head and stared down into her passion-glazed eyes. He appeared to be asking a question.

"I ache, Colt," she whispered.

"I know, honey," he said. "So do I."

Twisting around so his body covered hers, Colt pushed her legs apart. And then his mouth devoured hers again. Twining her fingers through his dark hair, Amelia urged him closer, imitating his movements, touching her tongue to his, swirling, then retreating.

Colt's breath came in ragged gasps, as though he'd been running for hours, when he finally lifted his head.

"More," she breathed huskily, an expression of absolute bliss on her face.

His dark eyes gleamed with something that looked suspiciously like satisfaction. "Gladly," he groaned. He nipped her neck with his teeth, then moved upward to press soft kisses on her cheeks, her ears, and all the while his hands were working magic on her nipples, teasing the taut peaks that had become so hard they ached with desire.

"It feels so good," she moaned. "Don't ever stop."

Colt turned his attention to her breasts, pushing aside the thin chemise that had been covering them and exposing the creamy mounds. He lowered his mouth and began to suckle.

Amelia cried out, arching her back to increase the contact. She clutched his shoulders, her fingers digging into his muscled flesh, moaning with the pleasure he was creating.

As though urged on by her moans, Colt slid his hand lower, found the tie of her bloomers and released it, pushing the garment aside easily.

Amelia barely had time to realize her bloomers were gone before Colt's palm was cupping the mound at the apex of her thighs.

She stiffened immediately.

"Easy," he said. "I just want to touch you."

She sighed and relaxed against him, but moments later, with his mouth on her breast and his finger in the folds of her soft flesh, she was aching again, moaning and thrashing beneath him as she tried in vain to quench the flame that threatened to burn her alive.

"Help me, Colt," she moaned. "Make it stop burning."

It was all he needed. The words that Colt had been waiting for. He quickly divested himself of his garments, whisked her chemise away, then poised himself over her. As he plunged downward, Amelia stiffened momentarily; then, as she felt the swelling heat of him buried deep inside her innermost being, she tightened muscles that had never been used before around him.

"Don't," Colt said quickly.

But it was already too late, he realized. He might just as well have been trying to stop a runaway train. His body would not be denied. He lifted himself slightly, then plunged deeply, quickly, almost frantically. And as he did, Colt felt his seed gathering. Although he tried hard to slow things down, knowing it was too soon for Amelia, he could not stop what was happening. He was losing himself, climbing to that far distant peak where he would find blissful satisfaction. Moments later he was there, on top of that incredibly high mountain, waiting for the sweet bliss that he knew would soon follow.

When the release came, Colter threw back his head and gave a mighty roar. His mouth stretched tight over his teeth as though he were in extreme pain for a long moment; then he was spiraling downward.

In that grand moment of surrender Colter slumped against Amelia, covering her body completely with his own. He was utterly spent, yet more relaxed than he'd ever been in his entire life.

He lay there for a long moment, quivering with remembered pleasure. Then, realizing that he must be heavy on such a winsome female as Amelia, Colter rolled to one side and gathered her close against him.

Kissing her softly on her love-swollen lips, he closed his eyes and sighed with pleasure.

"Maybe I'll be able to get some sleep now," he said gruffly.

Without another thought, Colt sank into that deep quietness that preceded sleep, and when he had almost achieved that state, he heard her voice.

"Colt?"

"Hmmmm?"

"Is that all there is to it?"

Colt's eyes flew open as he realized that Amelia sounded almost disappointed.

Almost, hell! he silently swore. Amelia *was* disappointed. But why? He had enjoyed their lovemaking so much that he'd just naturally thought she would have, too. Had she expected something more, something he'd failed to give her?

That thought caused a curious sense of inadequacy to flood over him. He couldn't help but feel that he hadn't measured up to what Amelia had expected.

But what in hell *had* she expected?

He leaned up on his elbows and studied her flushed face. Her lips were red and swollen from his kisses, and to him she appeared to have been thoroughly loved. But then, what did he know? he thought crossly.

He frowned at her. "You didn't like it?"

Her answer was a long time coming, as though she were choosing her words carefully.

"It's not that I didn't like it, Colt, but . . ."

"What?" he asked sharply.

"Well, you know . . ." She looked down, hiding her gaze from him. "You seemed to enjoy it, Colt. Quite a lot, in fact."

"Of course I enjoyed it," he growled. "Otherwise I wouldn't have done it." When she remained quiet, he said, "Didn't you enjoy it?"

"I guess so, but—"

"Hell, Amelia," he growled. "Either you enjoyed it or you didn't. There's no two ways about it."

Again she was silent.

He watched her for a long moment, wondering what she was trying to say. He'd never had any complaints before. Not from anyone. Every other woman he'd bedded had always seemed to enjoy their sexual encounters as much as he did. So why hadn't Amelia? Granted, he'd never made love to a virgin before, but he'd been as gentle as he could with her. And he had held back as long as possible before he spent himself. So why were they even having this conversation?

Crossing his arms behind his head, he stretched out again, planning to go to sleep, but he continued to worry the problem over in his mind. Finally he could stand it no longer.

"Amelia?"

"Hummm?"

"Are you asleep?"

She laughed softly. "No. I don't think so."

"What didn't you like about it?"

"I didn't *not* like it. At least, not exactly."

He gritted his teeth. "Then what *did* you like about it?"

"Well, the buildup was nice."

"The buildup?"

"You know."

"No. Tell me."

"Oh, Colt." She covered her hot cheeks with her hands and looked anywhere but at him. "It's so embarrassing for me to talk about things like that."

He laughed huskily, his hand cupping her bosom while his thumb played with her nipple. She drew in a sharp breath at his touch. "You shouldn't be embarrassed," he said softly. "Not with me. And not after what just happened. Go on. Tell me what you liked about it. You mentioned something about the buildup."

"I—I w-was talking about what—what you're doing to me right now," she said huskily. "About the way you're touching me."

He smiled widely, a glimmer of understanding seeping through his undoubtedly thick skull. "You like the touching?"

"Um-hum. It's real nice, Colt."

"But you didn't like the last part."

"Not really."

He laughed softly. "You have to know that touching is not enough for a man, Amelia."

"That's all right," she said sweetly. "I guess I can stand it if you want to do it again."

His movements halted abruptly. "Stand it?" he choked. "You guess you can *stand* it?"

"Um-hum," she said. "If you really like doing that, then I won't object. Not if you touch me like you were doing before. And the kisses were real nice, too."

"Amelia," he grated. "*Food* is nice. *Kisses* are not supposed to be *nice*. And neither is what I've been doing to you. The soft touches here"—he tweaked her nipple—"and here"—he cupped her Venus mound—"are supposed to get you all hot and bothered and make you want more of the same thing."

"Oh, they did." Amelia realized her voice held a slight quiver and knew that it was his fault. He was still cupping the secret place between her thighs. "It's just that since I've already had the 'more' and I know what it's all about, Colt, I would rather concentrate on the touching and kissing. And afterwards, you can go ahead and do whatever you want. I won't object."

"Dammit, Amelia!" he exclaimed, removing his hand from her body. "I don't feel like doing anything else when you talk that way."

Her eyes widened, and disappointment flooded through her. "I'm sorry, Colt," Amelia said softly. "I didn't mean to hurt your feelings. I'm sure you must be an expert lover and—"

"Obviously not," he grumbled. "Not if you didn't enjoy it." He was silent again, then said, "Exactly what wasn't good about it?"

"Well," she replied, knowing she had to be honest with him, even if his feelings were tender. "It *hurt*, for one thing."

"It won't hurt you again," he reassured her. "You're not a virgin anymore."

"I'm certainly not," she said with a husky laugh. "You took care of that little problem."

"You said, 'for one thing,'" Colt remarked mildly. "So I gather there were other reasons why you didn't enjoy it."

"Well . . . it wasn't quite . . ." Amelia wondered how best to say it, then just allowed the words to come out in a rush. "You finished so fast."

He grinned wryly, feeling almost exultant. What she was obviously saying was that she *did* enjoy his loving, but he hadn't held out long enough to satisfy her.

Well, hell! That was a situation he could remedy easily enough.

Curling an arm around her, he clutched her to him, rolled over, then pinned her beneath him so quickly that she gasped in startled surprise.

"What are you doing?" she asked breathlessly.

"I'm going to show you what you've been missing," he growled.

Lowering his mouth to hers, he kissed her deeply, parting her thighs as he did so, and cupping her femininity in the palm of his hand. He rubbed her gently while his tongue worked its magic in the sweet moistness of her mouth. And as she began to moan with each stroke of his tongue, he entered her body and began a slow, rhythmic movement that she found extremely pleasurable. He continued to stroke her, both inside and out, as he sought to give her the pleasure he was so obviously feeling himself.

Amelia matched his movements as he stoked the fire that burned within until the flames were finally burning out of control. And when she thought she could stand no more of the pleasure he was creating, she cried out his name and they plunged together over that high distant peak that she'd never even known existed before.

Afterwards, they lay together, completely sated, their

bodies soaked with sweat as each of them fought to control their breathing.

It was Colt who finally broke the silence. "Was that better?" he asked dryly.

"Much," she said softly, reaching up a hand to stroke his beard-roughened face. "In fact, I think I could become addicted to such pleasure."

"That's good," he growled, pulling her tighter against him. "Because I most certainly have."

Amelia laughed softly and snuggled closer against him, tucking her head beneath his chin. Shortly thereafter she fell into a deep sleep, and when she awakened the sunshine was streaming through the top of the cavern.

As Amelia remembered what had passed between them during the night, an embarrassed flush warmed her cheeks. Things looked different in the cold light of day.

But Colt, who was obviously used to waking with a woman in his bed, appeared to take it in stride. He pulled her tight against him and let her feel the strength of his desire.

"Colt," she pleaded, laughing unsteadily as she pushed at him. "We have to get up."

"Why?" he asked softly.

"Because we won't be safe as long as those outlaws are looking for us."

He sobered instantly, a frown pulling his dark brows together. "You're right, Amelia," he said heavily. "For a minute there I forgot all about them."

His expression was so grim that she wished she'd never mentioned the outlaws. But they couldn't afford to forget about them. To become careless might prove fatal to both of them.

"Do you think they might have stopped searching for us?" she asked hopefully.

"I don't know. But I intend to find out today." Colt slid into his breeches and donned the undershirt, his only other garment since he had given her his shirt. "I'll go outside and have a look around. And I'll see about trapping us some breakfast at the same time."

"All right," she replied, reaching for her chemise and pantaloons. "But don't be gone long."

"I won't."

But he was. It seemed like hours before Colter returned. And when he did, there was a somber look on his face.

"What's wrong?" she asked quickly.

He tossed a brace of rabbits on the floor. "Seems we weren't drifting downstream like we thought, Amelia," he said. "Somehow we wound up on a tributary. A creek that flows into the main one."

"What does that mean?"

"Means we'll have to backtrack to find our way out of here."

"Backtrack." Her breath caught in her throat. "But won't the outlaws find us if we do?"

"I hope not." Colt began to lay a fire. "We need to cook these rabbits," he said grimly. "We might not have a chance to trap any later, and I expect we'll need the food before we find our way out of here."

"Do you really believe we can find our way out . . . before the outlaws find us?'

"Yeah," he replied. "We'll do just fine, Amelia. But we're gonna have to keep moving."

Despite his reassurance, she was still worried. "We don't know which direction to take, do we?"

"If we follow the main stream, we're bound to eventually leave the forest."

"I guess." She sounded despondent.

Colt cupped her chin and made her look at him. "Believe me, Amelia," he said gruffly. "We *will* get out. You can be certain of that."

She forced a smile to her lips. "I believe you," she said.

And she did. She believed he *was* certain they would get away. But Amelia didn't feel that same certainty. And she knew, even if he did not, what the results of her attempt at escape would be if they were caught. Jude was an evil man. The devil himself. And he would not deal lightly with either of them.

Chapter Nineteen

The water was sluggish, barely flowing, and if Colt hadn't been paddling, the canoe would have remained motionless in the stream. At least that was what Amelia thought until she saw the alligator.

"Colt," she said quickly. "There's an alligator over near the bank. Oh, God, there's another one. And they're both headed this way." The panic in her voice told him just what she thought about the creatures that were obviously bent on investigating the humans who had entered their domain.

"Alligators are just naturally curious creatures, Amelia," he soothed. "They won't bother us. Not as long as we stay in the canoe."

Although Amelia realized that Colter was bound to know more about the creatures than she did, she remained rigid with fear until the alligators suddenly swerved aside and glided toward one of the nearby cypress knees, a strange protuberance that reached up from the depths of the murky stream.

The swamp was alive with sounds from unseen creatures that alternately screeched, barked, or growled, which made Amelia glad that she wasn't alone.

As the boat glided smoothly through the water, she saw a deer watching them from the bank. A chattering sound from high above jerked her head up, and she saw an opossum hanging from a limb.

It was an enchanting place, this Big Thicket through which they traveled, yet there were also many dangers. Even so, Amelia hated to be leaving, and might even have begged Colter to stay longer if she hadn't been so worried about the outlaws that were probably still searching for them.

Soon they left the channel and entered the main stream. Colter turned the canoe in a northerly direction.

"No, Colt," Amelia protested. "Don't go that way. Upstream is north and we headed downstream. Away from the outlaws."

"We have to go this way, Amelia," Colter told her. "We need Thunder. And I left him near the northwest edge of the forest."

"But what about the outlaws?" she protested. "They'll find us if we go that way. And there are far too many of them for us to fight."

Us. Colter liked it when she linked the two of them together like that. So she planned on fighting the outlaws with him. He smiled at the image that presented. "I imagine they've stopped looking for us by now."

Remembering Jude Tanner, Amelia had to disagree with him, but she remained silent, yielding to his better judgment. After all, she reminded herself, Colter had spent four years fighting in the War Between the States and had undoubtedly survived countless horrors during that time.

She could depend on Colt. He wouldn't let her down. Somehow he would see them safely through this danger. And there was always the chance that he was right. Perhaps the outlaws *had* given up on the chase. She certainly hoped they had.

Amelia didn't know her hope would soon give way to despair.

By the time the sun had reached its zenith, they'd traveled upstream to a point just short of where they'd entered the creek. When Colt turned the canoe toward the bank, Amelia thought he must have forgotten where they'd found the canoe.

"This isn't the place, Colt," she said, her gaze searching the marshy ground where cypress trees hung with moss grew in such abundance. "Don't you remember? We found the canoe farther upstream."

"I know," he replied, dipping the oar into the water and pulling it toward him. His efforts were rewarded as the boat slid over the water as easily as a greased pig through human hands. "But I recognize this place I know I've been through here before. In fact, if I'm not mistaken, there should be a marked trail just a few feet from here that leads straight back to Thunder."

"There is? You really marked a trail?" At his nod, her expression brightened. She was completely amazed at his foresight. "Why didn't we go that way before?"

"We couldn't choose our path when we left that cabin," he reminded her. "We were running for our lives. And in doing so, we lost our way."

"But you're sure about where we are now?"

"Yes." His smile was reassuring. "Trust me, Amelia. We've got it made now."

A worried frown creased her brow. "I don't know. The outlaws might have found your marks and wiped them out.'' She knew she was playing the devil's advocate, yet she couldn't help voicing her worries.

He laughed at her fears. ''I'm no amateur, Amy. The sign I left won't be easily noticed. You'd have to know what to look for.''

''And what is that?''

''I stripped a few inches of bark off the north side of the small pines—the saplings that were six inches or so thick—in a place that would be mistaken, if spotted, for the mark of an animal that had been rubbing against the tree. And where there were no trees, I scratched a mark in the dirt.''

''That's very clever of you.'' Amelia smiled at him. ''I'm so glad you're with me. I'd be lost on my own ... or a prisoner in that cabin with that evil man.'' Amelia shivered at the thought of being in Jude Tanner's clutches again. ''You're sure you won't have any trouble following them back to your horse?''

''No,'' he chided gently. ''Now stop your worrying before you put permanent lines in that pretty forehead of yours.''

Her eyes opened wide. ''Colter Morgan. I think you just paid me a compliment.''

''Is that such a surprise?''

''Yes,'' she told him. ''It is. I don't think you're a man who gives compliments to a woman very often.''

''You're not just any woman,'' he said gruffly.

Amelia flushed beneath his gaze. It would take time to get used to their changed circumstances, she decided. But she was going to enjoy getting to know the man who had become her lover.

Lover.

She'd rather use the word *husband.*

Afraid he might be able to read her thoughts, Amelia decided a change of subject was required. ''Where did you learn a trick like that, Colt? That thing about scratching marks on trees.''

His mouth thinned instantly, and something flickered in his dark eyes. ''A man learns what he must to survive, Amelia.''

Amelia wished she'd kept her mouth shut. It was apparent that Colter was remembering the long years he'd fought during the war. He was sure to recall battles where men had died, where brothers had fought against brothers, fathers against sons. It was a horrid war, one that never should have happened. And she silently cursed herself for making him remember.

''It's a good thing you're in charge here.'' She bestowed a glowing smile on him, hoping to chase away the darkness that hovered around him. ''I would never have thought of leaving a trail behind me.''

Although Colter made no reply, the muscle had stopped twitching in his jaw and the grim expression had faded. He beached the canoe moments later and jumped out on the creek bank, wrapping the rope around the limb of a cypress tree to secure it. Then he turned to help Amelia out.

The canoe wobbled when she stood upright, and she sucked in a sharp breath as fear pimpled her flesh. The swamp was alive with danger—hungry alligators that could bite a grown man in half, cottonmouth water moccasins with venom so deadly it would mean certain death to its victim—and mere moments in the murky water might very well prove fatal to her.

''It's all right,'' Colter soothed, grasping her hand in his much larger one to steady her. ''I've got you, Amelia. You're not going to go overboard.''

She gasped as he pulled her forward with one mighty heave. And then he was holding her close against him, smoothing her hair back from her forehead and wiping away the beads of sweat that had gathered there.

Amelia shuddered against him, her arms tight around his waist, her head nestled close beneath his chin. She was safe now, she told herself. Safe in the arms of the man she loved.

That thought brought her head upright and she gazed up at him. She did love him, she realized. There was no use in denying it anymore. Somehow during their time together—was it only a few short days?—Colt Morgan had become her reason for living. She didn't know the exact moment when it happened, only knew that it had.

Oh, God, she *did* love him!

Amelia opened her mouth to tell him of her love, but at that moment she heard a sharp crack that sounded like a branch snapping underfoot.

Her eyes widened in fear. She didn't have to ask Colt whether he'd heard the sound, because he was already reacting to it.

Shoving her toward the trunk of a thick cypress tree, Colt motioned silently for her to hide there, drawing his six-gun at the same time and moving in the opposite direction, obviously intent on drawing attention away from the place where she was hiding.

Amelia opened her mouth to protest, but he shook his head vigorously and glared at her, again motioning her toward the cypress.

Reluctantly she obeyed, unwilling to be parted from him yet knowing she could be putting them both in even more danger if she didn't do as he asked. Amelia crept behind the cypress tree and dropped down to her haunches. She remained poised there, silent, yet ready to leap out and run at the slightest command from the man to whom she'd given her heart.

* * *

Colter crept forward, easing his way through the heavily wooded forest as he put as much distance as possible between himself and Amelia. He felt a great need to get whoever was out there—and he was almost certain it was the outlaws—farther away from her, lest they find her hiding place.

Another sharp crack broke the silence, this one coming from his right, and he realized that he had more than one man to deal with.

How many were there? he wondered, ducking beneath a branch that was blocking his way.

Colter knew that if he could locate them quickly, he might be able to take down two of them, maybe even three or four, before they found him. But it would only happen if he was able to take them by surprise.

A heavy thud alerted Colter that someone had managed to get behind him. He swung around, his six-gun extended outward. Nothing. He backed away slowly, his gaze searching the wooded area for an enemy.

The blow, when it came, was completely unexpected. He was aware of pain exploding behind his eyes. Then nothing more.

Amelia heard a thud, then a heavy voice. "I guess that took care of him."

Oh, God! Amelia shoved her fist into her mouth to keep from screaming. The outlaws must have found Colt. But what had they done to him? Was he dead?

"Yeah," said another voice that was vaguely familiar. "But the girl's still loose. The boss ain't gonna be too happy if we come back without her."

"You're right about that, Nelson, but this ol' boy ain't

gonna tell us nothing. You hit him too damn hard. Why'd you have to go and do that anyway? You probably cracked his skull open. Now how's he gonna tell us where the girl is hiding?''

Amelia felt chilled at their words. *Oh, God, what did they hit him with?*

"Frank," growled the man they'd called Nelson. "Dip your hat in that creek and douse him with water. That oughta bring him around."

"Why in hell don't you dip your own damned hat?" Frank said sharply.

"Dammit," responded Nelson. "If you don't do what I said, you're gonna find yourself in that swamp with the alligators."

Footsteps approached Amelia's hiding place, and she slid quietly beneath the nearest bush, holding her breath as she waited for a shout of discovery. But Frank didn't even glance in her direction as he knelt beside the water and filled his hat. Moments later Amelia heard a loud splash, followed by a groan.

"Wake up," Frank growled.

"Go to hell," Colt responded grimly.

The sound was music to Amelia's ears.

She heard a coarse voice laugh harshly. "You'll be headed there soon enough if you don't tell us what we want to know," Frank snarled. "Now quit stalling. Where did you leave the girl?"

"Someplace where you'll never find her," Colter said curtly.

The sound of a quick thud sent a stab of pain through Amelia. It was obvious that Colt had been struck again. She swallowed around the lump that had lodged in her throat. If she came out, would they stop beating him? She rose silently to her feet.

"You can beat me to hell and back, but there's no way

you're ever gonna find the cave where I left her. Dammit!"
Colt swore softly, as though he'd given something away
that he'd been trying to keep secret.

Frank's voice sounded exultant. "A cave, huh?"

"No," Colt said quickly. "She's not there anymore. We
left the cave together, and I sent her on ahead to show
the posse the way back to the cabin."

"Like hell!" Frank growled. "You got her stashed away
in a cave somewhere. Only a fool would have turned her
loose in the thicket. And it's my guess you ain't no fool."

"You're wrong," Colt said coldly. "Amelia's following a
trail I blazed when I first came into the thicket."

"If she was, you damned sure wouldn't be telling us
about it."

Why was Colt telling them about the trail he'd blazed? It didn't
make sense, Amelia knew. Not when he'd taken such pre-
cautions to hide her from them. He certainly wouldn't put
her in danger now. Not even to save his own life.

"Bring him back to the cabin," Frank said gruffly. "Jude
will make him talk soon enough. It won't take him long
to find out where that damned cave is where he left the
girl."

Amelia heard the sounds of a struggle as the outlaws
forced Colt to go with them. And although she wanted to
confront them, to pound them with her fists and make
them release the man she loved, she knew that exposing
herself would only put them both in even more danger.
If they found her, they would have no reason to keep Colt
alive.

But why had he told them about the trail?

Then the answer came to her. Colt wasn't talking to
them. He was speaking directly to her. He was telling her
to follow the trail to the place where he'd left his mount.

But could she do it?

Even as that thought occurred, she knew she could do

whatever was necessary to free Colt. She eased around the cypress tree, ready to spring away if danger in the form of one of the outlaws suddenly appeared.

But there was no one there except herself. The forest was quiet, as were the creatures that lived there. And during that unnatural silence Amelia began her hunt for the marks that Colt had made. She stopped at every pine tree that fit Colt's description of the ones he'd marked. And soon her efforts were rewarded. She found the trail he had blazed.

Although she'd thought that finding the trail would get her out of the forest quickly, Amelia soon discovered she couldn't have been more wrong. She had to stop every twenty feet or so, sometimes searching several minutes before she found the trail again.

The land was darkening with shadows by the time she found the glade where Colt had left his mount.

The stallion was grazing placidly, seeming unaware of her presence until a stone rolled beneath her foot. He looked up then and saw her; then he nickered softly in greeting.

Amelia had almost reached the Appaloosa when a stranger stepped out of a nearby pine thicket and stood watching her with hooded eyes. He was dangerous-looking, with his unshaven cheeks, untidy hair, and rumpled clothing that appeared to be torn in several places. He was either a tramp or one of the outlaws.

Amelia turned to flee, but was stopped short by a hard wall of flesh.

Chapter Twenty

Iron-hard hands gripped Amelia's upper arms, holding her captive as she looked up into dark eyes that held her mesmerized.

Like the other man, his jaws were rough with several days' growth of beard, but he wasn't nearly as sinister appearing as his companion. And the expression in the man's eyes was definitely sympathetic.

"Whoa, there," he said gently. "We didn't mean to startle you."

"You—I—What are you doing here?" she asked breathlessly.

From the corner of her eye she saw the other man approach Thunder, and she jerked away from the man who'd been holding her so tightly. "Get away from there," she exclaimed. "That's my horse! I'll thank you to leave him alone."

"I beg to differ with you," the rough-looking man said.

"Thunder is *my* horse. Although I haven't seen him since my brother rode out on him last year."

"Your brother?" she breathed, her heart giving a leap of hope. "Colter Morgan is your brother?"

"Yes." The man crossed the distance between them and extended his hand. "I'm Matthew. That's brother Ben you just bumped into. And it's my guess you must be Colt's wife. I'm afraid we don't know your name."

"It's Amelia Spencer," she replied, taking his hand in a firm grip. "And I'm not Colt's wife." *Even though I would like to be,* she silently added.

"You two aren't married?" Ben's surprise at that bit of news was evident.

"No," Amelia replied. "But never mind about that. I need your help to free Colt. I was just going to ride to town for the sheriff."

"Where is Colt?" Matthew asked quickly.

"The outlaws have him," she said in a trembling voice. "They were taking him back to the cabin, and there's no telling what Jude will do to him when they get there." Tears suddenly blurred her vision. "I'm afraid for him, Matthew. It took me all day to get out of there."

"Don't worry, Amelia," Matt said gruffly. "We'll go after him." He turned away from her. "Let's go, Benjamin. It sounds like we don't have any time to waste."

Blinking rapidly to dry her tears, she said, "Wait! I'm coming with you."

"Like hell you will!"

Amelia raised her eyebrows at Matthew's tone. The brothers were alike in more ways than one.

"I'm going back," she insisted. "It's because of me they have him in the first place. And Jude is an evil man. He's sure to have ways to make people talk." She shuddered with fear, and tears welled up again, overflowing to rain down her cheeks. "It's my fault they captured him. Now I have to help you save his life."

"And he damn well won't appreciate it if we take you with us," Matthew said gently. "Do as he wished, Amelia. Don't make his sacrifice have been in vain."

"Oh, God," she cried. "I'm so afraid for him."

"Don't worry." Matthew squeezed her shoulders gently. "Colt's going to be okay. Just get on that stallion and head straight for Nacogdoches. Maybe when that damn sheriff sees you, he'll get that posse together again. There's a good chance we're gonna need it when we come out of that forest again." He swept a hand over his eyes. "Don't know what in hell happened to Blake."

Ignoring the last part, since she had no idea what he meant, Amelia continued to protest. "But you don't even know where the cabin is!"

"We know," Matthew growled. "Brother Ben has been there twice already. But since the outlaws hadn't caught either of you, he came back to report." He shoved her toward the stallion. "Go on now. Hightail it out of here and get that sheriff on the move."

They waited until she had mounted and reined Thunder around; then the two men faded into the thickly wooded forest.

Please God, she silently prayed. *Let them be in time to save Colt.*

Then, leaning over Thunder's neck, Amelia urged the stallion forward and soon they were racing toward town at a ground-eating pace.

The brothers made their way swiftly to the same rock where, only a few days before, Colter had watched the cabin hoping for a sight of Amelia.

Unlike Amelia, Colt was easy to find.

Spread-eagled between two poles that had obviously been driven into the ground for that purpose, Colt hung by his arms, his head hanging limp against his chest. He gave every appearance of being dead.

It was the pain that brought Colter back to consciousness.

Sharp, burning pain that seemed to cover every inch of his back, caused by the whipping he'd endured. Pain that made him grit his teeth to stifle the moan that was slowly working its way up his throat.

He wouldn't utter a sound. Damned if he would give them that satisfaction. He was determined that nothing they did would make him reveal the direction Amelia had taken.

Oh, Lord, he silently prayed. *Please let Amelia reach safety. Don't let all this have been in vain.*

Although Colter tried hard to ignore his pain, tried to concentrate instead on his surroundings without letting the outlaws know he'd regained his senses, he found it almost impossible. With his head hanging down the way it was, he could see nothing except a small patch of ground.

And even that was blurred, he realized, becoming aware in that instant how swollen his eyes were. His right eye was almost completely shut. And his vision was hazy, obviously affected by the swelling. But he'd been hurt worse before in his life.

Colt strained his ears, listening for voices, but there was nothing. Only silence.

He guessed the outlaws must have gone inside when they finally realized that an unconscious man couldn't possibly tell them what they wanted to know. But if they knew he was awake, they would surely be on him like bees on a honey bear who was trying to rob their hive.

If he hadn't been listening so hard, Colt might have missed the sound, because it was soft, merely a quiet displacement of air somewhere close by.

"Ughhhh."

The sound of a human voice was followed by a thud, as though something heavy had struck the ground.

Unable to contain his curiosity, Colt carefully swiveled his head on the stem of his neck so he could search for the source of the sound. The body of a man lay crumpled in a heap nearby.

Colt stared stupidly at the fallen man. A knife protruded from his back, and if he wasn't mistaken, it was an Arkansas toothpick.

And, dammit! The knife looked exactly like the one he'd given to Benjamin on his twelfth birthday. But it couldn't possibly be the same one or it wouldn't be stuck in the outlaw's back.

Another man entered Colter's line of vision and knelt beside the dead man, swiftly drawing the blade out of the outlaw's back and wiping the blood off on his shirt.

Colt felt a tug on his wrist and managed to stifle the groan of pain that threatened to erupt. He must be utterly silent. The outlaws must not be alerted to the fact that he had regained consciousness.

Another tug at the ropes and his right arm was free, making him fall to one knee. The only thing holding him upright now was his other wrist, tied to the stake. The strain on his left shoulder muscles was almost beyond bearing. He felt as though his shoulder was being wrenched out of its socket.

Perhaps it was another torture the outlaws had devised for their pleasure.

He wondered what they had in mind as the man behind him sliced through the bonds on his left wrist, freeing him completely.

Although Colt waited for the impact of his fall, it never came. Instead he was caught beneath the arms and legs and picked up off the ground.

"Is he alive?" a hoarse voice whispered.

A grunt was the only answer, but it too was low, as though the men were trying to keep from being heard. But it had to be a trick. Had to be.

"We're risking a lot for a dead man," said the first voice.

The timbre of his voice was curiously like Matthew's, Colt realized. But it couldn't be his brother, could it?

Opening his eyes to mere slits, he stared into eyes that he'd known all his life. Those of his oldest brother, Matthew.

"It's about time you quit playing possum and helped us get you away from here." Although Matt's voice held some amusement, his expression was dead serious.

"Then put me the hell down," Colter croaked.

"Can you walk?" Matt asked.

"I can run if I have to!" Colt claimed belligerently.

"Like hell you can." Worry made Benjamin's voice gruff. "You took a lot of punishment back there, Colt. You're gonna be weak as a newborn kitten when we put you on your feet."

"We're not going anywhere very fast with the two of you carrying me," Colt said grimly. "Just put me the hell down and we'll see how it goes."

They stood him on his own feet then, holding him upright for a long moment. Benjamin kept a close watch, looking behind them, making Colt aware that his brothers were anxious to be away before they were discovered.

"Dammit," he said softly as his legs crumpled beneath him.

"Never mind," Matt said, looping one arm around his brother's chest. "Just hang on to us, Colt. We'll get you out of here."

"Amy . . ."

"She's safe," Matt said, answering the unspoken question.

"Thank God!" Colt breathed.

"Let's get the hell out of here," Benjamin growled.

They made their way through the forest, at times carrying Colt, at other times dragging him along. And before they'd gone very far they heard the sound of pursuit.

The outlaws were coming after them.

Blake was in the sheriff's office, arguing with him and silently cursing his broken leg, when he heard the thunder of hooves. A horse was being ridden hard.

Going quickly to the window, he saw a woman astride a big Appaloosa stallion that looked mighty like the one his brother Matthew had loaned Colter.

His eyes widened as he realized it *was* Thunder. Relief flowed through him, then was washed away just as quickly as it had come. The woman riding the Appaloosa appeared in a mighty big hurry. She reined the stallion to a quivering halt in front of the sheriff's office, then dismounted quickly. There was something definitely wrong. Colter must be in trouble.

The woman rushed into the office, then stopped abruptly just inside the room. Her gaze flickered between them, pinpointing the stars fastened to each man's vest. Then she looked at the splint on Blake's right leg and apparently decided that the man with both legs intact was the one who could help her the most. She turned her attention to the sheriff.

"You've got to help me," she said. "I know where to find the outlaws who robbed the bank."

The sheriff's expression was mild, as was his voice. "Do you now?"

"Yes! And we have to get there as quickly as possible. They have a captive! They're holding Colter Morgan against his will."

Blake's gaze narrowed sharply. "The outlaws have my brother?"

She spun toward him. "Your brother? Colt is your brother? Then you must be—"

"Blake Morgan," he said abruptly. "Now, about Colt . . . You said the outlaws have him."

"Yes!" Amelia was exasperated that the men didn't appear too concerned that Colt was being held captive. At least the man with two good legs didn't. "We have to hurry," she said, turning back to the sheriff. "There's no telling what Jude Tanner will do to him."

"Jude Tanner?" The sheriff snapped to attention. "Tanner is holding Morgan captive?"

"Yes. He is." Why wasn't the sheriff already moving? Didn't he realize how desperate Colt's situation was? "We have to hurry," she exclaimed. "There's no telling what he'll do to Colt."

"I've heard of Tanner," Blake said grimly. "He's one mean son of a bitch." He threw a quick glance at Amelia. "Pardon me, ma'am. But Jude Tanner is so mean, he would sell his own mother if he thought anybody would buy her."

"Yeah," the sheriff muttered. "And he wouldn't even hesitate." His eyes were cold when he looked at Amelia. "Do you think you could lead us to their hideout?"

"I believe so. I know I could get you real close to the cabin if we use the trail that Colt blazed."

Blake stumped toward her, the splints on his leg thumping hard against the wooded floor. Taking her arm in a tight grip, he said, "Let's get on with it, then."

"You can't ride with that broken leg," the sheriff said mildly.

"Just gather the damn posse, Sheriff," Blake snapped, having run out of patience. "Don't worry about me."

Later, when they rode out of town, Blake was riding with them.

Colt was barely aware of the noise they made as they raced through the forest with his brothers half dragging him in their attempt to escape the outlaws.

The sounds of pursuit were getting closer with every passing moment. Colter could hear the shouts behind them, could distinguish every word uttered by the outlaws. Most likely they were only moments away from being caught.

As they broke through the clearing where his brothers had left their mounts, Colt heard the sound of a shot and the whiz of a bullet as the air was displaced beside his head.

Another two inches and it would have been over, he realized, as he heard the sudden *crack, crack, crack* of a six-gun being fired. One of the bullets was sure to find its target before he and his brothers could mount up.

Suddenly Matthew was shoving him on top of a gelding, then mounting quickly behind him.

"Go on, Matt!" Ben cried. "Get him outta here!"

"We go together!" Matt roared. "Together! Or not at all! Get on that damned horse, Benjamin!"

"Damn your stubborn hide!" Ben shouted. But even as he spoke, he was vaulting onto his mount, reining the sorrel around and sending shots off toward the pines where the outlaws were.

Colt tried to hold himself upright so Matthew could use his energy to fight off their attackers, but despite his every effort, he was too weak to do so. Matt had to abandon any thought of retaliation and concentrate instead on getting them to safety.

As he reined his mount around, Colt felt a burning pain in his chest and realized he'd been shot. He gripped the saddle horn tightly, managing to keep that information to himself for the moment. Matthew had enough to deal with, keeping ahead of the outlaws.

Although Colt tried to stay alert, he knew he was fading fast. His vision had blurred even more, and he felt a wet, sticky warmth flowing down his chest and knew that his lifeblood was slowly oozing away.

Amelia, he silently cried, and then he knew no more.

Chapter Twenty-One

Colt faded in and out of consciousness for two days. When he finally awakened, it was to find Matt leaning over him.

"Matthew?" Colt's voice was raspy, dry. He licked his lips; they felt swollen, cracked. Perhaps that was what made him realize how thirsty he was. His mouth felt as though it had been stuffed with cotton.

"Yeah," Matt said huskily. "Welcome back, Colt. We thought for a while there we'd lost you."

Alarm surged through Colter as he remembered how he'd come to be where he was, flat on his stomach with pain stabbing through his back and chest and almost every other part of his body. "Amy?" he whispered urgently.

"Amy? Are you asking about Amelia?"

Colter nodded.

Matthew hastened to reassure his brother. "Amelia's doing just fine, Colt." He squeezed his brother's hand. "She's been worried to death over you, though. Wouldn't leave your side for one damned minute until we forced her. The doctor told us she was on the verge of a nervous breakdown if she didn't get some rest." He grinned. "We didn't think you'd appreciate waking up to find her that way . . . not after all the trouble you took to rescue her . . . so we banned her from the room. Told her she couldn't come back until she'd had some sleep."

Although Colt was glad they'd made her rest, he couldn't help wishing she'd been there when he woke up. He swallowed around the lump that had settled in his throat. "So thirsty," he croaked.

"You need some water?"

At his brother's nod, Matt reached for the silver pitcher on a nearby stand and poured water into a glass. Then, sliding an arm beneath Colt's arms, he lifted him enough so he could drink.

Colt swallowed the cooling liquid, and when he'd had enough, he lay back against the pillow, trying to ignore his throbbing back. "The outlaws?" he rasped.

"Most of them are dead," Matthew replied. "But their leader, Jude Tanner, survived. He's in jail waiting for the circuit judge to come through."

Colt clasped Matt's hand, his gaze steady on his brother's. "Watch him, Matt." His voice sounded strained, weak. "Make damned sure that devil can't get to Amelia."

"He won't," Matt promised. "The sheriff's got him locked up tight, Colt. He won't be getting out anytime soon. And I expect he's gonna be stretching a rope before very much longer."

"Make sure—"

Colt broke off when the door was suddenly flung open and Amelia rushed in. She looked at his torn back, and tears dimmed her eyes. "Oh, Colt," she whispered. "I'm so sorry."

"It's nothing," he said hoarsely.

"Nothing?" She knelt beside him and caressed the hair at his nape. "How can you call it nothing? They beat you so badly. I thought you were dead when they brought you in."

Colt patted her shoulder, offering the only comfort he was capable of.

"I'm so sorry, Colt," she whispered. "I hurried as fast as I could, but I kept losing the trail and I knew all the time that that outlaw—Jude Tanner!—that terrible man was making you suffer for helping me get away."

Colter threw Matt a beseeching look as Amelia's tears overflowed and began to stream down her face.

"Now, Amelia." Matthew squeezed her shoulder. "Don't take on so. We went to a lot of trouble to save this boy's life. We don't want him drowned with your tears."

Amelia's eyes widened with dismay. She released her hold on him. "I'm sorry," she whispered. "I wasn't thinking. I was just so glad that you were . . . that you would recover. I went out for a walk, and when I returned, the hotel clerk told me you were awake. He said the doctor told him you would recover, and I was just so happy that—"

"Amy," Colter interrupted. "I'm fine."

"You don't look fine. You look . . ." Tears filled her eyes again. "Oh, Colt," she cried, reaching out to touch his swollen jaw. "Your poor face. Your eyes are ringed with purple. And your lip is split. And your back! You must be in terrible pain. What did that monster do to you?"

"Amelia." Matthew reached toward her again, but Colter's voice stopped him.

"No!" His gaze met that of his older brother's, daring him to interfere as he reached out a hand to hold Amy in place. When he spoke again, his voice was stronger. "It's all right, Amy. It's really not as bad as it looks."

Amelia wrapped her fingers around his. "I'll never be able to thank you enough for getting me out of there,

Colt," she said. "And I am so sorry"—the tears that had been her constant companion since they'd brought him overflowed again—"so sorry that you had to endure so much pain because of me. There's no way I can ever repay you."

"You don't owe me anything," he growled, brushing her tears away with the back of one hand. "Now stop crying all over me. You're gonna drown me in tears."

Amelia sniffed and took the handkerchief Matthew offered, but she continued to kneel beside Colt and gaze at him with those damnable blue eyes in that way she had. It was enough to make the whole world aware of her feelings. And he could do nothing except lie helpless in bed with his brother watching them.

Had Matthew guessed what had happened between Amelia and himself while they were in hiding?

He hoped not. Colt hoped they'd be able to keep that episode a secret between the two of them. He had no intention of ruining her reputation, of making her fodder for gossip-mongers.

Colt smoothed his palm over Amelia's silky hair and looked up at Matthew, silently begging his brother for help in dealing with her.

Matthew's gaze that had been so warm only moments before had suddenly become cool, reserved, and when he turned his eyes on Amelia, there was compassion as well as a measure of frustration in his look.

Colter groaned, realizing his brother had correctly read the situation. On the one hand, Colt wanted to deny what had happened between himself and Amelia, wanted to protect her reputation from idle gossip. But he knew that their secret would be safe with Matthew. With any of his brothers, for that matter.

Suddenly Matthew relented. With a heavy sigh, he bent

and clasped his hands on Amelia's upper arms and lifted her to her feet.

"He's going to be just fine now, Amelia," Matthew said gently. "No need to worry about Colter anymore. A man as ornery as him just naturally can't be killed. Not easily anyway."

She smiled up at Matthew, and he was struck dumb by the expression on her face. She was beautiful, totally feminine, with a smile so sweet, so loving, that for a moment he thought that feeling was directed at him. And he gloried in her love.

But suddenly he realized he'd misread the smile. It wasn't directed at him, but was a leftover from the look she'd given his brother.

"Thank you for saving him, Matthew," she said softly. "Thank you so much."

Rising on tiptoes, she pressed a soft kiss on his cheek, and Matthew stood frozen, unable to utter a word as he wallowed in the sunshine of her smile and wondered what his wayward brother had ever done to deserve a woman as lovely—in face as well as spirit—as Amelia.

Finally he found his voice. "You're quite welcome, Amelia," he said huskily. "Now, why don't you go to your room and rest for a while? I know you haven't slept properly since we got back to town. And more'n likely not since those outlaws took you."

For the first time, Colt noticed the dark shadows beneath her eyes. "He's right, Amy. You need to sleep. You look like you've been through hell."

She laughed shakily, her eyes meeting those of the man on the bed. The man who had come to mean so much to her in such a short time. "Now, those words are most definitely not designed to woo a woman," she joked lightly.

"Woo a woman?" Matthew's look challenged his brother. "Is that what you've been doing, Colt? Wooing

Amelia? Is something going on between the two of you that I should know about?"

Matthew hadn't noticed the opening door, but Colter had. His gaze flickered to the man who stood there, bag in hand, and guessed him to be the doctor.

Had the newcomer heard his brother's question? He could most certainly have done so.

Worry darkened his brow as he sought to remedy the harm that Matthew's question might have done to Amelia's reputation. "Not a damn thing, Matthew," he said gruffly. "You've got the wrong slant on things. I've just been helping Amelia out of a rough situation."

"Oh?" Matt's gaze swung to Amelia, who had become motionless, silently watchful. "That wasn't exactly my take on the situation."

"Well, it's the truth," Colt growled.

As the newcomer closed the door behind him and crossed the room to a nearby table, Colt explained how he'd met Amelia.

Matthew listened in silence, and when Colt stopped speaking, he asked the question that had been uppermost in his mind. "Where on earth did folks get the idea the two of you were married?"

"It's what we told them," Colt replied stiffly. "Figured it was the best, since we were traveling together. It cut down on speculation and went a long way toward saving her reputation."

Matt sighed heavily. "So there's nothing between the two of you?"

Although Colt's cheeks reddened slightly, he shook his head in denial. "Nothing," he muttered. "Except we've become mighty good friends. At least I hope so." His gaze found Amelia's, and there was something in his eyes that demanded she go along with his explanation.

"No," Amelia said woodenly, determined to keep the

pain she was feeling hidden from both men. "We're just good friends."

"Um-hum," Matt said. "Well, I must admit I was hoping for something different. Guess we jumped the gun because we wanted a woman around the place so bad. The house on Morgan's Creek is getting mighty shabby these days. And the food is not much better."

"You don't have to worry about that anymore," Colt said, flashing a smile at Amelia. "Because she's going home with you."

Matthew arched a dark brow and met Amelia's eyes before he looked at Colter again. "Is she, now? Well, that's wonderful news. But how in hell did you manage to talk her into that?"

"It was easy, since she had no other place to go."

"So we get her by default?"

Amelia flushed beneath Matt's appraisal. "I could probably find work here at the hotel," she said. "You don't have to be stuck with me, Matthew."

"We'd love to have you," he said gently. "I was just wondering about your family, though. Won't they be worried?"

"She has no family," Colter told his brother. "Not anymore. That damn father of hers sold her to one of the Kincaid brothers. Grady Kincaid. Anyway, even if that weren't the way of it, she still couldn't go back to Louisiana. There's a good chance the law's looking for her."

"For killing Kincaid?" Matt asked.

Colt nodded, and closed his eyes as pain streaked through his temple at the movement. He groaned softly and pressed his hand to his temple. "Damn! That hurts." He opened his eyes and saw the two of them staring at him, and he felt curiously hurt that neither of them had offered him a word of sympathy.

"Amelia should get a medal for killing the skunk," Matt said.

"My thoughts exactly," muttered Colt. "But the law may not see it that way."

"I'll have Blake make some inquiries," Matthew said. "He'll know how best to handle the situation."

"She'll be safe enough on Morgan's Creek," Colt told his brother.

Amelia had stood silently by and listened to them as they discussed her future. But she could remain there no longer. She felt stifled, needed to get out of the room before she broke down and allowed her feelings to erupt in tears again.

She'd been so certain that Colt loved her. So certain that he cared. But it was obvious now that she'd been fooling herself. That he'd only been using her as a vessel for his lust.

Lust! Dammit! He was no better than Kincaid!

No! She silently chastised herself. Colt Morgan was a good man. He hadn't forced her into anything. And he most certainly wasn't responsible for her thoughts. Or her hopes and dreams. He'd never claimed to love her. Never. She had taken comfort from his arms, and she had imagined that he loved her. But that wasn't his fault. There was no reason to blame him. No reason at all.

She sighed heavily and wiped a hand across her eyes. "I believe I'll go now and get some sleep," she said huskily. "I'm so tired . . . never knew I could be so weary."

"Of course you are," a deep voice boomed out.

Amelia gave a start of surprise, noticing the doctor for the first time. She summoned up a smile for him, weak though it was. "I didn't see you come in," she told him.

"I'm not surprised," he replied. "I gather you didn't mind me, young lady, when I ordered you to sleep."

"I couldn't," she replied. "Not until I knew Colt was out of danger."

"Well, you can rest easy now," he said gruffly. "He's on the road to recovery." He turned to Colter. "I suppose you've got a powerful headache, young man."

Amelia started toward the door, but Matthew reached it before she got there and opened it for her. He followed her into the hallway.

"You go straight to your room and crawl into bed," Matthew ordered. "And don't get up again for the next ten hours. I'll be here to see that Colter is taken care of, so don't worry about him."

Amelia returned to the room Matthew had rented for her and yanked back the covers and sprawled across the bed. She was too tired to consider her future now. But if she could find work elsewhere, she knew that Morgan's Creek didn't figure into it. No matter how much they needed a woman there.

To be around Colt and forget what had passed between them was an impossibility. Anyway, after what had occurred between them, there could be a babe on the way. And, if there was, then Matthew would probably insist on a wedding.

And there was no way in hell she was going to force marriage on Colter Morgan. Not when it was obvious he had no desire to wed her.

At that thought, the tears she had been holding at bay welled up and burst free.

Amelia cried for the future that she'd never have with Colter now. She cried for the child that might already be growing inside her. Then she cried for her mother who'd been gone for so long. And finally she cried for herself. When she finally had no more tears left, she curled up into a fetal position and fell into a deep sleep that was untroubled by nightmares.

* * *

After listening to what Matthew told him about Amelia's predicament, Blake headed for the telegraph office and sent off a wire to the constable in New Orleans. Within the hour he had a reply.

Judge ruled Kincaid's death self-defense. No warrant on Amelia Spencer. No bounty. If you know her whereabouts tell her to get in touch with me. Her father has been mortally injured.

Blake stared down at the message. Would Amelia want to return home when she learned about her father? If so, that could complicate matters. Blake was almost tempted not to tell her about her father. To keep that part of the message secret. He'd accomplished what he'd set out to do in learning she wasn't wanted by the law. That fact would relieve her mind. But the part about her father was sure to bring her pain.

Even so, Blake knew he couldn't keep the news from her. She had a right to know. And since there was a farm, there might be an inheritance at stake, for surely she would be the new owner.

There was nothing to do, he decided, except to tell her.

Chapter Twenty-Two

Amelia was surprised to see Blake when she opened her bedroom door at his knock. She listened quietly to what he had to say, and when he had finished speaking, she stood motionless, wondering why she couldn't work up a little sympathy for her father's plight.

Try as she might, Amelia could find no compassion in her heart for a father who'd turned his back on his only daughter, who had even sold her as easily as he would have sold off his livestock.

Blake watched her closely as though he expected her to fall apart at any moment. But she remained dry-eyed, completely calm, unaffected by the news of her father's impending death.

How could it be otherwise, when her father had proven what she'd always suspected . . . that he cared nothing for her well-being?

Realizing that Blake was waiting for some kind of

response, Amelia said, "I don't suppose the constable told you how he came to be hurt?"

"No. Just that it was serious. That your father was mortally injured. He gave me some good news too, Amelia. He said Kincaid's death was ruled self-defense."

"Thank God," she murmured. "Whoever saw him attacking me—I think it was Joseph, his manservant—must have come forward and told the sheriff what he'd seen."

"Someone actually saw you being attacked and didn't try to stop him?"

"Joseph was born a slave," she said softly. "He would have been too frightened to interfere."

"At least he came forward in the end." Blake studied her through narrowed eyes for a long moment, then said, "Do you want to go back there, Amelia?"

"I must."

"I imagined you would," he said gruffly. "After all, the farm will be yours now. As soon as Colt's able to travel, I'm sure he will take you there long enough to decide what's to be done about the farm."

"I can't wait for Colt to recover, Blake. I have to go now."

He frowned at her. "Why?"

"I need to see my father. To talk to him before he dies."

"That bastard doesn't deserve to see you, Amelia," Blake said harshly.

He'd been appalled when Matthew had told him her story, how she'd been sold to Kincaid by her own father. He remembered what his own family had suffered at Kincaid hands. They were evil incarnate. Every damned one of them! And as far as he was concerned, Amelia's father was cut from the same cloth.

"I'm not going back for my father's sake," Amelia replied. "I have to go for myself. And right away. I have so many questions that need answering. And he's the only one who can help me.''

Blake frowned at her. "You can't go yet, Amelia. Colter isn't well enough to travel.''

"It makes no difference,'' she replied. "I have no problem with traveling alone.''

"Maybe you don't, but I imagine Colt will have a problem with it,'' Blake said sternly. "He won't allow you to go off on your lonesome without a soul around to look after you.''

She smiled without humor. "Colter Morgan has nothing to say about what I do, Blake.''

"I thought—''

"I know what you thought,'' she interrupted. "What all of you thought. But it's not so. There's nothing between us. Colt and I are just good friends.''

Blake looked skeptical. "Are you sure, Amelia?'' he asked softly.

"Of course I'm sure.'' She moved away from him and picked up the extra day dress Matthew had insisted on buying for her. When she'd allowed him to do so, she'd been under the impression that he would soon be family. Perhaps she should leave it behind.

Realizing that the gown couldn't possibly be returned since it had already been worn, she shoved it into her reticule, then looked up at Blake. "Do you know what time the east-bound stage leaves town?''

Instead of answering her question, he said, "Don't be so hasty, Amelia. You need to talk to Colt before you think about going anywhere. I'm almost certain he wouldn't approve of you leaving like this. A woman alone is easy prey.''

She laughed softly. "I've been alone for a long time, Blake. Most of my life, in fact.'' She threw him a quick smile that didn't quite reach her eyes. "Don't worry about me. I'll be just fine."

"Maybe so," he said grimly. "But you're not going anywhere until you speak to Colter."

Seeing that Blake wouldn't be budged on the subject, Amelia tried to ease his mind. "I wouldn't dream of leaving without telling Colter good-bye."

"You promise?"

Since it was obvious that Blake had no intention of leaving until she gave him her word, Amelia quickly obliged. "I promise, Blake. I won't leave without saying good-bye to Colter."

A smile lightened Blake's features, and he felt his tension ease. He knew his brother well enough to know that Colt would never consent to Amelia traveling so far without an escort. "All right then," he said. "Colt should be waking up real soon. You can talk to him then."

"Is Matthew still with him?"

"No. He went down to the restaurant to eat."

"And Benjamin?"

"He went to the Rocking M Ranch to look at a stallion they're wanting to sell." He smiled at her, believing he knew her reasons for asking. "Colt should be alone now, Amelia. It's a good time to talk without interruption."

"Thank you," she said sweetly. "I'll just go along to his room now."

Blake smiled at her again, glad to put the problem of Amelia in Colter's capable hands. Colt knew her better than any of them. He would know how best to bring her around to their way of thinking.

Amelia entered Colter's room quietly. As she'd hoped, he was still fast asleep. Now she could keep her promise to Blake and still leave without anyone trying to stop her.

She knelt beside Colt and studied the features of the man who had come to mean so much to her in such a short time. He looked so awful, his flesh so bruised and swollen, even though it had been two days since he'd been beaten so severely.

Amelia knew she'd never forget him. Not if she lived to be a hundred years old.

Colt. Her love. Her *only* love. Amelia felt certain of that fact, because there would never be another man for her. Not as long as she lived. When she left here, she would be leaving her heart behind.

But perhaps she wouldn't always be alone. If she was lucky enough to have conceived a child, then she would have part of him to love.

Oh, God, please let it be so!

"Good-bye, Colt," she whispered, brushing her lips against his. "I'm going home."

Having kept her promise to Blake, Amelia rose quickly to her feet and left him there, stopping at her room long enough to fetch her valise before making her way to the small building that housed the stagecoach office.

Amelia purchased a ticket on the east-bound stage, waited patiently while the clerk counted out her change, then dropped the coins into her change purse.

Although she was aware of the opening door, she paid no attention, her mind already occupied with the long journey that lay ahead.

"Amelia?"

Hearing her name spoken, Amelia looked up to find Blake standing in the doorway frowning at her.

"What are you doing here?" he asked harshly.

"Waiting for the stage."

"Dammit, I told you to see Colter first!"

"I did see Colt," she said evenly, holding his gaze. "I

told him where I was going, Blake, just like I promised you, and he had no objection to me doing so."

"That's damned hard to believe."

"Believe it or not," she said flippantly. "It doesn't matter either way."

His gaze held hers for a long, silent moment. Then he said, "I don't like this, Amelia. Not even a little bit. You have no business going anywhere alone."

"You have no right to dictate to me, Blake." Suddenly she relented, standing on tiptoe to kiss his unshaven cheek. "It is sweet of you to worry about me. But there's really no need. I've been taking care of myself for a long time. I just lost sight of that for a time. But with Grady Kincaid gone, and my father no longer a threat . . . well, surely you can see that I'll be just fine."

At that moment the stage rolled to a stop outside, and Amelia picked up her reticule and gave Blake a brilliant smile. "Tell your brothers good-bye for me, Blake. And make sure they know how terribly grateful I am for the kindness they've shown me."

"My brothers?" His gaze was sharp as a knife. "Colter too, Amelia?"

"Stop worrying," she said softly. "I *did* tell him good-bye, I promise. And he didn't have one single objection to me going home alone." She repeated the words, all true as far as they went. But Amelia knew she needed to get out of town before Blake discovered Colt had been asleep when she told him good-bye.

Amelia didn't worry about Blake coming after her. Once she was gone, he would forget about her. After all, she was nothing to him. Nor to Colt. He had made her his problem . . . for a while. And he had stolen her heart during that time.

Colt. He might feel a slight pique that she had left while he was sleeping, but he would get over it soon enough.

After all, she meant nothing to him. They were only friends. She'd heard him say so.

And that still hurt.

She was on the verge of stepping around Blake when the stage driver entered the room and looked at the clerk behind the counter.

"Howdy, Luke," the stage driver said. "You got any passengers going east?" His faded blue eyes flickered around the room, stopping on the man and woman beside the door.

"Just one," Luke replied. He jerked his thumb toward Amelia. "That lady over yonder. She's going to New Orleans. She's the only passenger." He shifted his gaze back to the old man. "You gonna take time to eat?"

"No." The stage driver's answer was abrupt. "Got no time for chow. I'm already running behind."

"It's not like you to miss a hot meal when you get a chance at it."

"No," the old man said. "It damned sure ain't. And it's the company's fault I'm missing it this time. Had a busted wheel that needed repairing or I'd have been here early enough to enjoy one. They better come up with a new wheel, since the old one won't take much more repair." He turned to Amelia. "You ready, ma'am?"

"Yes." She smiled up at Blake. "Stop worrying about me," she chided. "I'm going to be just fine."

Blake's gaze touched on the stage driver. "You watch out for her, hear?"

"She'll be fine with me," the driver said gruffly. Bending over, he lifted Amelia's satchel. "This all you got in the way of baggage, ma'am?"

"Yes," she replied. "That's all."

"Come on then."

Amelia followed the driver outside, then quietly waited while Blake—who'd followed them outside—opened the stagecoach door. She would be traveling alone for a while, she realized, and she would welcome that solitude since she didn't feel like being sociable.

Tears stung her eyes as she turned for one last look at the hotel where Colter lay sleeping, but she quickly blinked them away, afraid that Blake would notice.

Leaving Colt behind was the hardest thing she'd ever done. But she had to do it. She refused to stay near him, knowing her love was hopeless.

Amelia allowed Blake to help her into the coach, then seated herself on the narrow bench. Then she lifted her gaze to find Blake watching her with narrowed eyes. "Good-bye, Blake," she said softly.

"Good-bye, Amelia," he said gruffly. "Don't be surprised to find me on your doorstep one day."

Her smile was sad. "I'd like that, Blake. One day." When she had time to get over Colt . . . if she ever did.

"Let me hear from you now and then. And if you ever need anything, just let me know."

Amelia nodded her head, too overcome by emotion to speak. Moments later the stagecoach rolled away from Nacogdoches, leaving behind the man who meant more than life to the woman inside the coach.

The hotel restaurant was crowded when Blake joined his brothers for a meal that evening. Night had long since fallen, and he'd been without food the whole day. For the past hour his stomach had been growling, so he ordered accordingly, then turned his attention to his oldest brother.

"How's Colt doing?" Blake asked, correctly assuming that his brother had just come from Colt's room.

"He's doing good," Matthew replied. "Chafing at the bit, but that's no surprise. He's not used to being bedridden. He was cussing so much this morning and threatening to leave the bed that the doc finally took mercy on me and fed him a dose of laudanum in a glass of whiskey." He laughed. "Colt never knew what hit him. He slept most of the day."

The waitress returned with their food, and the brothers busied themselves with filling empty bellies. It was Matt who finally broke the silence.

"Amelia must have been awfully tired," he said gruffly. "I haven't seen hide nor hair of her since early morning."

"Neither have I," Benjamin said. "But I've been looking over some horseflesh the last few days. Haven't had much time to get acquainted with her. I imagine I can remedy that, though, when she gets to Morgan's Creek."

"She won't be going to Morgan's Creek," Blake said abruptly.

"But Colter said—"

"I know what Colter said. But he must have changed his mind. Amelia left town today."

Blake hadn't thought to inform his brothers of Amelia's decision since he'd spent the day looking through the sheriff's Wanted posters.

Matthew's gaze narrowed. "Why in hell didn't you say something, Blake?"

"I got busy," Blake replied with a shrug. "Anyway, I'm telling you now."

"Where did she go?" Ben asked.

"Home," Blake replied.

"Home?" Matthew's gaze darkened. "Dammit, Blake! Amelia doesn't have a home! Didn't you hear a word of what I told you? Her father sold her to one of the Kincaid brothers! And on top of that, the law could damned well be looking for her."

"They're not."

"How in hell do you know that?"

Blake explained about the telegram.

"That's a relief, then," Matt said gruffly. "At least she won't be jailed when she gets there."

Benjamin set his fork carefully on his plate. "Colt's not going to like this," he predicted. "Her sneaking out on him like that."

"She didn't sneak," Blake growled. "Amelia told him she was leaving. She made her good-bye."

"You're sure of that?" Matt asked.

"Saw her go in his room myself."

"That doesn't mean she told him," Ben pointed out.

"I know," Blake replied. "But later, when I saw her at the stagecoach office, I asked her about it, figuring she must not have told him."

"And?" Matt said.

"She claimed she'd told him. And I believed her."

"And he had no objection to her leaving?" Matt asked.

"I asked that too. And she said he didn't object."

"I'm surprised," Benjamin said. "I didn't think he'd want her going anywhere without him. I kind of got the idea they loved each other . . . the way she took on over him when he was brought in."

"Yeah," Matt said. "I guess we all had that idea. But Colt assured me they were just friends."

Benjamin shrugged. "I guess he oughta know better than anybody else. But I still don't like it . . . her going off alone like that. If I'd known what she was about, I'd have rode along with her."

"I would have felt better about the whole thing if you had," Matt muttered. "But if she's bent on living there . . . well, dammit, Ben, you know you couldn't have stayed there forever."

"Yeah, I know," Benjamin replied. "But I could've made sure she got home without any trouble."

"Hey, you two," Blake chided. "The stage driver said

he'd take good care of her. There's no need to be worrying about her safety.''

"I guess not,'' Matthew replied. "And it's not like she's too young to take care of herself. Amelia is a mighty plucky lady. She proved that when she followed Colt's trail out of the Big Thicket to find help for him.'' He turned his attention to his food.

Amelia would be just fine, he told himself. *Otherwise, Colt would never have agreed to her leaving Nacogdoches alone.*

Chapter
Twenty-Three

Amelia was weary beyond belief when the stagecoach reached New Orleans two days later. It was late afternoon and she'd just endured a grueling journey that was not over yet.

After leaving the stagecoach, she picked up her satchel and strode quickly down the boardwalk, making her way to the nearest livery stable, where she rented a horse. She left town and rode toward the north, where the Spencer farm was located.

During the long ride, Amelia had plenty of time to consider the questions she would put to her father if she were given the chance. But it might be too late for questions. Her father might already be dead.

With that thought came a sudden need to hurry, to reach the farm as quickly as possible.

There was a carriage outside the house when she arrived. And lamplight streamed through the windows.

Amelia felt a flicker of hope. Perhaps she wasn't too late. It was obvious that someone was in the house.

Reining her mount up outside the house, Amelia dismounted, then hurried up the rickety porch steps, noticing that they were in bad need of repair.

She shoved open the door, then paused, her gaze wandering around the familiar room.

There was her grandmother's chest against the far wall, just where it had been since her mother had placed it there. And there on the mantel was the oil lamp, and the tintype of her father and mother made the day they were wed.

She sighed deeply. It was all so familiar, so dear to her heart.

A flicker of movement to her left caught her attention and she turned to see an elderly man seated gingerly on the settee.

"Who are you?" she asked.

"I might ask the same of you." He was a big man, as she saw when he rose slowly to his feet. His brown hair was shot through with gray. His faded gray eyes were red-rimmed, set deep in their sockets, as though it had been a long time since he'd had any rest.

"I'm Amelia Spencer."

The stranger wiped a tired hand across his brow before he spoke again. "I'm glad you've finally come, Miss Spencer." He stretched out a hand and grasped hers. "Your father is very ill. It's doubtful he will last through the night."

"You're the doctor?"

"Yes. The name is Silas Willoughby." He sighed heavily. "And right now I'm the only doctor around."

"I suppose he's in there?" She nodded at her father's bedroom.

Willoughby nodded. "Yes. And he's awake. If you want to speak to him, you'd best do it now."

"Is he able to talk?"

"Yes," Dr. Willoughby replied. "At the moment. Can't say how long that will last, though."

Amelia didn't want to see her father, but she needed some answers before he died. She walked stiffly toward the bedroom where her father lay, opened the door, and looked at the man who lay on the bed with his eyes closed. The man who'd caused her so much misery. And she felt nothing. No compassion, no sympathy whatsoever. Nor did she feel the hate that had dwelt within her ever since she'd learned he'd sold her to keep his farm.

As though sensing her presence, he opened his eyes and looked at her. "So you've come back, have you?"

"Yes," she replied, approaching his bed. "I've come back."

"Guess you're after your inheritance."

"Why else would I have come back?"

"Why else." He closed his eyes wearily, then opened them to look at her again. "Guess you know what I done . . . how you came to leave home."

"If you're talking about how you sold me to Grady Kincaid, then, yes, I do know."

"Figgered you did." He fingered the patchwork quilt that covered him to the waist. "Heard you killed him."

"Yes. I did."

"Good. He didn't deserve to live."

Neither do you, she thought. But she said instead, "Would you answer my questions now, Pa? Would you tell me why you sold me?"

"Needed the money," he said.

"More than you needed me?"

"Hell, girl. I didn't need you. Never needed you. Now, if you'd been a boy, then we could have made the farm work without me having to sell off my daughters the way I done. But you weren't a boy. Neither was any of the others.''

Her heart skipped a beat. "Others?"

"Yeah," he replied gruffly. "Lorrie never gave me nothing but girls. Three lousy girls that didn't have the strength to help me make it and—"

Amelia's eyes widened. "Three girls?" she asked. "I had two sisters?"

He laughed. "Didn't know that, didja? Thought you had just the one." A grin curled his mouth. "Well, you was wrong. Dead wrong. Your ma had another girl, all right. She was just a few years older than the two of you. But we got in a bind and needed money real bad. Guess that was what started the whole thing. If those people hadn't got a look at that little red-haired girl and wanted her so bad . . . well, I never would've knowed any of you was worth real money, now would I?"

He frowned suddenly. "It was hard on me and your ma both. Parting with her like that. Firstborn and all—even if she was a girl. But a man's gotta do what he's gotta do. And your ma knew that. Sure, she was mad at me in the beginning. Railed and ranted like a crazy woman for more'n a month, trying to make me tell who took her.''

He smiled widely. "But I never gave in. Nope. Held my ground real good. And finally she stopped crying about the kid. Just got real quiet. Too quiet, maybe, 'cause she never was the same after that. And when the two of you finally came along, well, I figgered she was gonna be all right." He looked away from her. "She must've got over it too, because when I sold your sister, she never said a word about it to me. Just lay there on this bed I'm in right now and looked at me. Never even shed a tear."

Amelia looked at him in horror. She'd never known him, this man who talked so casually about selling his

children, about his wife who had lost her reason for living.
How could he be so evil, and not realize what he'd done?

"Didn't you ever love her?" she asked.

"The sister?" he asked. "She warn't nothing but a girl
nohow. And she was real small. Like you. Wouldn't have
been much use on the farm."

"I was talking about my mother," she said coldly. "And
wondering if you ever loved her. But it's obvious you
couldn't have done so. If you had, you wouldn't have taken
her children away from her."

"Hell!" he exclaimed. "I didn't take 'em all away from
her. There was two of you. And I knew it was the good
Lord's way of looking after us, kinda like he was just giving
his permission for me to sell one kid for the money we
needed to keep us going. Anyway, it didn't come as no
surprise. Your ma knew from the day she borned you both
that she'd have to choose between the two of you when
the time came. Only she couldn't seem to do it. In the
end, I had to be the one to choose."

"So you kept me," she said coldly. "Was there any particular reason why you kept me instead of my sister?"

"No reason," he said gruffly. "Since you were twins, it
didn't seem to make a difference."

"Twins?" she gasped. "I had a twin sister?"

"Yeah. Didn't I say so? I'm surprised you didn't remember. You was old enough when it happened. Anyway, you
asked about your sister for a long time. And it always set
your ma to crying. That was the reason I'd take the strap
to you at times like those."

Amelia remembered the whippings. And she'd always
associated them with questions about her sister and finally
stopped asking about her.

"Where are they?" she demanded. "Who did you sell
my sisters to?"

"I ain't right sure where they are," he replied. "But the

oldest one went to a family named Cobb. They were headed for Texas at the time.''

"Where in Texas?'' she demanded.

"Don't rightly know,'' he replied. He coughed, spat up blood, then sank weakly into the pillow again. "I'm done talking now, daughter. Need to rest.''

"No, Pa!'' Amelia was determined to get her answers now . . . while there was still time. "You can rest in a few minutes. But first you must tell me her name.''

"Told you I didn't know,'' he mumbled. "Your ma just called her Velvet.''

"No, Pa,'' she said again. "I want to know my other sister's name. Your firstborn child. Surely you remember the name of your firstborn child.''

"The first baby?'' he asked, closing his eyes weakly. "Yeah. I remember her name. Should remember, since we named her after your grandma. It was Rachel.''

"Rachel.'' Relief flowed over her. She finally had a name. "And my twin?'' she whispered.

His eyes flew open. "Dammit, girl! I told you I don't know!''

"I'm not asking for her name now, Pa. I want to know what happened to her.''

"Sold her to the Johnson family that owned the farm west of here.''

Amelia frowned. "I don't know them.''

"No. You wouldn't know them. They left for parts unknown a couple of years later,'' her father replied. "Don't know where they went either, so it won't be any good to ask me.''

She stared at her father. He had a lot to answer for when he met his Maker.

* * *

The darkening twilight lengthened the shadows in Colter's hotel room, where he lay abed cursing his inability to stand on his own two feet for more than three minutes at a time.

It wasn't as if he hadn't tried, because he had. In fact, it hadn't been more than half an hour since he'd left the bed and crept, weak as a newborn babe, to the chair beside the window. He hadn't been able to sit there long, though, to keep the vigil that he'd intended by the window. But it was long enough to know that Amelia wasn't out there among the throng of women who hurried around town, doing their shopping and greeting their friends and neighbors as he'd thought she might be.

But where in hell was she? It had been two whole days since she'd been to see him. What in hell had she been doing all that time?

Granted, she might have been coming while he was sleeping—he'd been doing a lot of that since he'd been shot—but nobody had even mentioned her name lately, and he worried about that.

Colter wanted to see her. The need to be with her was like an untended wound that festered with each passing moment. He missed her more than he'd ever thought it possible to miss anyone.

Amelia. She was like a sunrise on a dark horizon.

Amelia. Her name was a lyric, her smile a beacon in the dark corners of his mind.

When had it happened? No matter how hard he tried, he couldn't pinpoint the exact moment when his reason for living had become Amelia. She was a woman-child, an enchanting, fey creature that had completely bewitched him.

And he loved her.

That thought stabbed through him with the quickness

of a knife. Sharp. Piercing. And the realization made him weak as a kitten.

He sank against his pillows, his pulse racing wildly as though he'd been trying to outrun the wind.

Amelia. Dammit! How could he have fallen in love with her and not even known it? His goose was surely cooked now. At that thought, a smile twitched at his lips. If he had to go and fall for a woman, then he was damned grateful that the woman had been Amelia.

But where in hell was she anyway?

It was a question that needed answering now.

A sudden thought caused momentary panic. Matthew and Benjamin had left for Morgan's Creek that morning. Had they taken Amelia with them? If so, why hadn't they told him?

Come to think of it, when his brothers came to say good-bye, they had seemed unusually silent, had not lingered long at his bedside. Colt had thought, at the time, that they were just worried about his health. But upon reflection, he realized there could have been another reason.

Colt was cursing his inability to search for her when the door opened and the doctor walked in.

"How is my patient this evening?" the man asked, setting his bag down on a table.

"Damned tired of lying in this bed," Colter growled.

The doctor chuckled. "I imagine so. But you're gonna have to stay there awhile longer, Morgan. Otherwise you might just pull those stitches out and start it bleeding again. If that happened, you'd be ripe for an infection."

"I know that!" Colter snapped, rising to his elbows to glare at the doctor. "Why in hell do you think I'm still in this bed? I saw enough wounds in the war to know what can happen if they're not dealt with properly."

"Now settle down, Morgan," the doctor soothed. "Or else I'll have to give you something to make you sleep."

"Like hell you will!" Colter roared. "You already done that once and I slept around the clock. I don't like being that way, and I'm not drinking anything else you've prepared."

"Take it easy. You're not—"

"What in hell is going on in here?"

The harsh voice jerked the heads of both men around to see Blake Morgan standing in the doorway. He stepped inside the room and closed the door quietly behind him.

"Somebody gonna tell me what's going on?" he asked, his gaze flickering between his brother and the doctor.

The doctor spoke first. "I was just advising your brother that he'd have to settle down or I'd give him a dose of laudanum."

"And I was telling him what I thought of the idea," Colter snarled.

Blake laughed huskily. "I didn't catch the words, but I sure as hell know what you thought about the subject."

The doctor completed his examination, then put a new bandage over the wound.

"How's he doing, Doc?" Blake inquired.

"The wound's doing better than he is," the doctor said cheerfully. "Shouldn't be but a few more days before he's up and around."

"That's good," Colt growled, relaxing against his pillows again. "I'm getting damned tired of being laid up." He eyed the doctor for a long moment, then asked casually, "I hope Amelia recovered from her ordeal without any problems."

The doctor smiled at him. "She wasn't hurt. Just shook up a bit. Mighty plucky young lady, that one. Has more courage than most men I know." His brows pulled together in a heavy frown. "I did hate to see her leave like that, though."

"Leave?" Colt jerked up on his elbows, groaning as pain

shot through his sore ribs. "What do you mean, leave? Where in hell did she go?"

"Easy now," the doctor soothed, pushing Colt back against the pillows. "You're going to pull them stitches out if you're not careful."

"What is he talking about, Blake?" Colt demanded.

"He's talking about the stitches," Blake explained. "If you jerk around like that, you'll—"

"Dammit, man!" Colter exclaimed. "You know what I'm asking about! Where's Amelia?"

"In New Orleans, I expect."

Colt's pulse was leaping a mile a minute as he struggled to take in the information that Amelia had left town . . . without even saying a word to him. How could she have done such a thing, and why would she do it?

"She can't go back there," Colter said bleakly. "She'll wind up in jail if she does."

"Don't worry about it," Blake said, watching the doctor measure out a dose of medicine into a glass. Laudanum, if he wasn't mistaken.

"How in hell can I keep from worrying about it?" Colt grated harshly. "Amelia's out there alone, and I can't do a damned thing about it!"

"What you need is a drink," Blake said mildly.

"You're damned right I do," Colter said, "but you pour it. The last time I asked for one, that damned doctor poured some laudanum in the whiskey."

Colter's mind was whirling as he tried to find a way to go to Amelia. He formed and discarded one plan after another as Blake poured the whiskey he'd requested. And, although it was his brother who was handling the liquor, Colt watched the medical man to make sure he didn't doctor the drink with a sedative.

When Blake handed the glass of whiskey to Colter, he

swallowed the contents in one huge gulp. "Another," he said, holding out the glass.

"Better not," the doctor said, closing his medical bag with a snap. "I recommend whiskey for dulling the pain during an operation, but otherwise, it's best to lay off the stuff until the wound heals."

"Go to hell!" Colter snapped.

The doctor took no offense at his patient's words. He'd been sworn at before. And some of his patients had even thrown a punch at him. Men! They made the worst patients.

But Colter Morgan could rant and rail all he wanted to. The laudanum he'd put into the man's glass had been enough to put him under for a good twelve hours. There'd be hell to pay then, but, meanwhile, the wound would be healing.

He was still grinning when he bade the two brothers farewell and went out the door, closing it softly behind him.

Chapter Twenty-Four

Despite Silas Willoughby's prediction that her father wouldn't last through the night, he was still hanging on the next day.

As the sun rose in the eastern sky, topping the oak trees with a golden burst of color, Amelia set the basket of eggs she'd gathered on the table and went outside again to enjoy the sunrise.

Seating herself on the uppermost porch step, she folded her legs, looped her arms around her ankles, and rested her chin against her knees. She sighed deeply, feeling a sense of satisfaction that she'd finished the chores so early. The cow had been milked, and the stock fed and watered. All the eggs had been gathered, and the chickens fed. Now there was nothing to occupy her mind. Nothing except her sisters . . . and Colter Morgan.

No matter how she tried to put him out of her mind, thoughts of him kept intruding. She remembered their time together in the cave and wished they'd never left there. It had been a magical place and a magical time. A time when she'd thought he loved her, and had gloried in that love.

But she had been mistaken. Amelia's lips quivered with pain, and her blue eyes misted. How could she have been so mistaken? She should have known better. Colter Morgan was a loner. He would never give his heart to any woman. Most certainly not a woman such as herself.

That thought caused a stab of pain. If only her circumstances had been different. Perhaps then he might have loved her.

The sound of hooves jerked her head up, and she narrowed her eyes on the approaching carriage. It was Silas Willoughby, obviously coming to check on her father.

The carriage rolled to a stop beside the corral, and Willoughby stepped down and looped the reins over a post before reaching for his medical bag.

"Well, young lady," he said, striding toward her. "How are you doing this morning?"

Amelia rose to greet the doctor. "I'm doing just fine."

"And your father?"

"He made it through the night." She pushed a hand through her copper curls and shook the wrinkles from her skirt. "He appears to be in a lot of pain, Dr. Willoughby. I was wondering . . . what happened? How did he come to be injured?"

Amelia realized that her questions should have been asked when she first arrived, but at that time she'd been more intent on getting answers to her questions before her father passed on.

"His mount stepped in a gopher hole," the doctor explained. "He was crushed beneath the horse, and vital organs were pierced by his broken ribs."

"I see." She sighed heavily.

"I keep him dosed with laudanum," he said gently. "It

helps. If you're staying here, I'll leave some with you." He raked a hand through his shaggy hair. "Lord knows I could use the extra time, if you're willing to take over his care."

"I'm perfectly willing to do anything I can," she said quickly. "But what if he needs more care than I can give him?"

"In that case I will most certainly return." His faded eyes were kind as he studied her. "You look tired, my dear. Did you get any rest last night?"

"No. I couldn't sleep."

"Perhaps if you had a sedative—"

"No!" she said quickly. "I don't need anything."

"As you wish." He mounted the steps. "Now let's have a look at the patient."

After he'd tended to his patient, Silas Willoughby motioned Amelia outside. When they were beyond the patient's hearing, he said, "It's only a matter of time. I'm surprised he's lasted this long. The only thing we can do now is make him as comfortable as possible."

From that moment on, Amelia took over the task of ministering to her father. Even though she hated every moment she was around him.

As the day passed slowly by, she found herself searching for excuses for him, trying to find a reason for what he'd done to them. Surely there was one. He must have had some redeeming qualities, once, or her mother would never have married him.

That thought continued to plague her as the afternoon waned. And since her father was the only one who would know the answers, Amelia spoke aloud her thoughts while she was feeding him that evening.

Scooping a spoonful of thin gruel—the only nourishment her father could take—out of a bowl, she said, "You know, Pa . . . I've often wondered why you chose my mother for a wife."

Although his gaze had been fixed on the gruel, it flickered to her before he spoke. "Your ma loved me. Only woman who ever did."

"Open," Amelia said, and when he did, she dumped the gruel in his mouth, then went back for more. "Did you love her?" she asked.

He thought about that for a long moment, waiting until he'd swallowed the next spoonful of gruel before he answered her question. "I don't rightly know what love is, girl. But I needed your ma. Knew she'd help me make a go of this place." He sighed heavily. "We'd have got along just fine, too, if it hadn't been for that damned war." He coughed, and groaned with the pain it caused. "It's the damn Yankees' fault what happened. They come in here and stole our stock and—"

"Ma died a long time before the war," she reminded him coldly.

He narrowed his eyes against another spasm of pain, and his body seemed to shrink into the mattress. "Yeah," he sighed. "I guess she did. I kinda forgot about that. I've been thinking lately, though, that it was them damned Yankees that killed her."

"It was you who killed her," Amelia said coldly.

"That's a damned lie!" he snarled, and there was more strength in his voice than there had been since Amelia arrived. "I never done no such thing, girl. It was losing her babes that made your mama give up on living."

"And who made her lose her children?" she asked stiffly. "Who besides you, Pa?"

"She knew it had to be done," he whined. "There wasn't nothing else we could do. And they went to good folks. Your ma was friends with the Johnson family. And she thought they'd be staying close by so she'd be able to see Velvet grow up."

His voice turned bitter. "Then they had to go and move away from here . . . clear out of Louisiana. Took the heart right out of your mama when they went, too. She never was the same, even though she had you left." He narrowed his eyes on her. "Guess I made a mistake letting 'em take Velvet instead of you."

"Velvet?" Amelia licked lips that had suddenly gone dry. "But that wasn't her real name, you said."

"No. That's just what your ma called her. Her twins were like satin and velvet, she said, the day the two of you were borned. And those names kinda stuck with the both of you. Her ma called her Velvet and she called you Satin . . . until the day the Johnsons took Velvet off where she couldn't never see her again."

"What was her name, Pa?" Amelia asked softly.

He brushed a trembling hand across his eyes. "Velvet. That's all I remember. It ain't right a feller should forget his own daughter's name."

And it's not right that same father should sell his daughter, either, she thought. But she kept her thoughts to herself, unwilling for some reason to speak the words aloud.

Her father had enough to think about during his last few days on earth. Dealing with her anger would only shorten his life, and she had too many questions left that needed answers to want to see him die now.

Anyway, despite everything he had done, he was her father, and when he was gone, she would have no one.

Her thoughts turned inward, to the man she'd left behind in Nacogdoches and to the dreams that had been hers for such a short time. Then, knowing that such thoughts only increased the longing she felt for Colt, she locked them away in a secret place deep in a corner of her mind.

There would be time enough later to take those dreams

out again, to relive every precious memory of their time together.

Yes. Later. There would be time enough then.

Colt fought against a peculiar dizziness as he glared up at his brother in horror. "How in hell could you let her leave, Blake?"

"Dammit, Colt," Blake snapped. "She told me you didn't have any objection to her going. How was I to know she was lying?"

"Amelia wouldn't lie," Colter snarled, jerking upright and dragging his legs off the side of the bed. The action set his head to spinning so wildly that he was barely aware of the pain that stabbed at his shoulder. But suddenly it struck him and he groaned aloud.

"Dammit!" Blake snarled, his gaze fixed on the bandage that had begun to turn bright red with fresh blood. "Now look what you've gone and done, Colt. You've got that blasted wound bleeding again. You've probably torn out some stitches."

Gripping his brother's shoulders, Blake shoved him back against the bed and held him there. "Now stop that," he ordered when Colt struggled to gain his release. "Look what you're doing to yourself. And for what, Colt? It's too late to stop Amelia. She's long gone. And your efforts are all for nothing."

"It's not for nothing," Colt snapped, squeezing his eyes shut as he fought to clear his mind of the fog that was slowly pulling him under. What in hell was wrong with him anyway? His mind was fuzzy as though . . .

He opened eyelids that seemed incredibly heavy. "Did you put something in my drink?"

"The doctor put a dose of laudanum in the glass," Blake replied bitterly. "For all the good it did. He's probably going to have to sew you up again now."

"Damn the doctor," muttered Colt in a slurred voice. "I have to go after Amelia."

"You're in no shape to go after anybody," Blake said gruffly. "Hell, you can't even make it out of this room. You'd fall flat on your face if you tried."

His brows were drawn together in a worried frown as he waited for that fact to sink into his brother's hard head. And when Colt finally ceased his struggles and sank back onto the pillow, Blake grunted, "Good. I see you've still got a little sense left. Now you stay put while I go after the doctor."

"I don't need . . . no damned doctor," Colt said, forcing the words out. He could feel his brain slowing down, and struggled to express his thoughts. "I have to . . . go after Amy . . . before she gets . . . in trouble." His eyes closed; he needed desperately to rest them, to succumb to that restful state that awaited him . . . to sleep.

Becoming aware that he was sinking deeper into a laudanum-induced state, Colter managed to jerk his eyes open again. "The law's after . . . Amy," he said. "Go—"

"No," Blake said gently. "The law doesn't want Amelia."

Although he wasn't sure if his brother would understand his words with the laudanum taking hold the way it was, Blake went on to explain the reasons Amelia had left town. He finished by saying, "She knows what she's doing, Colt. That's some smart woman. She'll be just fine."

"No," Colt mumbled. "She'll get in . . . trouble."

"You've got to stop worrying about her, Colt," Blake said gently. "Amelia will be just fine. Nothing's going to happen to her. But you . . . well, you're another thing. If you don't concentrate on getting better and stop pulling such stupid stunts—like getting out of bed and pulling out your stitches—you're going to wind up with an infection in that shoulder. Then you won't be able to help anybody, let alone yourself.''

Prophetic words, Blake realized several hours later when the wound began to show signs of infection. And sometime during the night Colt's temperature escalated, and Blake, along with the doctor, was kept busy applying cold rags to his brother's heated flesh.

Throughout the night Colt wavered in and out of consciousness. He tossed and turned, continually crying out for Amelia. He remained that way for two days; then the fever broke and he fell into a deep, untroubled sleep.

It was finally over.

The afternoon sun beamed down on her as Amelia stood beside the open grave, watching silently while the grave diggers shoveled dirt onto the pine coffin that held her father's remains. He had lived longer than they'd expected, and she'd stayed with him until the end, hoping that by doing so she'd learn more about her sisters.

And she had. Because her father had finally remembered the name they'd given to Amelia's twin: Sarah.

How on earth could a father forget his daughter's name? Amelia wondered, as she'd done so many times before. It wasn't as if he'd had so many of them that he'd lost count. Three. That was all there'd been, and yet he'd forgotten her name.

Her ma called her Velvet, he'd said. *And she called you Satin.*

When he'd told her that, Amelia remembered the sound of her mother's voice. So sad, so tearful. And the look in her eyes . . . a pain almost beyond bearing.

It was when her sister disappeared that her mother began calling her by her proper name. Amelia. And Amelia remembered how she'd felt at the loss of the pet name, as though she'd done something to displease her mother.

In retrospect, though, looking back, Amelia realized that the sense of loss she'd felt was probably because she'd lost a part of herself when she lost her twin.

But she would find her, Amelia thought grimly. She would find both her sisters.

Their neighbor, Silas Bascomb, had made a good offer on the farm, and Amelia had decided to accept it. And she would use the money to find her sisters. If it was the last thing she ever did on this earth, she would find them.

She turned away from the grave then ... turned her back on the man who, in life, had been her father, the man who'd turned his back on his children.

He was dead and buried now. Unrepentant to the last. But his Maker could deal with him now. He would exact punishment for her father's sins.

He was beyond the reach of the living now.

And perhaps that was best, too. Amelia wasn't sure what she'd have done had he lived. But her hatred for the man knew no bounds. And she would never forgive him for what he'd done.

Never! As long as there was breath in her body, she would hate him and everything he stood for.

Colt's nostrils twitched at the pungent smell of hay when he entered the stable to saddle up the stallion. It had been two long weeks since Amelia left town, and he was anxious to see her again.

He would already be with her if his wound had not become infected. The fever had raged within his body, and he'd wavered in and out of consciousness for several days, all the while—so he'd been told—calling out Amelia's name.

Even when he'd regained his senses, he was forced to wait, too weak to do anything except follow the doctor's orders. It had seemed forever before he regained his strength, since the fever had left him weak as a newborn babe.

But now, nothing could stop him from going to her.

As though he'd tempted fate with that thought, Colter heard boots thudding quickly against hard-packed earth outside the stable door.

He looked up as Blake rushed in and paused momentarily, his gaze searching the shadowy interior.

"What in hell's eating you, Blake?" Colter growled.

He was still angry at his brother for allowing Amelia to leave town, and it showed in the tone of his voice.

"I was hoping to catch you before you left town," Blake said. "I just came from the telegraph office, and you'll never believe what happened, Colt."

"No," Colt sighed. "I probably won't, so why don't you tell me?"

"I've been corresponding with several other U.S. marshals since you've been laid up . . . and it finally paid off."

Colter tightened the cinch on his saddle, waiting for Blake to continue. He didn't have long to wait.

"I found them, Colt. Dammit, I can hardly believe it, but it's true. I damned well found out where they are!"

A cold chill slid down Colter's back. "You found who, Blake?"

"Well, hell!" Blake exclaimed. "Who've you been looking for the past year?"

"The Kincaids?"

"Damn right," Blake replied. "They're down near Laredo. Hiding out on a ranch down there." He snatched his reins off the wall and fastened them on his horse. "Good thing you're all saddled up, brother," he said.

"Won't take me but a few minutes. Then we can be on our way."

Colt frowned heavily. Any other time he would have been as excited at the news as Blake obviously was. It had been a long time coming, but the Kincaids had finally been run to ground.

But what about Amelia?

"Hurry up, big brother," Blake growled, striding quickly toward his own mount, which occupied the last stall. "We've got a long way to ride before nightfall."

Yes. It was a long way. Laredo was clear on the other side of Texas . . . which would put Colter even farther away from Amelia.

Yet Colter knew he couldn't just ignore the Kincaids and go to Amelia instead. The Kincaid gang must be brought to justice; had to be made accountable for their deeds.

And it wasn't as if Amelia needed him. Hell! Blake had been in contact with the constable in New Orleans several times and he'd been told that Amelia was caring for her father.

If asked, Amelia would surely tell him to go on, to bring the men who'd murdered his family to justice.

He knew where to find her when he and Blake had dealt with that gang of vipers. She might be mad as an old wet hen at the delay, but she'd understand why he'd had to go there first.

If there was one thing he'd learned about Amelia during their time together, it was how understanding she could be. Yeah. She'd understand why he had to go.

Having come to that conclusion, Colter slid his six-gun from the holster and spun the cylinder. It was loaded, as it should be. He'd have to practice his draw during the journey, since his shoulder—left stiff by the wound—was likely to slow him down. But there would be plenty of time. It was a long ride. Would take most of a week to get there.

Swallowing his disappointment at the delay in fetching Amelia, Colter mounted his stallion and rode out of the stable. A moment later Blake joined him, and together they rode out of town, eager to find the men they had vowed to destroy.

Chapter Twenty-Five

Although Colter and Blake were anxious to reach Laredo—and the men they had been searching for so long—neither of them was willing to push their mounts too hard. Both brothers were aware that good horseflesh was not easy to come by, and they knew that a strong, healthy mount might very well make the difference between life and death. It was for that reason they decided to stop overnight in Madisonville.

It had rained hard the night before and the Trinity River was in full flood, so they boarded a ferry to reach the other side, then rode to the livery stable. After seeing to their mounts, the brothers headed for the hotel to get a good night's sleep.

Colter lay abed long into the night, listening to the rinky-tink sound of the piano coming from a nearby saloon, unable to sleep for thoughts of Amelia.

Amelia. The image of her rose in his mind, the way she'd looked after they had made love. Her tousled curls had been spread around her, making her skin look almost translucent. Her blue eyes had been dark with passion, a deep blue in color. And her lips, swollen from his kisses, were almost pouty, as though they were begging for more. She *had* begged for more. Pleaded with him, more times than he could remember.

Oh, God! How could she walk away from him so easily after all they'd shared together? And what if she was pregnant, carrying his babe?

Dammit! Did she think she could raise his child on her own? Was she planning on depriving the babe of a father? Or maybe she intended to find herself another man, to pass his son—or daughter—off as another man's child.

Well, he damned well wouldn't allow it! As soon as he'd dealt with the Kincaids, he'd head straight for New Orleans. And he would drag her away from the farm by her hair if he must. But he would have her!

Colter lay there in bed, his anger rising as he continued to think about Amelia and the way she'd left him. And even though he knew he was being absurd, he found the anger easier to deal with than the pain that had lodged in his heart the moment he realized she was gone.

He didn't sleep much that night. And when Blake woke him the next morning, Colter's mouth was grim, his eyes dark and cold. Blake took one look at his brother and decided to wait awhile before he told Colt what he'd learned the night before while visiting with the local sheriff.

Blake never did get around to that conversation. By the time he judged Colter approachable, he'd forgotten all about the sheriff in Madisonville. It wasn't until they reached their destination that he finally remembered.

That first night after her father's funeral, Amelia lay awake for long hours listening unconsciously for the sound of his voice. She had become so used to tending him that it seemed strange she was no longer needed.

She realized for the first time that tending her father had kept her so busy she had no time to dwell on her lost love. Colter Morgan. She ought to hate him for taking her innocence when he had no intention of making their relationship a permanent one. But, she realized, it hadn't been entirely his fault. She had wanted him just as much as he'd wanted her. And in the end, she'd begged him to make love to her. It was the cause of her shame. If she was with child—as she suspected—then it was her own fault that the babe would have no father.

Oh, God, how would she deal with that? An unwed mother. The babe would surely suffer for her sins. He, or she, would be branded a bastard, would hear the name flung at him or her through the years and would eventually come to hate her, as she'd come to hate her own father.

Hate. It was a cruel word. A horrible feeling. And if she didn't come to grips with her feelings, it could ruin her life, as well as that of her unborn babe.

Amelia knew then that she must forgive her father for his misdeeds. He was gone now, and it was too late for her to say the words to him, but perhaps, wherever he was in that eternal life beyond the living, he would know and it would grant him peace.

"I forgive you, Pa," she whispered. "I forgive you for everything."

As she uttered the words aloud, Amelia felt a sense of peace wash over her, and she closed her eyes and fell into a deep, restful sleep.

It was late afternoon when the Morgan brothers sat astride their mounts and looked down on the ranch below.

The barn was large, dwarfing the small house that stood nearby with smoke curling from the rock chimney.

"Looks like they're there," Colter said grimly. "And from the looks of the horses in that corral, they've got company."

"Dammit!" Blake growled, eying the horses—a dozen or more—in the corral. "I forgot about the cousins."

Colter turned to his brother. "Cousins?"

"Yeah," Blake replied. "The sheriff in Madisonville told me some Kincaids had come through there. He overheard one of 'em saying they were going to join their cousins in Laredo."

"Dammit, Blake," Colter snarled. "How could you forget a thing like that?"

Blake removed his Stetson hat and shoved his fingers through his dark hair. "Damned if I know," he growled. "I was going to tell you the next morning, but you looked so damned grim that I decided to wait. We've been traveling so hard since then that I just plumb forgot it."

Colter sighed heavily. "We can't take on all of them alone. We're going to need some help."

"Yeah," Blake agreed. "Guess I'd better send off a telegram to Matthew."

"I don't suppose the law would be interested in helping."

"No." Blake's voice was grim. "There's no warrants out for them in Texas, Colter. We're the only ones looking for them here. The law won't interfere. And," he added warningly, "if we don't work this right, we're likely to find ourselves accused of murder."

"Not if they start shooting first."

Blake grinned. "That's what I'm counting on."

The two brothers parted then. Blake rode off to send a telegram to Matthew, while Colter settled down to keep watch on the ranch where the Kincaid gang made their headquarters.

Blake hadn't been gone more than an hour when the door to the cabin opened and several men stepped outside. They talked together on the porch for a few minutes before most of them headed for the corral, leaving one man to watch from the porch.

Colter's muscles tensed as he watched the men saddle their horses. Where in hell were they going?

Knowing he couldn't stop them alone, Colter could only watch as they mounted their horses and rode away in a flurry of dust. And when they were gone, there was only one horse remaining in the corral.

One horse. One man.

Perhaps luck was finally on his side.

Using the bushes for cover, Colter made his way down the slope and cautiously approached the cabin, keeping away from the window that would expose him to anyone who might be watching.

Then, feeling certain of victory, he rounded the side of the cabin and bent low as he made his way to the front door.

His muscles were tense as he readied himself for attack. He gripped his six-gun tightly, his finger on the trigger, ready to use if necessary. He hoped it wouldn't be, though. He had questions that needed answering, and a dead man couldn't talk.

With a grim smile, he rose to his full height and kicked open the door, glaring at the man who jerked upright so quickly that his chair was flung halfway across the room.

"Who in hell are you?" the startled man asked.

"Colter Morgan!" Colt replied grimly. "And I've come to send you to hell!"

"What the hell—"

The startled exclamation from beyond the room jerked

Colter's head around. He'd been mistaken, he realized, as he sent off a shot toward his rear. One horse hadn't equaled one man. It was a mistake that could cost him his life.

A bullet tore through his sleeve and he felt a stinging sensation. Dammit, he'd been shot!

Colt fired his weapon and made a dive for the door, striking the porch with a heavy thud that almost knocked the breath out of him. But he couldn't wait to recover his senses. His reflexes took over and he rolled quickly, landing on the balls of his feet as he struck the ground and scrambled toward the nearest bush large enough to provide cover.

The acrid scent of burnt gunpowder hung in the air as he crouched there, cursing himself for leaving his rifle with his horse. Hot lead whined around him like angry wasps whose nest had been disturbed.

A bullet ricocheted off a fence post, sending fragments of wood toward him, and he crouched lower, hoping to present an even smaller target to the men who were holed up in the cabin.

Dammit! he silently cursed. He'd been a fool for busting down that door without making sure there was only one outlaw inside. Something moved near the window, and he sent off a shot, then ran in a zig-zag motion toward the barn, where he could find more cover.

A quick succession of gunfire told him the outlaws were determined to keep him from reaching the building. He turned and sent off a shot, then made a dive for the wide barn door, which was kept open during the day.

Then, with his breath coming in short spurts, he settled down to wait inside the barn.

Minutes passed and silence settled around him. Colter wondered if there were more than the three outlaws he'd already seen. He sure as hell wasn't going to take anything for granted anymore. He'd already made a mistake that could have cost him his life, so he'd take it for granted there were a dozen or more guns in there until he knew for certain he was wrong.

A sudden snapping sound spun Colter around, just as a booted foot struck his six-gun, sending the weapon spiraling toward the wall. Colt was on the point of reaching for it when he saw the pistol aimed straight at his middle. He knew there was no way the red-haired man who confronted him could be kept from blowing a hole in his chest if he wanted to.

"Hold it!" the man snarled. "You make one wrong move, mister, and you're dead."

Colt studied the man through narrowed eyes. It was obvious he was one of the Kincaid clan.

"Move easy like and kick that six-gun over here," the man said. "And keep your hands high while you're doing it. I get nervous real easy, mister. And when I'm nervous, my fingers tend to shake." He smiled, but there was no humor in his eyes. "I got some questions that need answering, and I don't want to have to kill you before you and me have a little talk."

Colter remained motionless, warily silent.

"Do it!" Kincaid snarled.

Realizing he could do nothing else, at least for the moment, Colter complied, reaching out a booted foot to kick his six-gun toward the other man.

"Did you come here alone?"

"Go to hell!" Colt said grimly.

"I prob'ly will," the red-haired man laughed. "But you're sure as hell gonna beat me there." His gun hand never once wavered, and Colt thought it likely the outlaw was right. "Now answer me. Are you alone?"

"Of course not," Colt replied, deciding he might be able to put the fear of God into the man and come out of this alive. "I'm not that stupid. I came with my brother. He went to town after the sheriff. I imagine they'll come back with a posse."

Colter looked through the doors toward the western sky, where the sun was setting in a blaze of glory. "Shouldn't be much longer before they get back, either. Blake's been gone for several hours."

The outlaw's eyes flickered toward the wide opening in the barn, as though he suspected a posse might already be sneaking through the bushes growing beyond the corral, just waiting to catch him unawares.

Although Colter watched warily, hoping to catch his opponent off guard, there was no time. Even while the outlaw scanned the underbrush outside, he appeared totally aware of the man he held at gunpoint. It would only take a tightening of his finger to blow a hole through Colter. And Colt had sense enough to know that.

Apparently deciding there was nobody else around, the outlaw turned his attention to Colter again. "What do you want here anyway?" he growled. "And why should I be afraid of the law?"

"You figure it out." Colt shifted slightly, his action moving him closer to the man who faced him. "I'm sure if you try real hard you'll come up with plenty of reasons why the law would be after you . . . why other men—like myself—would want to see you hanging from a tree."

"I don't know what you're talking about. And I don't believe anybody came here with you."

Colter shrugged. "Believe what you will. It won't matter in the end."

Kincaid shifted uneasily, then stepped closer to gain a better look outside. And when he did so, Colter was quick to take advantage. He kicked out and knocked the six-gun from his opponent's hand.

With a snarl of rage, the outlaw leaped toward him, striking Colter a hard blow on the jaw that sent him reeling.

Before Colt could recover his senses, Kincaid snatched a knife from the sheath around his waist and made a quick stab at his opponent.

Colter leaped aside, avoiding the deadly blow.

The outlaw grinned widely. "Now we're gonna have some fun." He waved the blade back and forth, bent on taunting Colt. "Maybe you'll be more inclined to talk if I slice off one ear."

Then with a laugh the man lunged at Colt and lashed out with the knife. Colt leaped aside again, and the blade swished through the air, only inches from his head.

The outlaw circled his prey again, darting forward and lashing out, slicing through the skin of Colt's forearm with such speed he was gone before the bright blood beaded forth.

A sharp, stinging pain was the only notice Colt had that he'd been wounded. The outlaw closed in again and Colt jerked aside, reaching out quickly and gripping the outlaw's wrist before he could escape.

Then Colter applied pressure, squeezing hard enough to make the man drop the knife. The outlaw resisted for several long moments as Colt continued to apply pressure, making him wonder if he'd have to break Kincaid's wrist to make him release the knife.

"Arghh!" the outlaw grunted and opened his fingers. The knife fell to the ground, and Colt closed in with a doubled fist and struck the outlaw a hard blow on the chin. The outlaw's head snapped back and he staggered.

Quickly taking advantage, Colt lowered his head and butted into the outlaw's belly.

Kincaid grunted and lost his footing. Colter struck again with his right fist, then followed it quickly with his left, snapping the outlaw's head from one side to the other.

Howling with pain, Kincaid went down, and Colt followed him, smashing the man's nose with his fist, striking his face over and over again as he remembered the three graves on the lonely hillside back on Morgan's Creek.

Chapter Twenty-Six

Colter dropped to the ground, his breath coming in harsh gasps as he stared at the unconscious man. He didn't know how long he'd been pounding on him, but he did wonder if the outlaw was even alive.

When he got his breath back, he decided, he would look for a pulse. But now he was just too damned tired to do anything but sit there.

He remained motionless for several minutes, and the other man did not move a muscle during the whole time.

Colt's shoulders sagged as every last ounce of energy he possessed drained away. With a heavy sigh, he leaned back against the barn wall and closed his eyes, planning to rest for just a moment.

But a rustling sound jerked him upright, and he narrowed his eyes on the outlaw, who appeared completely unconscious. If it wasn't the outlaw who'd made the noise, then who was it?

Colt sat there, his muscles tensed, straining his ears for

another sound. And then it came. A quick rustle of movement nearby, followed by a mewling sound.

"What the hell!"

A tiny tabby kitten, not more than a month old, strolled into view.

Colter laughed unsteadily. His muscles unknotted and the tension left his body. With a sigh, Colt leaned his head against the wall again.

The kitten dug its claws into Colter's britches and climbed up his leg. Then, curling up on his lap, it started licking the blood off Colter's knuckles.

"There's plenty more where that came from, kitty," Colt muttered. "If you like that kind of thing."

When Colter got his second wind, he found his pistol and jammed it into the holster at his hips. Then, realizing the outlaw had been unconscious for some time, Colt knelt beside him and felt for a pulse. It beat strongly.

Using the outlaw's belt, he bound the man's wrists together, then settled down to wait. The other outlaws would probably come looking for their brother. And when they did, he would be ready for them. But perhaps he would get lucky and Blake would return before that time.

As time passed, Colter began to see the mistake he'd made by beating the outlaw senseless. Not that he had any sympathy for the fellow, but he might have learned something about the other men in the cabin.

Cursing himself for a fool, he resumed his watch on the cabin. It wasn't long before he saw a flicker of movement at the cabin window.

And then a voice rang out. "Shorty! You okay out there?"

The shout was followed by a long silence.

"Shorty! Give me a holler if you can."

Colter looked at his captive and grinned wryly. "Shorty ain't able to holler," he muttered. "In fact, Shorty can't even hear you."

Although Colt continued to watch from his vantage point, there was no further movement around the cabin. Were there only two men left? he wondered. If so, he might be able to take them out alone.

But suppose it was a trap. If there were several, instead of two, then Blake might come back to find his brother dead and the outlaws gone again.

A movement nearby caught his attention, and he turned to see his captive stirring. He waited silently until the man groaned, then opened eyes that were swollen almost shut. Then Colt knelt beside the outlaw and gripped the neck of his shirt, jerking the man's head and shoulders off the ground.

The man groaned again, blinked at Colter, then began to swear. "You damned near killed me," he growled, spitting out a tooth that had been knocked loose. Along with the tooth came a goodly amount of blood.

"You're lucky I didn't kill you," Colt said. "But you're not home free yet, Kincaid. If you don't cough up some answers, you just might find yourself on a fast trip to hell."

"What do you want with me anyway?" the man asked.

"I already told you," Colter growled. "I want some answers."

"I ain't heard no questions yet," Kincaid muttered.

"How many men you got in that cabin?"

Something flickered in the dark eyes. "Enough to keep you pinned down here until the rest of my brothers come back home."

Hell! "I want numbers, Kincaid. And I'll have them if I have to beat them out of you."

"Why should I tell you anything?"

"Because if you don't, I'll have no good reason for keeping you alive."

Kincaid thought about that for a while, then asked a question of his own. "Are you kin to the Carters?"

"I don't know any Carters," Colt said coldly. "My name is Morgan. Colter Morgan."

There was no recognition in the outlaw's eyes. "Is that supposed to mean something to me?"

"I thought it might," Colt replied. "But I guess you don't make a habit of learning the names of all your victims."

"Victims?" the man squawked, his eyes widening in their swollen sockets. "What victims?"

"My father and mother," Colt replied. "And my little sister, Annie, who was just ten years old. Remember her, Kincaid?" Colter's grip tightened around the man's neck. "Do you remember what you and your brothers did to my little sister, Annie?"

"I didn't do nothing to no little girl, mister."

"Don't lie to me," Colt snarled, slamming the man back against the ground before pulling him up again. "You know. And you damn well remember."

"No, I don't," the outlaw muttered. "Dammit, Morgan! I'd remember something like that. I never did nothing to no kid. I swear it."

Colt was determined to make the man admit what he'd done. "In the hill country, damn you. A big white house with a pillared porch running all the way around. There was a clear running stream nearby. Morgan's Creek. In Burnet County. When you and your brothers rode in that day, there was nobody around except for my pa and ma and little Annie. You killed my pa and raped my ma and then you killed her. And you did the same to my sister, Annie!"

The outlaw's eyes were wide with horror. "Dammit, Morgan," he howled. "I never did nothing like that. I'd know if I did that to a kid. I'd remember a thing like that, wouldn't I?"

"*I* would. But you're vermin, Kincaid. You're lower than

a snake's belly in a wagon's rut. Maybe vermin like you don't remember the horrors they've left behind."

"You gotta believe me, Morgan," the man babbled. "I never took part in that raid." His eyes narrowed. "When did it happen anyways. When did that raid take place?"

"A year before the war ended," Colter replied.

"There you have it, then, man!" the outlaw said eagerly. "I wasn't anywheres near Texas then. Didn't come to these parts until the war ended."

"I don't believe you," Colter said, his grip tightening around the man's throat.

"I can prove it," the man said eagerly. "My two brothers are here—in the cabin. They know. They were with me all through the war. None of us came here until about six months ago."

Colter relaxed his grip on the outlaw. "All right," he said. "Call your brothers out here. I want to talk to them."

"What guarantee do I have that you won't shoot them when they come out?"

"No guarantee at all," Colt said grimly.

"Then why in hell should I call them out?"

"To save your own skin," Colter replied. "To delay your own trip to hell."

The outlaw thought about that for a long moment, then said, "Clarence and Jimmy are the only brothers I got. It wouldn't be right if I got them shot just to save my own skin."

Colter arched a dark brow. "A Kincaid with a conscience? That's hard for me to believe, considering what the lot of you have been doing for the past few years."

"I told you I didn't have nothing to do with that!" the man snarled. "Who told you it was Kincaids that done it anyways?"

"Somebody whose word can be trusted," Colter replied. "A longtime family friend who recognized one of your brothers when they were riding out . . . after they'd destroyed my family." His hand squeezed the man's throat again, and it was all he could do to keep from squeezing the life out of the outlaw.

"Wait," the man gasped. "It must have been Blair's bunch who did all that."

"Who's Blair?"

"He's my cousin, Blair Kincaid."

A grin curled the edges of Colt's lips, but there was no humor in it. "And where is he, your cousin Blair?"

"He rode into town for supplies," Kincaid said. "He oughta be back anytime now." A cunning look crossed his face. "But if I was you, I wouldn't wait around. He'll have Luke and Jordan and the rest of his bunch with him, and there's no way in hell you'll take 'em all down."

Colter knew the outlaw wanted him to give up and go away, and although he knew it might be prudent to do so, he decided he had come too far to back out now. No, he'd wait where he was, and perhaps Blake would come back before the outlaws did.

Meanwhile, he would get some more answers to his questions, to determine if the man he was holding captive was telling the truth about his involvement.

"Exactly where were you in June of 1864?"

"I was fighting the damned Yankees, that's what I was doing!" the man snarled. "Just like you probably was!"

"Shorty," hollered a man from the cabin. "You out there, Shorty?"

Distracted by the other man's voice, Colt peered around the doorway, and his captive leaped to his feet and darted away. "Here!" he yelled. "I'm here, Clarence!"

Colt made a dive for Kincaid and quickly brought him down again.

"Shorty!" the man in the cabin shouted. "You okay, Shorty?"

"Hell, no, I ain't okay," Shorty muttered, spitting dirt out of his mouth. He glared at Colt. "I suppose you're gonna kill me now."

"I'm thinking hard about it."

"Well, go ahead and do it then," Kincaid snarled. "I sure as hell ain't in any position to stop you."

"No, you're not." Colt rubbed his chin, rough with two days' growth of beard, and studied the man, trying to gauge if he was telling the truth. "And I might do that very thing before it's all over. Unless I decide you're telling me the truth."

"I am," the man said eagerly. "Just ask Clarence and Jimmy. They'll tell you the same thing I did."

Colt laughed. "The moment I show my face to your brother, he'll shoot me dead."

"Not if you use me for a shield. We ain't like Blair's bunch, me and Clarence and Jimmy. Ma didn't want us to come out here. She said they'd lead us into trouble. And now it looks like they done exactly that."

"How long has Blair been gone?"

"A few hours," was the reply. "He left just before you got here."

Since Colter had been watching, he knew Shorty was telling the truth. "You said you weren't part of their bunch, that you didn't take part in their raids—"

"I didn't," Shorty said eagerly. "I swear it! And neither did Clarence or Jimmy."

"Maybe we better just find out before Blair Kincaid and his bunch get back here."

"You're gonna talk to Clarence, then?"

"Yeah. I'm gonna talk to him. And, like you suggested, I'll use you for a shield. But if you're lying to me . . ." He left it up in the air what he'd do in that event.

"I ain't lying," Kincaid said quickly. "You'll see. Just ask my brothers, and they'll tell you the same thing I did. We wasn't there with them when they did those things to your family."

"And yet you started shooting when I opened that door. Why?"

"Well, hell, man!" Shorty exclaimed. "You kicked that door open like a man bent on revenge. And you said you'd come to send us to hell. We figgered you meant what you said, and none of us was eager to go there."

Colter grinned. "I guess you wouldn't be."

Colter could see how he might have reacted in the same way, but he wasn't ready to turn them loose. First, he would see what the Kincaid cousins had to say for themselves.

Chapter
Twenty-Seven

Although Blake was in the sheriff's office when the riders rode into town, he paid no attention since he was busy trying to convince the lawman to organize a posse. He had no idea anything was amiss until several minutes later when a bow-legged man with scraggly gray hair and beard hurried into the office and stopped beside the sheriff's desk, swaying unsteadily as he tried hard to catch his breath.

"What in hell's wrong with you, Salty?" the sheriff growled.

"Sheriff . . ." the old man gasped. "Come quick!"

"Come where?" The sheriff rose to his feet and glared at the other man. "Is this another one of your jokes?" he growled.

"No! No," the old man said. "The bank . . . the bank's being robbed!"

The sheriff frowned and crossed to a window. When he saw the horses waiting in front of the bank, he turned to Blake. "Better get your six-gun ready, son," he said grimly.

"The old-timer's right. There's too many horses in front of the bank to suit me." He looked at the old man again. "Find Harley. Tell him to get the men in place."

The old-timer grinned widely. "Already done that, Sheriff. I saw Harley on the way over. When I told him, he lit off like a scalded cat. I reckon you don't have nothing to worry about."

"Let's hope you're right," the sheriff said gruffly.

He turned to Blake. "We knew we'd probably be hit sometime or other, so we made plans. If everything goes as it should, those outlaws won't get out of town."

His words proved true. Blake took up a position behind the water trough while the sheriff waited at the door. On top of each building a man watched, rifle at the ready.

A man ran out of the bank, saw the sheriff waiting and the empty streets, and shouted, "It's the law!"

"Throw down your weapons!" the sheriff shouted.

But the outlaws weren't interested in complying. They commenced firing as they fought to mount their horses. Only one man made it, for all the good it did him. Blake had him in his sights. A quick squeeze of the trigger and the outlaw slumped over his mount's neck. Only moments later he slid to the ground.

When all the dead were accounted for, there were more than a dozen of them. And only one man left alive. It was Blair Kincaid, the man the Morgan brothers had been searching for so long.

Amelia stayed at the farm for several days after her father's funeral. She tried to keep busy, to keep her thoughts off Colter Morgan, but no matter how hard she tried, his image continued to haunt her. Amelia remembered so well the gentleness of his hands in her hair as he stroked her the way he would a kitten. She could still feel the burning hardness of his mouth and the way his unshaven jaw had felt against her skin.

But it was useless to keep remembering, Amelia told herself. She had to put him from her mind, needed to think about her future instead.

With that in mind, Amelia cleaned the house from top to bottom, then decided to go through the trunk that had contained her mother's things.

Although she'd been through the trunk before, she'd always been in a hurry lest her father catch her at it and become enraged. He'd always been adamant that she keep out of the trunk, but he was gone now and she could browse through it at will.

It was hard, though. The faded dresses neatly folded inside brought back memories of her mother that she found painful. Memories of a quiet, sad-eyed woman who drifted through the farmhouse like a visiting ghost.

Had her mother ever been happy? Her father claimed she had, but to live each day with a man who'd taken away her children must have been horrible.

Oh, God! How had her mother been able to stay with him?

But even as that thought occurred, Amelia realized her mother had not in fact stayed with him. She had left in the only way she knew how, slowly drifting away from him, first in her mind, then taking her body with her when she finally gave up trying to live in a world that appeared so uncaring.

And she had left a helpless child to cope with an unforgiving father!

Amelia tried not to think of her mother's abandonment—for that was exactly what it was—but it was hard to put it out of her mind. Because her mother had been weak, Amelia had been raised by a father who despised her.

With a sigh of regret for what might have been, Amelia took each faded gown out of the trunk and laid it carefully aside. There wasn't much in the trunk. Just a few faded bits of clothing. And when they had all been removed, only a worn Bible remained.

Judging it to have been her mother's, Amelia opened it to the first page. The date and place of her mother and father's wedding were recorded there. And below that, Lorrie Spencer had registered the birth of each of her daughters.

Amelia traced the first name written there with her right forefinger. "Rachel Loraine Spencer. Born July 1, 1847."

Counting backwards, Amelia realized her sister would be twenty-one years old now. If she was still alive.

Entered on the next line was Amelia's own name. "Amelia Anne Spencer. Born May 2, 1850." And below that was written, "Sarah Jane Spencer. Born May 2, 1850."

Amelia's twin.

It was still hard to believe she had a twin sister somewhere. Although her father had told her so, her sister hadn't seemed real somehow.

Not until this moment.

Amelia ran her finger over the name again. "Sarah Jane Spencer," she whispered, her eyes moistening with tears. "Velvet." She blinked away the tears that were threatening to fall. "Where are you, Sarah Jane? Where did they take you?"

Closing her eyes, she tried to send her mind across the years, tried to feel her sister's presence beside her. But it was a useless effort. She remembered a girl . . . vaguely. But she could put no name to her, nor could she put a face on the shadowy figure. Her sister was a complete stranger. She could pass her on the street one day without even knowing they were related.

She closed the Bible and was about to set it aside when

she noticed a piece of paper sticking out from the middle. Opening the Bible to that page, she discovered three squares of paper, each folded to form a smaller square.

The paper was old, brown at the edges as though it had been there for many years, hidden in the old family Bible that had belonged to her mother.

Why had she kept it there? Amelia wondered, opening one sheet carefully, realizing how delicate the paper was. She was intent on keeping intact whatever her mother had treasured so greatly.

Amelia's eyes widened as she opened the paper and saw the bright lock of hair that her mother had cherished.

The curl was baby fine, a pale golden color, and it had obviously meant something special to her mother. Amelia looked at the paper in her hand and saw a name written there. "Amelia Anne."

Her fingers trembled as she opened another sheet. Again there was a lock of hair, and it was identical to the first one. She looked at the paper. "Sarah Jane."

Amelia could hardly breathe as she realized she was holding a lock of her sister's hair. *Oh, Sarah Jane,* she silently cried, wiping away the tears that would no longer be contained. *Where are you, sister? Where did they take you?*

But there was no answer to be had. And she realized that it was more than likely that she would never find her sisters, no matter how long and hard she looked for them.

She sighed and reached for the third folded paper, certain she already knew the contents. Moments later she was looking down at the bright red hair that belonged to her sister Rachel.

Her father's words came back to her. *If those people hadn't got a look at that little red-haired girl and wanted her so bad . . .*

So her older sister had red hair. Amelia stroked the silken lock. She'd only been three years older than the twins. And she must have been given away—*sold!* Amelia corrected herself—during the first three years of her life, because her father said he'd hoped the birth of his wife's new daughters would take away the pain of losing her first child.

God, what a monster he'd been.

During the time she'd spent with him as he lay on his deathbed there'd been times when she felt almost sorry for him. But she'd been wrong to do so, she realized. A man who could do that to his wife, to his own children, deserved no sympathy.

With another deep sigh, Amelia replaced the locks of hair in her mother's Bible and carefully closed the book. The Bible would keep them safe. And Amelia needed to know that, because those tiny locks of hair were all she had to remind her of her sisters. She might never know them. But at least she'd found the Bible that held her mother's memories.

And she *would* look for her sisters. Someone around these parts was bound to remember the Johnsons, since there were several farms located nearby. Surely one of the old-timers would remember the family and know where they had gone. One of her neighbors might even be corresponding with them now.

Amelia took heart at that thought. All was not lost yet. The Cobbs might have been strangers just traveling through on their way west, but not the Johnson family. Someone had to know their whereabouts. And if they did, then Amelia might eventually find herself reunited with her twin sister.

But first, there was something she must do.

Darkness had descended and Colter was fighting exhaustion when he reached the Spencer farm. He had ridden hard in the last few days, intent on reaching Amelia as quickly as possible and had rested only when his body refused to go on.

But now the journey was over. He was finally at Amelia's home, and soon he would be holding her in his arms.

His eyes glinted at the thought of holding her again. It was his intention to scold her first, to berate her for leaving him the way she had done. And then he would make love to her.

Colter's body became hard with tension when he remembered how it felt to hold her in his arms. God, he wanted to hold her that way again, to bury himself within her soft flesh as he'd done in the Big Thicket.

As he reined up beside the porch, two spotted dogs leaped out of the shadows and bared their teeth at him. They appeared to take their job as guards seriously, growling fiercely as he waited for Amelia to appear.

He would have dismounted immediately but he didn't want to frighten her; he knew he needed to identify himself before approaching the house.

Suddenly the door opened and a stranger stood before him, a rifle held in the crook of his arms. "What do you want?" the man asked gruffly.

Colt frowned at him. What was a man doing in the Spencer home? Amelia had no kin. And she sure as hell wasn't supposed to have a husband. "I'm looking for Amelia Spencer," he said.

"She ain't here," the other man said.

"Is this the Spencer farm?"

"Was," the man said succinctly. "Not now, though. It belongs to me."

Colter frowned at the other man. "You bought it from Amelia?"

"Just said so, didn't I?"

Colt didn't like the man's surly attitude. "No," he

snapped. "You just said it belonged to you. As far as I know, you might've stolen it from her."

The man eyed him grudgingly. Then he said, "Guess you might as well get down for a while. You look like you've been doing some hard riding."

"I have," Colt agreed, knowing he needed to rest, yet feeling a desperate need to find Amelia before he did.

"Then come on in. I'll heat up some beans and make a pot of coffee."

Wearily Colt dismounted and entered the house. "Coffee would perk me up," he admitted. "But I need to be moving along real soon. I'd be mighty grateful, though, if you could tell me where Amelia might be found."

"Don't know where she went," the stranger replied. "All I know is she's off someplace looking for her sisters."

"Her sisters?" Colter's brows drew into a quick frown. "I didn't know Amelia had any sisters."

The man gave him a narrow-eyed look. "It appears you might not know her very well, mister. Why are you looking for her?"

"I intend to marry her," Colt replied. "And I thought I knew her real well. But she never mentioned a sister."

"Maybe because they were sold off before she was old enough to know."

Colt's shoulders sagged. "My God," he muttered. "Her father actually had more daughters and sold them off like he did Amelia?"

The man's eyes narrowed. "He sold Amelia too?" He poured coffee for Colter and set it on the table. "Guess I oughta introduce myself," he said grudgingly. "The name is Silas Bascomb."

"I'm Colter Morgan." Colt curled his hand around the hot cup and took a long, reviving swallow. "Do you have any idea which direction Amelia was going when she left here?"

"Said she was going to Nacogdoches first," Silas replied. "Claimed to have some unfinished business there."

"Yeah, she did," Colt said grimly, raking a hand through his dark hair. "Me."

"You coming from there?"

"In a roundabout way. I left there and went to Laredo on some business of my own. And when it was done, I rode here to find her."

"Well," Bascomb said, "you got here just a few days too late. But maybe you can still catch her in Nacogdoches."

"I hope to hell I can," Colt said.

He drank his coffee and ate the beans offered him and then, after allowing his horse water and oats, mounted up and headed toward Nacogdoches again.

When Amelia reached Nacogdoches, she was dismayed to find Colter already gone. And according to the hotel clerk, it had been more than a week since he'd left town.

She took the news calmly enough, then asked, "Did he say where he was going?"

"No." The clerk pushed up his wire-rimmed glasses.

"But the other one—his brother—said they were headed for Laredo."

So he wasn't coming after her, Amelia realized. He had dismissed her so lightly, he probably wouldn't even remember her in a few months. But what had she expected anyway? She'd been the one to leave.

But she couldn't dismiss him as easily as he appeared to have dismissed her. Even if she didn't love him so desperately, she would still have to find him. To do otherwise would be a betrayal. To herself . . . to Colter . . . and to the babe she was carrying nestled beneath her heart.

Amelia was certain of it now. She was carrying Colter's child, and he had a right to know. And she would damned well find him, wherever he was, and acquaint him with that fact.

But it was a long way to Laredo. She would get a good night's sleep before beginning her journey. It never once entered her mind that he might be hard to find after she reached that town.

She just knew that she must go.

It was daybreak when Colter reached Nacogdoches. His eyes were gritty as though filled with sand, and his brain felt senseless, as though it had no more substance than a bowl of mush. As for his body, well, it had become an aching mass. He wanted to find a bed and give himself over to oblivion, yet he dared not. He had to find Amelia before he did anything else.

Pray God that she had not already left.

Amelia was coming down the stairs pulling on a pair of gloves when she literally bumped into another guest. She looked up indignantly, ready to express her disapproval, and her mouth dropped open as she realized the man who faced her was Colt.

But she'd never seen him look the way he did now. His eyes appeared to have sunk into their sockets, and the skin was stretched tightly across his cheekbones, as though he hadn't had a decent meal in weeks.

And he was staring at her like a man gone mad. She couldn't prevent her abrupt words. "You look like hell warmed over, Colt."

"I damned well feel that way, too," he snarled, curling iron-hard fingers around her wrist. "Where in bloody hell have you been, Amelia?"

"Why . . . I was upstairs in my—"

"Never mind!" he growled, pulling her up the stairs behind him.

"Stop, Colt!" she cried. "What are you doing?"

Amelia was aware of the disapproving looks cast their way by everyone they passed. "Colt," she hissed. "Stop dragging me!" She tugged hard at his wrist, trying to release herself from his strong grip.

But it was an impossibility, she quickly realized. It was obvious that Colter had no intention of releasing her anytime soon.

She was completely breathless when he finally stopped in front of a door marked number 7. He inserted a key and moments later pushed her inside. Kicking the door shut with a booted toe, Colt locked the door again and shoved the key into his pocket.

With his fingers still locked tightly around her wrist, Colter dragged her across the room and flung her on the bed amidst a swirl of petticoats.

"Don't!" he snarled when she tried to crawl away from him. "Don't even think about it, Amelia," he warned.

"What are you going to do?" she asked, watching him sink down on the bed. Her heart was beating double-time and a half-smile curled her lips.

"Sleep," he muttered, closing his eyes.

"Sleep?" she squeaked. "You're just going to sleep?"

"Damned right I am," he replied. "And don't you move a muscle while I'm doing it, either."

He curled his arm around her waist and snugged her tight against his side. Then, expelling a weary sigh, Colter closed his eyes and immediately began to snore.

Amelia's emotions were mixed as she stared at him. On the one hand, she was happy to be with him again, but on the other, she was frustrated at his attitude. She hadn't seen him in more than a month, and he had nothing to say about himself except that he wanted to sleep.

But even though he hadn't said so, it was obvious that he wanted her beside him . . . at least for a while. And she was encouraged by that fact.

With her free hand she traced the line of his mouth, taking pleasure in the feel of him against her skin. She nestled closer beside him. She had missed him so much and had thought she'd never see him again.

But here he was, sleeping beside her as though they'd never been parted. Somehow that made what she had to tell him a little easier to say.

She wondered how he would react.

Would he be glad? Or would he feel tied down, forced to marry her because it was the right thing to do?

Although Amelia wanted desperately for him to care enough to want both her and their unborn babe, she realized that might not happen. But he would do the right thing by her, she knew. Colt was an honorable man. And he would make her his wife.

But if he didn't love her, he might one day regret doing so. Even so, she could do nothing else, for there was the baby to consider.

And if she took pleasure in doing what was right for their child, then who could gainsay her?

Nestling closer to the man who meant so much to her, Amelia uttered a blissful sigh, closed her eyes, and went to sleep.

Chapter Twenty-Eight

Amelia didn't know how long she had been sleeping when a knock at the door woke her, but she thought it must have been several hours.

Tilting her head, Amelia looked up at the man she loved. He appeared to be resting peacefully, undisturbed by the sound. Or anything else.

Knock, knock.

Glaring at the door as though it were responsible for whoever was intent on disturbing them, Amelia tried to free herself from Colter's embrace so she could answer the summons. His arms tightened around her.

Knock, knock.

"Colt," she whispered. "Someone's at the door."

He slept on.

Knock, knock.

Whoever was on the other side wasn't giving up easily. Amelia tried to pry Colt's fingers loose from her waist, but they were locked so tight that she might have been caught in a vise instead of a man's arms.

Knock, knock, knock.

The sound was followed by a deep male voice. "Colter, come on. I know you're in there. Open the door."

Recognizing Blake's voice, Amelia tried again to loosen Colt's hold on her, but as before, his arms tightened around her. Darn it! If he didn't loosen his grip, he would squeeze the breath out of her. "Colt, wake up. You're holding me too tight. I can hardly breathe."

As though her voice had penetrated his subconscious mind, Colt's grip on her relaxed, but ever so slightly.

"Dammit, Colt!" Blake exclaimed from beyond the door. "If you don't open this door, I'll damn well kick it down!"

Amelia stared in horror at the door. Surely Blake was joking. He wouldn't really kick the door down. Would he? The thought of the door caving in and allowing the other guests to see her trapped in Colter's arms was enough to make her struggle harder to escape from his embrace.

"Colt!" she said loudly. "Let go of me!" She pushed at his massive chest, trying desperately to free herself, but it was useless. She was well and truly trapped.

Realizing she could do nothing and fearing that Blake was on the point of kicking through the door at any moment, Amelia did the only thing she could under the circumstances.

"Blake!" she shouted. "Don't you dare kick through that door."

There was a long silence; then Blake spoke again. "Amelia? Is that you in there? The desk clerk told me this was Colter's room."

Dammit, was it necessary for them to have this conversation through a door, where everyone in the hotel could hear them?

"Amelia?" Blake was obviously puzzled. "Did you hear what I said?"

"I heard you!" Amelia was certain that everybody in the hotel must have heard him. "Go away, Blake."

There was a long pause; then Blake said, "Amelia? I hate to bother you, but I need to speak to Colter. Is he . . . in there?"

The arms that had been holding Amelia suddenly released her, and Colter sat upright and glared at the door. "Dammit, Blake!" he snarled. "I'm trying to sleep in here. What in hell do you want?"

"I need to talk to you, Colt," Blake said, apparently undeterred by his brother's mood.

Muttering curses, Colter rose, dug into his pocket for the key, then inserted it into the keyhole. A moment later he faced his brother.

"Well," Colter snarled. "Talk."

"In the hallway?" Blake inquired mildly, glancing over his brother's shoulder to meet Amelia's eyes.

Her face flamed. What must he be thinking of her?

Colter stood back and allowed his brother to enter the room. "Well," he said again. "What in hell was so important that you had to have a shouting match with Amelia?"

Realizing she was still sprawled on the bed where Colter had left her, Amelia scrambled off and smoothed her skirts around her legs. Then she seated herself by the window and tried to tune out the conversation between the brothers.

It was hard to do, though. Especially when she heard the Kincaid name. Then she began to listen shamelessly.

"What in hell do you mean?" Colt said angrily.

"Just what I said," Blake replied. "He got away. The sheriff in Laredo said somebody killed the jailer and unlocked his cell. Somehow they got out of town before anybody noticed."

"Dammit!" Colt swore grimly. "I thought it was over."

"It won't be over until he's dead."

Colter sighed heavily. "I suppose you're right." He looked at Amelia. "I guess I was just hoping . . ." His voice trailed away, and he swept his fingers through his hair. "I'll need somebody to take her home."

"To New Orleans?"

"No. To Morgan's Creek. She belongs with me, Blake."

Amelia's heart lightened at his words. Then she gave a quick jerk as she realized he meant to send her there alone while he went off on some quest again.

"I won't go to Morgan's Creek alone, Colt," she said quickly.

Colter met her gaze. "You won't be going there alone, Amelia. Blake will take you there."

"No," she said firmly. "I won't go there without you."

Colt's mouth tightened. "You'll do whatever I decide, Amelia. And I've decided to send you home with Blake."

"I won't stay there."

"Dammit, Amelia." He crossed the distance between them and wrapped his arms around her, pulling her hard against his side. "Don't oppose me in this. I know what's best for you."

"I won't stay," she said again. "If you leave me, Colter Morgan, I won't be waiting for you when you decide to come back."

"We'll talk about this later."

"I won't be changing my mind," she said grimly. "Our baby needs a father who's there for him and . . ." She broke off, aware that she'd revealed more than she'd intended.

Both men were staring at her as though she'd suddenly developed two heads. Blake was the first to recover.

"A baby?" he said, a grin twitching his lips. "I'm going to be an uncle?"

Colter appeared to have lost his voice. He continued to stare down at her in apparent confusion. And then his expression changed, his lips flattened, and his eyes bored through her.

"A baby, Amelia? You're expecting my baby?"

"Are you denying responsibility?" she asked tartly, her face aglow.

"Dammit to hell!" he swore. "Of course I'm responsible! Why in hell didn't you tell me?"

"You didn't give me a chance!" she shouted, struggling to free herself from his arms. But her struggles were useless. His arms were like steel bands holding her captive, and the more she struggled, the tighter they became.

"I guess you two need some privacy," Blake said gruffly. "I'll be in the lobby when you're done." He left the room and closed the door behind him.

"He'll have a long wait," Colter muttered, tilting her chin to look into her eyes. "Where were you going when I stumbled into you, Amelia?"

"I was looking for you," she admitted. "I was hoping you'd be here, but you'd already gone."

"Silas Bascomb said you'd gone to find your sisters."

She smiled at him. "I was going to find you first," she replied. "I wanted you to know about the baby before I started looking for them."

"A baby," he said wonderingly. "I can hardly believe it, Amelia." He kissed her cheeks, her eyelids, then her forehead.

Amelia stood on tiptoe and pressed her mouth against his in a kiss so sweet it nearly buckled his knees. He responded to her touch like a match to tinder.

His eyes burned with raw hunger as he pressed her body to his in an agony of need, of wanting.

A flame began to burn deep inside Amelia, and she whispered his name with unbearable yearning, her arms clutching his waist tightly, convulsively.

"I love you," she whispered.

"Do you really?" he asked huskily.

"I wouldn't say so if it weren't true."

He nibbled at her lips, and when she opened her mouth he was quick to take advantage. His hands closed over her jaw to hold her in place, and his tongue sank deeply into the moist cavern of her mouth.

Amelia whimpered softly as he stroked the damp moistness he found within. Her lips were soft and pliant as he probed, plundered, plunging in and out in an age-old rhythm that made her ache with longing.

Shivering with the pleasure he was creating, Amelia caressed his jaws, his back, his buttocks, until he was groaning with the need to possess her.

And then his hands were at her throat, working at the buttons of her gown. His lips never left hers as he divested her of her clothing, then took care of his own. When they were both naked on the bed, his body covering hers, she remembered Blake, who was waiting for Colter to join him in the lobby.

"Blake," she said, her voice trembling with need. "Colt, he's—"

"To hell with Blake!" he gritted.

And then his mouth was on hers again, his knee prying her legs apart. His possession was swift. And although Colter had intended their next encounter to be slow and easy, he could not wait. He felt such overwhelming passion that he knew he was out of control. He slammed into her over and over again while passion raged through them like wildfire.

Amelia's nails dug into his shoulders as she urged him on, and when she felt that incredible pressure building inside her, she clung tightly to him, following him to that blissful place that only lovers know.

When Colter cried out his release, Amelia gave herself over to the sweet surrender of fulfillment. She knew, in that moment of time, that she had reached out and touched the stars.

Chapter Twenty-Nine

Blake leaned against the counter, watching the stairway as he waited for his brother to join him in the lobby.

"Reckon he went back to sleep?" the desk clerk inquired.

"I don't think so." Blake knew damned well his brother had more on his mind than sleep. "He'll be along in a while."

"You might as well wait on the settee," the clerk said. "Be more comfortable there."

Blake looked at the cherrywood sofa with rose velvet cushions. He'd had occasion to try it and knew it wasn't comfortable. The clerk shrugged his shoulders and went back to the ledger he'd been perusing.

A woman came in and looked at Blake curiously, but he ignored her, his gaze never leaving the stairwell.

"Colt?" Amelia muttered.

"Hum?" He snuggled her closer to him.

"Are you going to sleep?"

"Um-hum."

"You can't do that," she said softly.

"Why not?"

"Blake is waiting for you."

"Aw, hell!" he said, rolling away from her. "I guess I'd better go downstairs before he comes busting in here."

"That might be a good idea," she said. "We're hardly dressed for company."

He snatched up his breeches and tugged them on.

She leaned up on her elbows, and her breasts jutted out, her nipples taut from his lovemaking. "Colt?"

"Yeah?" He leaned over and kissed a pert nipple, then sighed and reached for his shirt.

"I love you."

"I know." He grinned. "You told me."

A hurt look crossed her face. "Don't you have anything to say?"

"What?" He looked puzzled.

She shouldn't have to say the words. "How do you feel about me?"

"Good," he said, a stupid grin on his face.

She sat up and snatched up her day dress, covering herself with it. Colt knew something was wrong then. Why else would she hide herself from him?

He stopped buttoning his shirt and sat down on the bed. "What's wrong, Amy?" he asked, reaching out a hand toward her.

She jerked away, avoiding his touch. "Nothing!" she snapped.

"Something's wrong," he insisted.

"Maybe I'm just tired of being used."

"Used?" He frowned at her. "What in hell does that mean?"

"Exactly what I said." Tears misted her eyes. "I thought you loved me, Colt. But you—"

"Is that what's wrong?" he asked gently.

Her lips quivered, and she wouldn't look at him. "It doesn't matter," she said. "I was foolish for believing you cared when—"

"Amelia!" He grasped her chin and forced her to look at him. "I do care about you. I care a lot."

"You don't have to say that."

He gripped her shoulders and shook her. "Dammit, Amelia. It's obvious you want the words."

"What words?" she asked stubbornly.

"You want me to say I love you!"

"Not if you don't mean it," she said stiffly.

"I do mean it!"

"You love me?"

"Of course I do." His voice was gruff. "I thought you knew that."

"No," she said in a small voice. "You never told me. And you told Matthew that we were just friends."

"Well, hell!" he gritted. "I was just trying to save your reputation."

"Are you sure?"

"Amelia . . ." He sounded hesitant. "I have to be truthful . . . When we made love in the cave it was because . . . Well, hell! I'm just a man, Amelia. I'm not a saint. And you were so damned tempting that I just couldn't resist."

Amelia smiled at him. "What are you trying to say?"

"Hell, I don't know. I guess I just wanted you to understand. When we made love in that cave, there was nothing on my mind except loving you. I never once thought of the consequences, never even considered the possibility that you might have a child."

"What are you trying to say, Colt?"

He raked his fingers through his dark hair. "I do love

you, Amelia. Please believe that. But I can't go home with you."

A chill swept over her. "Are you saying that you don't want me . . . or our babe?"

"No!" he exclaimed, pulling her hard against him. "Never! It's just that I made a vow, Amelia, to punish the men who destroyed my family. To hunt them down like dogs and make them pay."

"So you're leaving me." Amelia felt a fatalistic calm sweep over her.

"I have to leave," he said gruffly, smoothing back her hair. "But you have to know I wouldn't go if it wasn't absolutely necessary. When I've found Kincaid, I'll come home and we can—"

"What if you never find him?"

"I will." He tilted her chin and met her eyes. "I will find him, Amelia. Please believe that."

"How long have you been looking for them?"

He knew what she was asking. "It's been over a year, but this time—"

"You won't see your baby born." There was a certainty in her voice that shook him to the core.

"No!" he exclaimed. "I'll be back by then."

"No," she said. "If you go after Kincaid, you won't be back."

He sighed and tucked her head beneath his chin. "I promise I'll come back, sweetheart. You won't have to raise this baby alone."

Tears misted her eyes. "I don't want you to leave, Colt. Please. Stay with me."

"I want to. Amy. God, how I want to, but I can't." He tipped her chin and forced her to meet his eyes. "Don't you understand?"

He kissed her then, devouring her mouth with his kiss. Then he pressed heated kisses all over her face, her eyelids, her neck before returning to her mouth again, never drawing completely away from her as he worshiped her body in a way designed to make her understand how much he cared.

"I need to know you'll be waiting for me, Amelia," he said fiercely, running his lips over her jawline.

"No," she whispered. "I won't wait for you, Colt Morgan." She had to make him believe that, or he would go away and she'd never see him again.

A shudder racked his powerful body. "God, Amelia. How can you say that? You're tearing the heart out of me."

"Just the way you're tearing mine out." She pulled away from his embrace and met his gaze with a long look. "You decide right now, Colter. You can ride away from me or you can stay and make a home for our baby. The decision is yours."

"Hell, Amelia!" he snarled. "You leave me no choice."

With his mouth set in a grim line, Colt pulled on his boots and donned his six-gun. Then, with a long look at Amelia, he left her alone, slamming the door behind him.

Amelia felt stunned. She'd played out her hand and lost. Colter had chosen the path of vengeance over a future with her and his child.

Oh, God, how could she stand it?

With a heart-wrenching sob, Amelia threw herself across the bed and cried out her misery.

Blake knew the moment he saw his brother that something was wrong. Colt's hair was tousled, which wasn't a surprise, judging from how long it took him to reach the lobby. But he didn't look like a man who'd been tumbling his woman. He looked like a man who had been to hell and back.

"Something wrong?" Blake inquired.

Colt nodded abruptly.

"You gonna tell me about it?'

"Amelia said if I leave, she won't be waiting when I come back."

Blake studied his brother for a long moment. "I guess you've got no choice then, big brother."

"What do you mean?"

"You won't be going."

"Dammit, I made a vow and—"

"We all made vows, Colt. You don't have to be the one to do this. Anyway," he added, "it would probably be best if I took over from here."

"Why you?"

"Because I'm a lawman. I'm used to tracking outlaws." He gripped his brother's shoulder. "It's time to let go, Colt. You have a family to think of now. A woman to wed and a babe that will need caring for."

Colt raked his hand through his hair. "I feel like I'm letting them down."

"Our brothers?"

"No," Colt said softly. "Ma and Pa and Annie."

"You're not," Blake said gruffly. "You've done your part, Colt. It's time somebody else took over." He leveled his gaze on his brother. "Go on back to her now. She's probably crying her eyes out."

Colter's hands fisted at the thought. "Probably," he said grimly. "Hell, Blake! I never knew love could hurt so much."

Blake laughed. "I think you've got it bad, Colt. You better marry her as fast as you can."

"Just as soon as it can be arranged," Colter assured him. "You gonna stick around for the wedding?"

"If you have it today," Blake replied. "Come morning I'll be headed out. I don't want Kincaid's trail to get too cold."

The brothers parted then. And when Colter returned to his room, he found Blake was right. Amelia was sobbing so hard her body was shaking.

"Amelia."

Her head jerked up and she stared at him as though she couldn't believe her eyes. Then, before he could reach her, she flung herself in his arms.

"Oh, God, Colt," she sobbed. "I didn't mean it! I'll be here when you get back! I'll wait for you!"

"You won't have to," he said gently. "I'm not going anywhere without you."

Shivering with joy, Amelia slid her hands around his neck and threaded her fingers through his dark hair. The hunger she felt for this man was so devastating that she wanted to bury herself in his body.

"Love me, Colt," she begged. "Please, love me."

With a husky groan, Colt seized her head between his large hands and pressed his feverish lips against hers. He pushed his tongue into her mouth, darting in and out, tasting the sweetness he found inside. His breath was hot, searing her senses as his mouth moved across her face, down her throat to caress the pulse that throbbed at her neck.

And then he was moving lower, brushing the swell of her breast before capturing one taut nipple in his mouth.

Amelia shuddered and held him closer as he took suckle. His mouth worked at her nipple as his hand continued down her silken skin, stroking her stomach before moving along her inner thighs until finally he was cupping the mound between her legs.

"Colt," Amelia groaned.

Her senses swirled wildly as he parted the soft folds of her femininity and dipped one finger into the moistness he found there. He tormented her with his fiery caresses, and she responded to him with a vibrant passion that almost overwhelmed her.

"Love me, Colt." she whispered hoarsely.

Amelia felt completely immersed in the sensual pleasure he was creating. Every thought was gone from her mind except for him and her passion.

She shifted beneath him, almost crazy with longing as she tried to get closer to his throbbing masculinity, the instrument that would surely bring relief from the searing passion threatening to consume her.

And then he entered her, and she surrendered to the overpowering sensations that had tormented her. Colter moved inside her, slowly, then increasing his pace and force until the flames that he'd ignited became a furnace of passion.

Amelia's breath was harsh as she was carried with him along the path to that distant peak. They reached it simultaneously and clung together as they rode out the stormy waves of passion.

She heard him cry out her name and shudder; then he collapsed against her, his body quivering in the throes of passion.

Then, as though afraid he was crushing her, Colt rolled onto his side and held her tightly against him.

Amelia pressed a kiss against his perspiration-dampened skin. "Don't hate me, Colt," she whispered. "Please don't hate me."

"How could I hate you?" he asked gently.

"Because I'm so selfish. I know you want to go after Kincaid, and I won't stop you."

"I'm not leaving you, Amelia." He stroked her silky hair. "No matter how much you beg me to go, I'll never leave you. Not as long as there's breath in my body."

"But you have to find him!" she protested.

He laughed huskily. "No. Blake's going after him." He

grinned at her. "As for you and me, well, darling, we've got a date with the preacher man."

"We do?'

"Yep."

"When did you have time to ask him?"

"I didn't ask him yet. But he wouldn't dare refuse me." She smiled up at him. "He wouldn't?"

"Damn straight. If he even hesitates, I'll just show him my six-gun and I'll—"

"Colter Morgan!" she exclaimed. "You wouldn't dare. Not a man of the cloth."

"I'd dare anything to make you mine, love. Didn't you know that?"

"Just keep reminding me, Colt," she said. "In case I ever forget."

"Yes, ma'am," he drawled.

Amelia laid her head against his chest and smiled. Colter Morgan would probably prove to be a handful, but in the long run it would be worth it.

"Colt?" She lifted her head to meet his eyes. "While I was away I discovered I have two sisters somewhere."

He caught the drift of her thoughts. "We'll look for them, Amelia," he said softly. "And Blake can help us. He knows who to contact." He kissed the tip of her nose. "But first he has a wedding to attend."

She smiled with pleasure. "Blake is coming to our wedding?"

"Damn straight," he said. "And Matthew and Benjamin will probably put up a fuss because we didn't wait for them. But I feel a great need to make you my wife before something else happens."

"You do?'

"Yeah," he growled. "I most certainly do."

Those were the exact words he used later that day when the preacher asked his question.

Chapter Thirty

It had been a hurried affair, getting ready for the wedding.

Colter told Amelia he would not see her wed like some poor waif that nobody cared about. And although they could not wait for his family to arrive, they would have all the trimmings that a beautiful bride deserved.

He had commandeered Blake's services for the wedding preparations. Although Blake had groaned, saying he had no knowledge of weddings, within the hour—when Amelia had just stepped into a tub of warm water—a knock sounded on the door.

"Who's there?" Colter demanded.

"It's Mrs. Hawthorne-Vigny," a male voice replied.

Amelia's eyes widened. "Colt? That doesn't sound like a woman to me."

"It's not," Colt replied. "If I'm not mistaken, it's the hotel desk clerk."

Amelia slunk lower in the tub, as though she were afraid the desk clerk could see through the door.

"What does Mrs. Hawthorne-whatever the rest of it is want with us?"

"She's come for the—"

A female voice interrupted the desk clerk. "I've come for the fitting."

"Fitting?" Amelia whispered. "What fitting?"

Colt scratched his head. "Beats me." He eyed her for a long moment. "Do brides usually require one of those before their wedding?"

"Only if they are acquiring new clothes."

"Oh." Suddenly comprehension dawned. "Like a wedding gown. Blake must have sent her." He raised his voice. "Just a minute, Mrs. Hawthorne."

He reached for the lock, and Amelia squealed. "Colter Morgan! Don't you dare open that door! The desk clerk is out there, and the Lord only knows who else!"

"Well, hell, Amelia! How can she give you that fitting if she can't come inside?"

"Tell her to come back later."

He did so, then frowned at the woman's reply.

"Mr. Morgan," she said huffily. "I am standing in this hallway with two of my seamstresses holding four wedding gowns in their arms. I myself am carrying the accessories to each one, and the poor desk clerk is carrying a parcel containing numerous unmentionables."

A husky male voice joined in then, and Colter guessed it was the desk clerk protesting the parcel he'd been made to carry without knowing what the package contained.

"I cannot possibly return at a later time," the woman continued. "If you are interested . . ."

Colter closed his mind to the woman's voice and grabbed the folding screen that had been placed in the corner of the bedroom.

"Colter, what are you doing?"

"I'm hiding you," he said, stretching out the screen in front of the tub.

By the time the woman had stopped talking, Colter had the door open. He smiled at the middle-aged woman who stood before him, a grim look on her face.

"Come in, Mrs. Hawthorne," he invited.

"That's Mrs. Hawthorne-Vigny," she said coldly, managing to look down her nose at him. "And I am never kept waiting, Mr. Morgan. Never."

"Yes, ma'am," he said meekly, stepping back to allow the woman and her entourage to enter.

As the women spread the dresses carefully on the bed, Colter eyed them with trepidation. He wasn't easy with women's fripperies, and there seemed to be a lot of the damned things covering his bed.

"Where is the bride?" Mrs. Hawthorne-Vigny asked.

"Colt?" Amelia's voice was thin. "What's going on out there?"

"Just the uh . . . Hawthorne"—he looked at the woman for the rest of her name, which she quickly supplied— "Vigny. And her, uh . . . helpers." He ducked behind the screen and leaned down to give her a quick kiss on the end of her tip-tilted nose.

"Helpers?" she asked with lifted brow. "Colt, you didn't! How many other people did you let in my bedroom anyway?"

"I didn't count," he said quickly. "Two or three, I suppose."

"There are exactly four of us, counting the desk clerk," a cold voice said.

Amelia's gaze jerked toward the sound. A middle-aged woman came around the screen and stood before her, eyeing her attributes that showed above the water.

"Colt!" Amelia squeaked, making a grab for the towel. "The desk clerk! Get him out of here!"

"He's going," Colt said grimly.

Wedding or no wedding, he wasn't leaving any man in Amelia's bedroom when she was undressed. "And I'm going with him."

"You can't—"

"I can!"

And then he did, shoving the desk clerk ahead of him and shutting the door firmly behind them.

The next two hours were lost in a flurry of preparations. Amelia was fitted with each gown until she'd decided on a particular one. And then she was prodded and pinched, turned and stabbed with pins until the seamstress pronounced the gown perfect. But that wasn't enough. When Mrs. Hawthorne-Vigny, who had returned to her dress shop, was sent for, Amelia had to go through the whole thing again until the woman finally agreed that, yes, it really was a perfect fit.

The gown was a fragile thing. Amelia had never seen anything so beautiful. It was made of ivory silk satin that was cut in a long princess style with thousands of hand-sewn seed pearls adorning the bodice and long, flowing sleeves.

"You must wear the Irish lace veil with it," Mrs. Hawthorne-Vigny said softly. Tears misted her eyes as she looked at Amelia, who had somehow broken through the harsh exterior the older woman presented. "You will be the most beautiful bride this town has ever seen, my dear. Most beautiful."

"Thank you, Mrs. Hawthorne-Vigny."

"Call me Thelma, child," the woman said softly. "At least when we're alone."

Thelma. Amelia controlled a smile. The woman who seemed so proud of her heritage that she kept her maiden name along with her married one, had an uncommonly common name.

"Thank you, Thelma," she said, leaning over to kiss the woman's cheek.

"It's going to be a lovely wedding," the woman said. "Just lovely."

Amelia smiled at her. "Thank you so much for all your help. I just wish my mother . . ." She broke off and met the older woman's eyes. "I know we don't really know each other," she said, "but I have no family to attend my wedding." She thought about the empty church. "Colter will have his brother, of course, but if you'd like to attend the wedding, I would love to have you there. Perhaps," she went on, "you could stand in for my mother."

"Oh, lovey," Thelma exclaimed. "I would love to stand in for her." She tucked a stray curl behind Amelia's ear. "Thank you for asking me." She turned to the seamstresses standing by. "All right, ladies," she said briskly. "Let's get the rest of these things out of here and back to the shop. We have a lot of planning to do."

Amelia had no idea what Thelma meant, just supposed she was referring to work at the dress shop . . . until nearly sunset when Blake came for her.

She had been wondering where Colter was for the last two hours, had even considered that he'd gotten cold feet at the last minute and skipped town. She knew, almost as soon as the thought occurred, that it was not so. Colter loved her. She was positive of that fact. And yet, he'd been gone so long; ever since the women had arrived with the wedding gowns and he'd made such a quick exit.

Thelma was with her, attaching the veil among the bright curls that had been piled high on her head. Amelia gave a start when a knock came on the door.

Colter! It must be him. Oh, please, Lord, let it be him.

"Come in," Thelma shouted, her fingers pinching Amelia's cheeks to give them some color.

The door opened and Blake walked in, then stopped short to stare at her with jaw hung low. "My God, Amy," he breathed. "You're a sight to behold."

Amelia wasn't interested in his opinion at the moment, although it was always good to hear that one looked beautiful. At least she hoped that was what Blake meant. The only thing she was interested in at the moment was her absent groom.

"Colt isn't with you?" she inquired in a forlorn voice.

"No," Blake replied, his mind still trying to deal with the vision that confronted him. God, she was beautiful. No wonder Colter couldn't leave her alone.

Amelia's shoulders drooped and her eyes misted with tears. It was all she could do to keep her knees from buckling. "You've come to tell me he left town, haven't you, Blake? Colter decided he didn't want to marry me."

"Hell, no!" he exclaimed, wondering where she'd got such an idea. "If he did change his mind, I'd be mighty quick to take his place, Amy. But there's not a chance in hell that he will."

"Then where is he?"

"At the church. Where he was told to wait."

"Told to wait?" Her eyes widened at the thought of anyone telling Colt to wait and him actually doing it. "Who told him to wait there?"

"I did, lovey," Thelma said. "It's unlucky for the groom to see the bride before the wedding."

"But Colter had already seen me."

"That was before I took over."

"You took over?" Comprehension dawned. "Oh, you mean before you undertook to fit me with a gown."

"She took over," Blake said, his eyes glittering with amusement. "Literally."

"I don't understand."

"You will."

Suddenly Amelia heard the sound of a distant organ and crossed to the open window. "How strange," she said, staring down on the empty street below. "The organ is playing in the church." She turned back to Blake. "It's not Sunday, is it?"

"Nope." He grinned and crooked his arm. "Take my arm, Amelia. It's time for your wedding."

Feeling as though she were dreaming, Amelia placed her fingers on Blake's arm. Together, with Thelma leading the way, they left the hotel and walked the short distance to the church. As they approached the open door, the music swelled.

Several boys were waiting outside the church, and as Amy neared the door, one of them stepped forward and shoved a bouquet of wildflowers in her hand, then bowed low before her.

"Why, thank you," Amelia whispered. "It was sweet of you to gather these for me."

The boy grimaced and stepped back. "It ain't sweet neither," he said. "He"—he nodded at Blake—"paid me to bring 'em."

Amelia smiled up at Blake. "Thank you so much, Blake. For everything you've done."

Something flickered in Blake's dark eyes, and he was tempted to mount the nearest horse and ride away with her. He would have done so if her groom had not been his brother. He pushed the thought aside and continued to walk beside her into the church.

Amelia's eyes widened as she got her first look at the church. She was so surprised that she stopped short just inside the door. Every available space in the church was covered with wildflowers. There must have been thousands of them. Where had they all come from anyway? And the people . . . the whole town must have crowded into the room.

As though sensing her thoughts, Blake leaned closer. "The flowers came from the fields around the town, Amelia," he whispered. "When the boys heard I wanted flowers gathered, they all wanted to join in."

He didn't have to say that each one of them would expect to be paid for his efforts; Amelia already knew. She looked up at him with misty eyes. "Are you responsible for the people, too?"

"No." He grinned at her. "That was Thelma's idea."

Amelia's gaze slid around the room, moving over the smiling faces of those who had come to attend her wedding. Then her eyes fastened on one particular face . . . that of the man whom fate had decreed would be her husband. He stood beside the altar, looking uncomfortable in formal wear.

What in hell is going on? Colter wondered, staring at the vision who had just entered the church on his brother's arm. It wasn't enough that he had to stand there, in a suit that must have been designed for a dead man to wear. And the collar was so tight, starched so heavily, that he could hardly breathe. He could hardly wait for the wedding to be over so he could take Amelia home.

If she'd only walk down that damned aisle and marry him.

From the looks of it, though, she appeared to have changed her mind. She just stood there at the door, clutching Blake's arm as though she were afraid to let go. And that damnable woman, Mrs. What's-her-name, had invited the whole town to watch his shame at being abandoned at the altar.

But he wouldn't have it! No, Amelia had promised to marry him, and wed him she would. He started toward her, but the preacher grabbed his arm and shook his head.

Colter was on the point of shoving the man away when the organ player started a different tune.

The wedding march.

As though that were the signal she'd been waiting for, Mrs. What's-her-name started down the aisle toward him. What in hell was happening here? Surely that woman wasn't coming to be his bride. His hands clenched into tight fists as he looked past the woman—who was throwing flowers on the floor with every step she took—at Amelia, who continued to stand beside Blake.

Was it Blake's intention to wed her? Dammit, he'd strangle the life out of his brother before he'd allow him to steal his bride.

He frowned at the two of them. He'd seen neither one since that damned woman had come to the hotel room. He'd been waylaid on his way to the saloon and taken to another hotel room, where he'd been pinched and prodded and fitted with this new suit that Mrs. What's-her-name had deemed right for a groom. He'd seen nothing of Amelia or Blake, but he'd seen more than he wanted of the snobby woman who was coming toward him now. Even as that thought occurred, the damned woman smiled at him . . . actually smiled.

Dammit! Something fishy was definitely afoot. He jerked his arm away from the preacher's grip and started toward the door. He'd be damned if he would stand here and—

Ah! Amelia had started down the aisle toward him. She was coming after all, and the other woman, Mrs. What's-her-name, had seated herself in the empty space in the front row.

Colter knew he'd never seen a woman more lovely than Amelia. She looked like an angel in her wedding gown, appeared to be completely untouched, but he knew better. He had touched her, more than once.

And then she was beside him, her face radiant as she

met his eyes. Colter was vaguely aware of the preacher asking a question and, believing it to be directed at him, said quickly; "I damned sure will take her!"

A smattering of laughter followed his statement, and Blake stared hard at his brother. "He wasn't talking to you, Colt," he muttered. "He was addressing me."

"Dammit, Blake!" Colter jerked Amelia toward him. "I should have known this would happen. You were always trying to steal my girls! Well, I won't have it! This one's mine! Take your hands off her and find your own!"

The congregation howled with laughter.

Amelia blushed wildly, and when she looked at Colter, there was no sign of the angel that he'd seen only moments ago. Her eyes were blazing with fury. "He's giving me away, you fool!" she snapped. "That was the preacher's question."

He frowned at her. "How can he give you away when you don't belong to him?"

The preacher cleared his throat. "You really should listen, young man. Just keep quiet until I ask you to speak."

Realizing he was making an absolute fool of himself, Colter clamped his lips into a thin line and waited for the preacher to go on.

"Who gives the bride away?" the preacher asked.

"I do," Blake said, his voice trembling slightly.

Colter directed a suspicious look at his brother. Was Blake laughing at him? He'd damned well better not be. He forced himself to wait quietly and listen to the preacher's every word. And then the preacher faced him.

"Do you, Colter Morgan, take this woman—"

"I do!" Colter snapped.

The preacher's lips thinned, but he turned to Amelia. "Do you, Amelia Anne Spencer take this man to be—"

"She does," Colter said.

"She has to say the words."

"I do," Amelia said, her gaze softening as her eyes met Colter's.

"The ring," the preacher prompted.

Colter fumbled in his pocket for the ring he'd bought at the mercantile and slid it on Amelia's finger.

"I now pronounce you man and wife," the preacher said, his gaze settling on Colter. "You may kiss the bride."

Colter did exactly that as the organ music swelled around them. And he made such a thorough job of it that when he lifted his head, Amelia's knees were in danger of buckling.

He grinned down at her, feeling proud of his ability to make her so weak-kneed with pleasure. And then, knowing Mrs. What's-her-name must have planned some kind of party to celebrate their wedding, Colter swept Amelia into his arms and carried her out of the church.

He strode quickly across the street and through the lobby, then up the stairs to their room. He didn't even pause until he had kicked the door closed behind them. And then he smiled into her eyes. "Hello, wife."

"Hello, husband." Her voice was soft, tender with feeling. She loved this man. And she didn't care who knew it.

They stayed locked in the room until morning, and when they woke the next morning, they discovered Blake had left town.

They didn't hear from him for two months, and then it was by way of a telegram that Skeeter brought out to the ranch. The message he'd sent was short. Only a few words, but it was enough to bring tears to Amelia's eyes.

The message was simple. It read:

Found Amelia in Kansas City. Going by Velvet Johnson. I'm bringing her home.

"What in hell is he talking about?" Colter asked, staring in amazement at the message. "You're not in Kansas City, Amelia. Why would Blake believe you are? And who in hell is he bringing home?"

"My sister." Amelia's eyes glowed with happiness. "Blake found my twin sister and he's bringing her home to Morgan's Creek."